TIRFO THUIN

By

Andrew Butterworth

TIRFO THUIN
Andrew Butterworth

Copyright 2011 Andrew Butterworth
Illustrations Copyright 2013 Hayley Ormerod
Cover design/typography by Andrew Butterworth

ISBN-13: 978-1469957982
ISBN-10: 1469957981

http://www.tirfothuin.com

Dedication

This book is dedicated to Jessica and Leann for their patience and support.

Table of Contents

DEDICATION	V
PROLOGUE	1
CHAPTER 1 – 15 YEARS LATER	5
CHAPTER 2	17
CHAPTER 3	25
CHAPTER 4	37
CHAPTER 5	47
CHAPTER 6	51
CHAPTER 7	65
CHAPTER 8	79
CHAPTER 9	87
CHAPTER 10	93
CHAPTER 11	97
CHAPTER 12	111
CHAPTER 13	119
CHAPTER 14	127
CHAPTER 15	131
CHAPTER 16	143
CHAPTER 17	151
CHAPTER 18	167
CHAPTER 19	183
CHAPTER 20	191
CHAPTER 21	193
CHAPTER 22	203
CHAPTER 23	207
CHAPTER 24	217
CHAPTER 25	223
CHAPTER 26	231
CHAPTER 27	251
EPILOGUE	257
ABOUT THE AUTHOR	261
ACKNOWLEDGMENTS	263
BONUS MATERIAL	265
A SNEAK PEEK AT PART II OF THE TIRFO THUIN TRILOGY – OUT AUTUMN 2014	267

"Civilisation begins with order, grows with liberty, and dies with chaos."

Will Durant - Historian

PROLOGUE

The sodden ground squelched underfoot as the combat medics hurried the injured Witches from the front line, their defensive orbs thinning to almost breaking point from the battering they had received.

Their destination was a medical tent four hundred yards behind the first trench. They couldn't help but show the deep sense of urgency and fear on their faces once they realised the injured Witche drifting in and out of consciousness below them was Niamhson, the Witche King. This fear was heightened by the four bodyguards running alongside them.

They entered the medical tent and carefully tipped the King from the makeshift stretcher onto the table and ran back into the melee of fire and death. The nerves they had once felt on the field were now shredded by the constant exposure to blood and gore. The country of Ysrir had been at war for nearly eighteen months now, with many casualties for both the Witches of Rusalimum and the Sorcerers of Adiabene.

Niamhson struggled to part his encrusted eyelids and found he was being manhandled onto his back. He stared up at the canvas ceiling as it rocked violently. In a dazed state, Niamhson observed a white-clad Witche doctor looking down at him. He rubbed his temples and coughed on the sweet smell of incense. He managed to steady his breathing to a slower rhythm, but the searing pain in his ribs was enough to take his breath away.

"Where am I?" he asked, as he coughed a little harder and sprayed blood on the doctor's already red-smeared apron.

"Lie back, Your Highness, and we'll have you moved

back to the castle in no time," she said, sounding worried. A nearby explosion caused the tent to rock and sway momentarily, and two of the guards slipped outside to monitor the situation.

Niamhson reluctantly laid his burnt head back on the worn, lumpy pillow. The dried blood of previous occupants crackled against his neck and the smell of sick and death was acrid. His hearing began to break free of the constant humming he had been suffering since waking.

Tortured cries and screams penetrated the flimsy medical tent and shot waves of realisation through his nervous system. He sat upright with a start and almost knocked the young doctor off her feet.

"Where is my wife?" he yelled. "Where is Magatha?" He swung his legs around and slid to his feet. One of the guards approached him, but appeared to change his mind.

Niamhson staggered as he left the tent; an image of complete devastation and carnage hit him. From his position behind the back line of trenches, he could see a savaged landscape. Freshly wounded and killed soldiers scattered the burnt earth, their hollow faces like a sea of white roses against a backdrop of red and black. Falling to his knees with fatigue, he wondered how long he'd been in and out of consciousness before the medics had found him.

It appeared there had been a push on their last line of defences since he was hit by a Sorcerer's spell and awoke in the medical tent. He dragged himself deeper into the field against the advice of his guards and the yelling doctor not far behind. As he stumbled from body to body, he frantically scanned the surroundings for his wife.

To his disgust, Niamhson saw brown rats gorging on

the dead – a sight that had become more common as the war dragged on and conditions in the trenches got worse.

Why? Why is this happening? These were good people!, he thought. A red arc of fire swooped from the sky in an almost majestic fashion and shattered to earth before Niamhson's feet, causing him to slide and then tumble head first into a trench.

He instinctively placed his hand to his side, where a warm red stain had seeped through his leather padding, and he realised how much pain he was actually in – not only physical pain, but pain for the loss of his people and, it appeared from his surroundings, the loss of his wife.

He screamed an unmanly cry of grief and sobbed. His guards attempted to steady him as he was caught in the shoulder by an explosion of red and orange fire. His mind became strangely distant and fuzzy. As he lowered his head, he realised he was standing over a badly scarred, blood-stained man lying face down in the mud. A Witche doctor was violently shaking him, and his guards looked on in shock. Her cries for help were drowned out by blasts and screaming from the melee taking place just yards away. He could smell burning oak as his hearing became muffled and then surreally silent. Silent but comforting.

The doctor managed to roll the man over and, to his horror, he found himself looking down at his own pale face, eyes rolled back and lips blue with cold.

"What is this trickery?" he demanded of no one in particular. He already knew the answer. He had one last look around for Magatha as things began to turn hazy, and he started out toward the growing white light on the horizon alongside hundreds of other pale-faced soldiers. *Seirim help us all,* he thought.

Chapter 1 – 15 years later

The rain lashed against the upper reaches of the scarred trees as Magatha, Witche Qwein of Ysrir, hurried along the dark route that she had committed to memory. Moving from tree to tree, she desperately sought dry patches in which to shelter. If there was one thing she hated, it was rain. She could cope with pain, curses and spiders, and even her annoying second-cousin Ariana, but not rain.

"But, Mother, I don't even want to come with you!' Niamh exclaimed. "Why can't I just stay at home? I just end up cold and wet and bored," Magatha heard behind her as she increased her pace and stumbled through another opening in the trees, attempting to brush away the wet leaves that had stuck to her legs.

The sky resembled a lump of black charcoal with occasional patches of light dancing between the clouds. Magatha was sure that a full moon shone with great brilliance behind them, but it had yet to make a proper appearance.

She was a relatively young Witche, as far as Qweins went. Aged 187, she remained the youngest to hold the much-worshipped Staff of Light in the many centuries that Witches had walked the land. Magatha looked at the muddy staff and felt disgruntled about never having unlocked the powerful secrets it was said to hold. She knew that many Witche Qweins never did, but she had hoped she wouldn't be one of them.

She had an old-fashioned, formal appearance, wearing a long black cloak that appeared just too short for her delicate, wiry frame. Below this were two oversized mud-brown boots reaching just above her ankles. Up each side, several silver buckles were strapped tightly to prevent water entering through the top. She also wore long, black lace gloves that reached to her elbow, and a headscarf that revealed her ill-tempered scowl when it flapped back in the wind.

This was in stark contrast to her daughter Niamh. At fourteen years old, Niamh stood nearly as tall as Magatha, but seemed to hold herself differently. Where Magatha would stand with shoulders straight and chin up, her daughter would stoop and mope about the place.

Niamh always seemed to wear the new style of cape that she had seen many youngsters wearing that fastened with a red jewel at the front. Despite most of the children Magatha had seen opting for all black clothing, Niamh preferred to stand out and more often than not wore a deep purple velvet cape with red under it and elbow-high tough black gloves. She had waist-length white-blonde hair that was hidden below the hood of her cape and young, delicate features. Magatha saw Niamhson in her every time she looked at her.

She missed her daughter greatly when on her Royal duties, but times like these, when they couldn't seem to find words that did not anger each other, made it hard for her to kindle any kind of relationship. She knew her daughter hated the time they spent apart, but neither of them seemed able to make the time together work.

Magatha growled up at the tops of the giant oak trees as an icy raindrop plummeted down the back of her neck.

"Every time I put up with this nonsense. Wouldn't even be too bad if I could see what I was standing on," Magatha groaned as she leapt for cover under the charred carcass of a lightning-struck tree, its black insides a reflection of the dark night sky above. She continued to the outskirts of the wood, careful to avoid losing her footing, and reached the final few trees to look out at the clearing ahead. In front of her was a small stream at the foot of a hill – the kind of hill that couldn't be classed as an achievement if conquered but neither would you climb for fun, she often thought.

Magatha knew this hill well, for she had climbed it many times before. She pondered over whether she had really been doing this for fifteen years. It felt like so much longer. Witches Mount had been used by the Witche Kings and Qweins for generations to summon the spirit of Seirim and see the will of the gods, and no matter how well the ritual was carried out, there was often nothing to see at all. To her irritation, this had been the case for the last three visits.

"I thought it might be nice to spend some time together," Magatha attempted, anticipating the usual barrage of abuse.

"Nice? Nice!" Niamh retorted. "What is nice about trailing in your shadow whilst getting soaked to the bone and standing at the bottom of a hill for an eternity while you consult with your 'friend'?" Niamh asked sarcastically.

Magatha ignored the obvious insult to their God, hoping He would too if he was listening, and pressed on. She contemplated whether Gods really could see and hear everything and hoped for Niamh's sake they could not.

"I do try, Niamh. I know I spend a long time away, but I do it to keep our people safe. To keep you safe. One day, hopefully, you will understand."

Magatha turned back to see Niamh concentrating on the words she had just spoken, the inner conflict between love and hate evident on her youthful face. It saddened Magatha to guess at Niamh's thoughts, and she wondered if they were always as bad as Niamh led her to believe.

They made their way to the small rocky bank, and rested for a second, silently watching the rushing water as raindrops broke the foamy surface. Magatha suddenly looked up, as though remembering her task, and began to cross the water. Hopping from stone to stone, she was careful not to slip on the moss-covered surfaces as Niamh followed reluctantly behind her.

"Why can't you just spend more time at home? With a fire and a blanket and a hot drink? Like a real parent?" Niamh asked.

Magatha stopped dead in her tracks and lowered her head. What more could she do? It was a difficult time for her people, and she had many duties to fulfill. She knew this meant neglecting her duties as a parent – and a single parent at that – but she knew Niamh was strong.

She gripped the solid silver chain around her neck and thought of her late husband Niamhson, and of how they hadn't even known she was pregnant when the last war came to an end and he was killed. *How things would be different now*, she often thought, *if Niamhson was still alive.*

It was such a wasteful end to all that loss of life, with Witches and Sorcerers simply retreating and giving up due to the high number of casualties and the death of both the Witche King and the Sorcerer King in the same night. Both sides tasted victory, assuming that the death of the opposing King would bring the downfall of the enemy. That was until news of their own King's demise filtered through the ranks. She had sobbed for what felt like days, surrounded by scores of dead Witches in the mud of the battlefield.

Her inability to cope as a single parent was her one weakness, and one she dealt with badly. With Niamhson gone, Magatha knew Niamh relied on Henry, her best friend from school, to be the sole male figure and companion in her life. Magatha was thankful for Henry, but also jealous of the bond they had. She longed for Niamh's affection, but knew that she understood little about her daughter's life. She had witnessed so very few of its precious moments.

As they began to climb, lightning forked up ahead, temporarily lighting the landscape to reveal a handful of abandoned thatched cottages dotted around the hillside. Surrounding the mount was the circle of towering trees that she had just left, their thick, haunting trunks casting malevolent shadows in the semi-moonlight. Ahead, a small oak barrel swayed from a wooden frame, iron spikes gleaming within. The spikes, a curious mix of rusty-reds, browns and oranges, glimmered slightly, and Magatha was sure they contained the images of many past Witches. This, Magatha knew, was a stark reminder of how Witches were once treated by humans when they first came to Ysrir. The ancient practice of hurling women down a hill in a spiked barrel seemed so barbaric. The ironic thing, she pondered, was that the women who miraculously survived were deemed to be Witches and burnt alive. "Strange times," Magatha said aloud to no one in particular.

Things had changed drastically since those days. Humans had feared magic and Witchecraft, and they still would if they knew it existed. Magatha was one of the few Witches to know that humans still inhabited Ysrir, and she was certain her people would be just as frightened to find out that barrel-hurling humans still walked the land. Whilst they had little defence against magic, they were thought to be a resilient race.

"Right, you stay—" Magatha began as Niamh interjected.

"Yeah, yeah, I know. I stay here, get wet and cold and miserable. You carry on, Mother," she said in an unreadable tone.

Magatha shook her freezing head and tutted as Niamh made her way to the shelter of a crumbling cottage, muttering under her breath. She wouldn't force her to come again, Magatha thought. She would rather Niamh be happy at home with Henry than forced on a miserable trip on which they argued all the time anyway.

Magatha continued with her climb, wiping the salty rain gathering above her eyes with the back of her glove. She stopped a little way up the slope to peer around above the tree line. In the far distance lay her hometown of Rusalimum, with the dark mass of sea glistening just beyond it. She surveyed the horizon with a look of distant hope. Even from this distance she could see that the earth beyond the Craggy Peaks was burnt; life extinguished. Even the sky had taken on a gloomy, oppressive look with swirls of black and red ripping the horizon apart. "It seems strange times are still upon us," she mumbled.

Magatha meandered to find a safer route than the time before as loose granite fell from beneath her soles and ricocheted off rocks into the fast-flowing stream below. The mount had formed many millennia ago, when it was said great giants moved ice glaciers in order to make room for settlements. The material left was shards of loose, crumbly stone that dislodged easily underfoot. Lightning flashed once again, and from the trees below came the muffled sound of bark splitting and another wooden victim crashing to the sodden ground.

As she approached the summit, out of breath and with fresh purple grazes on her palms and knees, she steadied herself and brushed away the rubble collecting in the bottom of her cloak. She began to rummage through her pockets for the vital items needed to summon the spirit of Seirim. She unveiled a small lime-green bottle, a wooden star and an oil-soaked candle giving off a strong scent that tickled Magatha's senses.

At the highest, most central point of the hill lay what looked like a small extension of the hillside. A slab of grey-black stone protruded from the floor at the exact geographical centre of the mount. The stone rose from the ground and opened into two sections, coming together once again to a point at the top, creating an irregular stone ring. At the tip of the rock, a small vertical hole the size of Magatha's fist had been made. The outside of the slab was artistically rendered with Witche runes denoting, amongst other things, the eight seasons of the Witche year. When she reached the stone, Magatha looked to the east-facing side and slowly bowed her head to the current rune, Lammas.

Around the stone was a roughly circular layer of turf. It was written that this turf had been brought together from the nineteen parishes of Ysrir by human priests in an attempt to rid their township of Witches many centuries ago. It was supposed to symbolise the humans coming together and warding off evil. This attempt did little to halt the spread of Witchecraft, but conveniently created a soft area to kneel on when preparing rituals.

Magatha groaned to her knees and, using the stone to steady herself, placed the star in the gap within the slab and attached the candle to a point protruding from its centre. She swiftly uncorked the bottle and took a long drink before wiping her mouth on her sleeve. She replaced the cork with difficulty, and thought about how she always found the cold more bearable with an alcoholic blanket.

Sitting on a rock a few feet away, she crossed her legs and sheltered her face from the storm. Focusing on the star, she began to hum. "Something's not right," she muttered. Getting to her feet, she looked around perplexed for a few seconds, then brought the palm of her hand to her forehead. "The candle," she sighed as she approached the slab. Rubbing her thumb and index finger over the wick, she lit the candle and resumed her position on her rock.

"Ooooo, spirits from above, grace me with your wisdom and fo—" She stopped suddenly and, with one eye still closed, looked around suspiciously. She knew nobody would have dared venture this far from the village walls, but she wanted to make sure Niamh hadn't made her way up the hill. As a youngster Magatha had always been self-conscious when chanting spells like this, and she believed this came from her younger days at St Guinevere's when asked to perform spells in assembly. As Witche Qwein and Commander of the Witches Front, she had soon gotten over this, though. She continued, "—foresight. Tell us what is to come and prepare us for what we do not yet know."

A break appeared in the dense clouds, revealing a dagger of moonlight that seemed to stab at the ground below and search for the top of the rock face. The light intensified tenfold as it streamed through the hole in the centre and onto the candle and star below.

Magatha watched as the light spread through the star to each of its six tips. The flame began to grow and shiver, appearing to be fighting the invisible forces of the wind to stay alight. Magatha quickly fell into a deep trance. Her arms fell loose and her head lolled back and around so that her chin rested on her chest. Her eyes looked up while her head remained down, and she saw the face of Seirim materialise from the blue flames, dashes of fire licking at the cold grey stone.

To the inexperienced eye, the face seemed to shift form every few seconds, but Magatha knew to look beyond the swirling blue-orange flames. Beyond the pulsating outer glow was a face seen by few but worshipped by many. He had a long drawn-out face and rigid bone structure, with deep-set eyes that bathed in the dark shadow of the eyebrows above. Two short, rounded horns extended from his temple. Magatha had always thought his skin looked like it was too small for his skull.

"You have been summoned," the spirit said in a deep, demonic voice. Magatha had always wondered whether it was in her head or spoken out loud. "Summoned to fulfill a task. There are great troubles at present with the inhabitants of this once rich land. This has angered the gods."

Magatha, now defenceless against the rain streaming down her face, blinked several times in an attempt to see the spirit more clearly. She was now chilled to the bone, and felt the flames caressing her skin as she was pulled upright and drawn nearer. She noticed the smell of the burning candle itch at her senses.

"The gods fought when the men came from the north. The gods sent to protect each land should not have been used for war. You must say goodbye to someone you love as they begin a journey to return an ancient peace keeper to his rightful place. She must repair the damage that has been inflicted on the soul of this land.

"You will send a courageous Witche. You must inform them of an object that they must seek, and its power, and then send them on their way. They should head north until reaching the coast line and a winding path down to the shore. Here, they will cross to a small island when the sea permits. It is here the gods will be reunited," the spirit said.

"How will I know who to send? Do I select someone I feel is worthy of the task? A warrior like Gerito, perhaps?" Magatha asked.

"Everyone has their path set before them. The One was chosen well before being born."

The flames began to flicker and jump in the wind. "Wait, wait!" yelled Magatha as she felt sensation return to her fingers. It slid through her limbs like water seeping down a mountainside after a storm such as this. The flames began to subside, and Magatha watched with intense concentration. As the spirit face faded, another began to appear, the flames metamorphosing from shape to shape until it settled on the face of a girl not much older than fourteen. Magatha looked around in horror as she felt full control of her body return. She uncorked her bottle for a final swig and continued to stare as the flames died down. The line of brilliant white light returned to the clouds to continue its battle searching for cracks in the cover. The rain suddenly began to ease and the rumble of thunder gained some distance.

Magatha shook her head several times, rain spraying from her headscarf, muttering to herself. "It can't be. It just can't! He must be mistaken." At these words, she cowered a little and looked up to make sure the spirit had actually left.

She fumbled for the star, threw what was left of the candle to the ground, and shimmied sideways down the hillside, cursing under her breath.

She would not yet tell Niamh of these events. She needed to consult the Council and had a feeling Seirim had not yet told her everything she needed to know to prepare Niamh for this journey. *Seirim help her*, she thought, and went to collect her only daughter, thinking of what may lay ahead for her.

Chapter 2

As the golden, hazy light seeped through the crossed windows of the main hall, Mrs Vlemicks studied the students crossing the courtyard. She mentally weeded out the ones she saw as successful, those who would be mediocre and those who would always be trouble. *Niamh definitely falls into the last category*, Mrs Vlemicks thought to herself as she shook her head in dismay.

She turned on her heels and moved to the board, tightening her necktie to a perfectly central position. She selected a new piece of chalk.

"HERBAL REMEDIES USING WILD BLUEBELLS."

Two sweeping underlines using the full force of her arm concluded the lesson's subject as she returned the now half-sized chalk to its place below the board and began neatly distributing paper sheets to the symmetrical desks.

Mrs Vlemicks knew she was considered the toughest tutor at St Guinevere's. She was a tutor not to be crossed. She took pride in her posture and appearance, which was always rigid and immaculate. Her brown tweed outfit always appeared perfect and she kept her hair up in a solid bun on the top of her head. Her only apparent fault was the oversized crooked nose she attempted to hide in shadow with her scholar's cap. This, however, was an ambitious task for the cap, which it failed at miserably.

The students trickled into the classroom with little enthusiasm. When the class was nearing its full capacity Mrs Vlemicks marched to the front and took her seat, gently raising her skirt as she sat. She opened the green, leather-bound book, lowered her spectacles down her nose and began to read down the list, looking up after each name to give the recipient a quick glare.

"Miss June?"

"S'Miss."

"Young Master Keala?"

"Yes, Miss."

"Miss Retalla?"

"Miss Retalla?" Silence followed for a few seconds as Mrs Vlemicks slowly lifted her gaze.

"Does anyone know the whereabouts of young Miss Retalla? Anyone?" She scowled around the room looking for guilty faces.

"Master Keala? Hmmm? Anything you would like to share with me? When one watches a pupil cross the courtyard in the company of yourself it is expected that both pupils are actually going to attend my lesson," Mrs Vlemicks spat, her cheeks reddening slightly to match the pink squares sewn into her tweed-checked jacket.

"Miss?" replied Henry Keala, intended as an innocent I'm-not-sure-what-you-mean-Miss, reply. Just as Mrs Vlemicks opened her mouth to bark a reply, the classroom door swung open, crashing into the shelves behind and almost dislodging a glass ball on the top shelf beside the evacuation poster. Eyes lit up around the room as the children waited, stomachs turning, for the onslaught to follow if the Insight Ball smashed. Luckily for Niamh it steadied. It did, however, mean there were now more objects for Mrs Vlemicks to choose from were she to start throwing things.

"May I ask, Miss Retalla, where you have been for the first five minutes of my lesson?"

"You may," replied Niamh with a cocky smile. Mrs Vlemicks imagined that beasts were fighting in the girl's gut at this bravery.

Mrs Vlemicks glared at Niamh, her left eye twitching slightly, and through gritted teeth she snarled, "Sit down, young lady. I will deal with you after class and for an hour every night until the end of term!"

Niamh, knowing when to quit, headed down the first aisle of desks to the far left corner of the musty, sun-drenched room and threw herself onto a small, three-legged wooden stool. Taking a quill from her cloth satchel she scraped her chair to the desk and dipped the quill in her ink. Poised, she looked up to see half the students gawping at her in admiration and half in pity for what was to follow after class. The short length of varnished birch glistened in the morning light above Mrs Vlemicks's desk, and Niamh clenched her fists tight to hide the scars she had already received that term.

Mrs Vlemicks stood staring at Niamh for several seconds with piercing grey-green eyes and continued her stare until Niamh finally said, "Don't let me stop you, Mrs Vlemicks. We only have fifty minutes left to learn about..." she glanced at the board, "...bluebells," she continued, adding, "Please do continue," in an imitation of her teacher.

Mrs Vlemicks chose to ignore this disobedience for the time being and began writing the ingredients to cure hiccups on the board. The students could see she was literally shaking with anger, but what they couldn't see was the wry smile creasing her face as she thought how far she could push school regulations on detention punishments.

One bluebell head, opened;
Three bluebell stalks, split;
One drop of beeswax;
One drop of toad's blood.

Henry looked across from the table near the front of the class and Niamh replied with a triumphant thumbs-up and an indication of an explosion with her hands. Henry laughed uncontrollably until Mrs Vlemicks whirled around to look directly at Niamh who, to her surprise, was looking straight ahead with quill poised.

"SILENCE!" she yelled. "This is important. This remedy can be used for a number of things. You should practise preparing it tonight. Not only is it the only documented cure for hiccups, it also repels Dhoohey attacks and, as a side note, is excellent for cleaning obstinate stains on your teeth." She stood for a second scanning the room, ensuring she had their full attention, then returned to the board.

A knock came at the door. As it creaked open, the belly of a short, round woman entered. This was slowly followed by her chest, head and, finally, behind. Mrs Triana was the school secretary and general dogsbody. She did, however, see herself as the most vital cog in the school mechanism. Without her, as she often told anyone who would listen, the school wouldn't run at all. Surprisingly, Niamh got on well with Mrs Triana. She also held the keys to the entire school and, more importantly, the chemics rooms and was easily bribed to look the other way when food was involved.

"Ahem," she cleared her throat. "Sorry to interrupt, Gertrude." There was a small murmur of laughter throughout the classroom. Mrs Triana gave a small sideways smile and a quick glance at the students and it was clear the revelation of the most hated teacher's first name would mean weeks of ammunition.

"Would it be possible for me to see Niamh for a while?"

"Concerning?" Mrs Vlemicks barked back, knowing full well that Mrs Triana wouldn't know. Asking questions like this often put the secretary back in her place.

"Erm, it's an important matter with the headmistress."

Niamh darted a worried look at Henry, who shrugged and bit a nail in response.

"Such as?" Mrs Vlemicks asked.

"Erm, can't help you with that one, I'm afraid. Top secret, hush-hush and all that. I'm assured it's urgent, though."

"In that case, why are you lolling around? Niamh, hurry along, please. Quick quick, don't dawdle. You will report straight back to me afterward, please, and no hanging around."

Niamh collected her things and strolled toward the door. Although she appeared confident on the outside, she was sure she'd been discovered. Maybe the headmistress had found it. What if it went off on the headmistress? This couldn't be any worse. For the first time since Samhein last year, Niamh was actually scared of being disciplined – or, even worse, her mother finding out.

Niamh had always been scared of her mother. She both admired her and hated her for who she was, and, one day, she would take her place. When she became Witche Qwein, she'd make sure her daughter wasn't singled out. Her daughter could have friends, lots of friends. Children wouldn't be scared to talk to her for fear of upsetting her; they would be climbing over each other just to see her. She strolled slowly down the wooden staircase and out into the warm morning air. Moisture still clung to the trees and cobwebs overhanging the courtyard from the wicked storm the night before. Unlike the other children in her class, she knew the reason for the regular monthly storms even in the hotter times of the year, and knew her mother had been at Witches Mount again the night before.

Niamh was glad of Mrs Triana's ample build at this moment. Her short body waddled slowly over the cobbled floor like a duck. *The longer this takes*, she thought, *the longer I have to think of an excuse.* They crossed to the north side of the courtyard. The huge circular structure of the headmistress's building basked in the heat. Constructed from white stone and marble, it had several levels of windows rising to the top, which Niamh had seen the inside of many times.

She had always known that being the only daughter and heir to the Witche throne would mean people wouldn't want to upset her. She would one day become the most powerful Witche in the Kingdom of Ysrir and be feared across all the land. She began to think, though, that maybe this time she'd gone too far.

As they approached the entrance, Niamh looked up, fascinated by the impressive architectural work evident in the ornate structure. Gold pillars rose to a circular dome to form the entrance. This was an entrance fit for a Qwein. For her.

On entering the hall, Niamh recognised once more the distinct difference between the rest of the school and this building. This building was grande. Majestic. There were statues of gold, coloured stained-glass windows and a marble staircase shooting upward from a central spot within the entrance and twirling off to all sorts of wonders as it disappeared from view on the first floor.

Although her mother technically owned this building and everything in it, she couldn't help but wonder why their home wasn't as magnificent as this. What value did her mother see in living in a normal house like everyone else?

She began to climb the south-westerly staircase. It seemed to rise forever and, unsurprisingly, Mrs Triana stayed at the bottom claiming she had 'important work to attend to. Vital if the school is to function properly'. *Yeah right*, Niamh thought.

As she approached the uppermost limits of the building, shafts of light speared across the entrance below and intersected at different intervals to create a network of coloured beams. She watched the light as it shifted between every colour of the rainbow, illuminating the dancing dust motes below. Niamh thought of a giant spider that could spin a web of colour, then shook her head at the thought as she stumbled after the top step, expecting another.

She tentatively knocked on the large, rounded mahogany door. Niamh was sure that centuries of untold history and discipline had gone on behind this door.

"Do come in," a voice from within called. This was an icy, elderly voice that would jolt you awake, screaming, in the middle of the night. It was a voice you would imitate when telling stories of a haunted castle in the northern lands. A voice that probably belonged to a warm, friendly character, but as a child you wouldn't notice.

The door creaked as she pushed it open. Ahead of her

lay a curved room that Niamh always thought of as being inside a quarter segment of a ring. The floors were wooden and the walls dark. Streams of light intruded from openings high above, illuminating objects that Niamh didn't recognise or understand – and wouldn't want to, for that matter. She wanted a quick punishment and to be on her way. The room felt oppressive and somber, and reminded Niamh of the smell of old bread.

She edged forward, her mind still working on conjuring an excuse. As she approached the desk, it became clear that another person was in the room. The top of a head sprang into view over the green, high-backed leather chair. Niamh heard sniffling from the direction of the head and received no acknowledgement. She knew before she even got close that it was her mother.

This was far worse than she thought.

Chapter 3

"Come. Come now," said the headmistress. The headmistress was nearing retirement, Niamh guessed, from a date on the initiation painting behind her desk. She estimated her to be about 250 years old, maybe even a little older. Her fine, white, wispy hair seemed unnaturally long for how delicate it appeared, and her eyes seemed to focus on two places at once. Her skin had an almost white complexion and her lips were taut and wrinkly.

"Do sit down," she said, pointing authoritatively at a cushioned stool. The order didn't leave Niamh with any hint of an option. She edged around the chair where her mother sat and tentatively took a seat.

"Hello, Mother," she dared, scanning her face for signs of anger.

"Good morning, child," Magatha replied with a sad, distant look.

"Well," said the headmistress, rubbing her bony hands together, causing what Niamh could only think of as unwanted friction. "I think..."

"Can I just say I haven't done anything wrong? All right, I had some Herby-lanex that I shouldn't have taken from the chemics storeroom, but it was only for a joke. It's Mrs Vlemicks, she..."

"Wait. Wait, child. I know nothing of this," the headmistress said, waving a hand dismissively.

"What you get up to down there is for your individual tutors to deal with. If Mrs Vlemicks can't handle a bit of charm defence or, at worst, spell reversal, she's in the wrong profession."

Niamh let out an immediate sigh of relief until the headmistress spoke again.

"No, child, what we need to speak of is of far greater importance than that."

A chill came over Niamh. The room, if it was at all possible, took on a whole new level of darkness. The walls felt as though they were contracting. Magatha stood, looked down at Niamh, and made her way to the window.

Niamh noticed out of the corner of her eye the old hunched-over cleaner who was practically part of the furniture in the headmistress's office. The cleaner moved off through the connecting door into the next room muttering under his breath.

Magatha looked back at Niamh, who was now looking at her nails at arm's length, already struggling to remain interested in what was going on – or at least probably giving that impression to her mother.

"Niamh, what do you know about the history of Ysrir?" asked Magatha.

"Err," she attempted, hoping somebody would fill the gap.

"It is not likely you will have covered it in past class," Magatha began, looking at the headmistress as though for confirmation of this fact and permission to continue. She received a subtle nod.

"You may have heard many myths about the formation of Ysrir. The common myth is often told as a bedtime story. I remember telling it to you as a youngster. The myth involves the ancient Petu Giants, who fought long hard battles many centuries ago. The Petu Giants, it is said, were the first living, colonial beings to walk on Earth." Magatha looked toward the window again and Niamh got the impression she was avoiding eye contact with her.

"These wars were brutal and persistent. Many countries were destroyed and divided due to the constant trampling and fighting on delicate pieces of land. Seas covered soil; new islands were formed," Magatha said as Niamh looked on in puzzlement.

She continued, "The gods were angered by this constant disrespect for their land and its creators. The Giants fell, and the gods punished them for their actions and banished them from the edge of the Earth. From that day, the gods sent a protector to watch each of the eight newly formed continents. These gods would no longer be allowed to return to the heavens but would be eternally grateful they were chosen by the One to protect his new creations."

Niamh looked at her mother and then the headmistress. She assumed the confusion was clear on her face as she began to wonder about the meaning of all this. She'd never seen her mother in this way. As disappointed as she had been in the past with the fact that they never really got on, she had never been in a room for this long and barely made eye contact. *And what is this she is waffling on about?* Niamh thought.

"Please, Niamh," the headmistress began. "I understand this is confusing, but please pay attention to what your mother has to say. It is vital that you listen." The headmistress looked at Magatha and nodded for her to continue, giving her a wrinkled wink with her left eye.

"Thank you, Bertha. Niamh, please concentrate. This is important. Each land had a god. He would always be there to protect the people of that land. Ysrir was blessed with the God of the Sea, or Manannán mac Lir, as He has been called.

"Manannán was able to protect our island from attack by conjuring a great mist. He could make men multiply in number and strength by a thousand times, and no force could defeat the races of Ysrir who lived peacefully then. The island was strong but the people were complacent. They thought, as did the people of every other land, that they would never be attacked. Until the men from the north, known as Norsemen, came with their god of fire and wind and began invading our shores.

"Manannán was unprepared when the Norse god attacked him, blowing his mist out to sea. The Norse Sorcerers made easy targets of our ill-prepared men and then our country was in enemy hands."

Niamh had, at this point, become visibly interested and was sitting on the edge of her stool as she leant forward balancing on two of the rickety legs.

"Well, what happened?" Niamh demanded. "What happened to our God?"

"He brought in a storm like none ever seen before or since. The skies parted and huge bolts of lightning crashed down as far as you could see in an attempt to drive the invaders away. Eventually the two gods clashed above the coastline at the furthest point north on Ysrir. Fire met thunder; rain met wind. Cyclones spun around them both as they clashed a hundred feet in the air. Waves rose over the land; fire burnt the trees below. Eventually Manannán couldn't hold on any longer and the Norse god struck him with his mighty axe, banishing our God from Ysrir forever."

"But gods can't die," Niamh said knowingly.

"It was thought that he vanished forever to roam the lands between this world and the next. He was paying the price for failing his duty to the Creator. It has come to light recently, though, that this may not have been the case. A human woman was fleeing the city of Nalbacca in the north when the invading force conquered the land. Her village was burnt and her people slaughtered.

"She fled to the hills in the hope of finding a safe shelter; somewhere she could hide from the Norsemen. On the cliff tops she saw a sight I believe no one else can claim to have seen. She witnessed a battle of almighty force, a battle between two ferocious gods. The sky is said to have lit up with the clashing forces of energy, a ferocious glow above the clouds that left her standing in awe and shielded by an overhanging rock face.

"At the point when Manannán was struck by the mighty axe, it is thought he was not banished from the Earth but from his physical form. At the exact moment he was struck with the axe he had summoned a huge lightning strike to end the battle once and for all. As he was hit, one of these bolts went through his body and struck the top of the cliff, sending a bolt of fierce blue light down through the rocks and into the necklace the woman wore. She was thrown out a hundred yards or so toward the edge of the cliff and left unconscious. The ground cracked where the thunder had hit and the land slowly began to creak apart over time, leaving a newly formed island just offshore.

"It is now believed Manannán's spirit is still very much alive within that necklace, Niamh. The woman survived the lightning bolt only through the protection of the necklace, having to wait until low tide to escape back to shore. It is also said she had good luck from that day on. She lived until the age of one hundred and thirteen, passing the necklace on to her eldest daughter as a good luck heirloom on her deathbed."

"One hundred and thirteen isn't old," Niamh jumped in.

"You have to remember this is a long time ago. People didn't have the resources we have today. These were human tribes. Few knew how to control the power of the land back then and people lived much shorter lives."

Niamh already knew a lot about humans. She actually had human blood on her father's side of the family – a fact known to no one except Niamh, her mother and Henry. Niamhson, her father, had a great-great-great-grandfather, Eubert, who chose to stay behind in a Witche village many years ago.

Eubert had strayed from his settlement when hunting and was ravaged by a bear. He woke, delirious, deep in the forest. Having no food or water, and no sense of direction, he'd wandered for two days until he came across an enormous wall of nothing – a blurred, swaying meadow beyond.

'It was hard to focus on, but there was definitely something there,' her mother had told her when recalling stories that she had been told. 'You couldn't see it unless you tried hard to look through,' she had said.

Curious about this phenomenon, Eubert sat to rest and began watching the polished wall as he ate churraberries from under a nearby rock. He threw the berries at the wall and could see them landing on the other side. They appeared redder, juicer – bigger, even – through the barrier.

Getting to his feet he walked to within inches of the surface and reached out. As his hand pierced it he was sucked through into a world full of magic and mystery.

He thought it a dream at first, but soon became settled, pretending to be dumb so as to not give away his origin. For six years he did not speak a word until, by chance, he met Lina the Witche Qwein, who soon became his wife.

Eubert managed to get by, and settled with the Witches. He learned a basic understanding of the magic of the land, but it was always weak with him. However, many lacked the skill and wisdom to wield it much better than he did.

Niamh had always been taught to keep her family ties a secret. The scandal that a Royal family had ties with another race would cause outrage. Most witches thought humans to be extinct, in any case.

Niamh remembered the shame she had felt in her past class exam when she read, 'Describe, using no more than one roll of parchment (both sides), how the Witches of around 100 AF were victimised by a race known as humans. For three extra points, describe three things that differ between our own people and the now-extinct humans.'

Niamh's mind appeared to have wandered, and this couldn't have gone unnoticed by the headmistress, who was looking at her sternly.

"But why did the Norse god attack the people here? Surely they are supposed to protect everyone?" Niamh said a little too enthusiastically but, the truth was, she was now interested in the story her mother was telling her.

"It is believed the Norse empire began invading its

neighbouring island, Gueterra, soon after King Dhogan came to the throne. The Norse kingdom is strong and, as I've told you before, consists of many evil Sorcerers," Magatha told Niamh.

"It is also now thought that the Norse protector, their god, was easily corrupted by the thought of being the only god on Earth, a god to rule all mankind. It seems even gods have a lust for power."

"Magatha, I think it is time," the headmistress prompted, looking at both the time and the interested look Niamh could no longer hide.

"Very well. Niamh," said Magatha, "as you well know, part of my duty is to consult with the Spirit of Seirim. I have even taken you up to Witches Mount a few times recently.

"I have seen many visions over the past six or seven months. Much of what I have told you this morning has been shown to me in pieces up on Witches Mount and from ancient scriptures we have recently discovered beneath Rusalimum Cathedral.

"The last few visits have been different, and in one of the more recent visits I was shown the reason for these visions, and the reason for me being told this information. It seems fate has drawn you into this story. I was shown a vision of you, Niamh. You have been selected by the gods to find this necklace. Once you have found it you must go and find the small island that was created when Manannán was imprisoned.

"The gods have shown this because it is what must be done. It is your destiny. If you are successful, this will return our Sea God to His rightful place and restore links with the gods that have since been severed.

"By following your destiny down this path I have foreseen you as a great leader; the greatest leader we have known."

Niamh sat there for a few seconds, mulling over what she had just heard. *If this is to be my destiny*, she thought, *I cannot fight it.* If there was one thing her mother had taught her, it was that you always ended up doing what you were meant to do, no matter how it manifested itself. *The greatest leader on Earth*, Niamh thought, and couldn't help smiling.

The bell rang in the courtyard below – a muffled ringing sound, then children's feet trampling in the playground below, along with the occasional 'poof!' from someone practising a charm without permission.

"Niamh. Niamh, dear. There may be a lot of people who have learned of this item. It may even be out of our reach already. Seirim only knows what would happen if the Sorcerers got hold of it. If anyone learns how to wield the power of a god, then they could create an army impossible to stop. A god's power without the wisdom and foresight of a god could be deadly. This journey will not be easy. You must leave at sun break tomorrow. I will pack your things tonight, then we shall talk some more," Magatha instructed.

"We cannot allow the Sorcerers to gain more power than they already have. After the old battles, the gods had to devise another way to keep peace throughout our land. They created barriers – not physical barriers, but spiritual barriers. It is impossible for a person to cross a barrier line into another race's land without being split from their spirit. This is what Eubert encountered but somehow bypassed. The gods thought it impossible for different races to mix in peace and harmony, so separated them many moons ago."

"What about the wars, though? How have the Sorcerers

been attacking us?" Niamh asked.

Magatha turned again to the window and dropped her head. "We do not know, Niamh. I have passed these boundaries myself many times before, but to do it on the scale that the Sorcerers have done is inconceivable. It took me days of preparation to cross the borders myself and visit the human settlements for research. The Sorcerers seem to be able to bring whole armies through the line. Whether they hold great knowledge of the land's magical powers or they have discovered a weakness, we do not know."

"Is that why we have never attacked them?" Niamh asked.

"Yes and no. We are not aggressive people. The magic we have should be used sparingly. It is not for violence. We have learned costly lessons from the stories of our ancestors. However, it is the reason why all the fighting has occurred just beyond the Craggy Peaks. That is the point where our land crosses to theirs."

Niamh began to picture the heavy defences surrounding her village and strict rules on leaving the outer walls and, now more than ever, was grateful for them. Around Rusalimum stood a heavily guarded, fifteen-foot wooden wall, a half mile line of wooden spikes followed by a final outer perimeter fence. It had always been forbidden to leave the first wall of the village. Witches were taught that an unseen force kept their race within their grounds. Stories of monsters and beasts so horrible they couldn't be described, lying in wait outside, were always thought of as just that - scary stories. They never dared prove them false, though.

"Niamh," Magatha said "It is important that you do not mention this to anyone, even Henry, for now. We will talk more tonight. Now you must return to your normal day."

"Yes, Mother," said Niamh, still a little in shock but ecstatic at the chance to go and explore. She had always wanted to go on a real adventure. Now she could.

"Niamh, we have much to prepare here now. Why don't you go down and play with your friends? You don't have to worry about any homework you receive today," explained the headmistress.

"OK." Niamh's eyes briefly lit up as though she was five again. Niamh hated homework and rarely got a good grade for her attempts.

Although Mrs Vlemicks would hate to admit it, Niamh thought she could actually be quite a talented student if she could put her mind to it, but initiative had never been her strongest point.

When most would picture the strings of ancient symbols that combine to create power spells, she would rely on the ways of humans. Niamh's mother had always put it down to the human blood in her.

Witches didn't rely on the land's magic to solve every problem, but had started to use it more and more for trivial tasks. Magic was once restricted to battle and to solve tasks deemed to be impossible without its help.

Whilst it was far more common now to use it day to day, she'd found, to her disappointment, that the majority of her classes so far at St Guinevere's had taught her nothing more than herb and potion mixing and learning how to channel premonitions.

Magatha looked at her, and Niamh realised her mother probably didn't see her as a little girl anymore. If she completed this journey successfully, she would be Witche

Qwein.

Niamh was dismissed, and she rose to leave the room, a lot more dazed than she had entered. She looked back to find her mother and the headmistress deep in conversation over a map that had appeared on the desk. The meeting had passed; now was not the time for questions. As she came out into the huge circular landing, she walked around the edge to a window overlooking the courtyard to watch the children playing. Looking out she saw a huge blast of purple smoke blow the doors to main hall open. This was shortly followed by Mrs Vlemicks with hair singed, face smudged, clothes ruffled and nerves on edge.

"Yes!" Niamh cheered, punching the air as Mrs Vlemicks slowly staggered to her feet, steadied by three students.

However pleased Niamh was with her latest prank, she had more pressing matters on her mind, and she descended the staircase to head for lunch and tell Henry everything.

From the shadow of a recessed doorway on the top floor, the hunched cleaner watched Niamh descend to the courtyard.

Chapter 4

Oddvard crossed the Great Chamber at speed and pulled his armour vest off over his head as he moved. The clatter of the overlapping iron rings echoed through the halls as he threw them to his feet. The protective runes shimmered in the distorted moonlight from the large, semi-opaque coloured glass high above.

He moved to the upper balcony as the smell of fresh fire and sweat carried from the outer ward where Oddvard looked down. Outside the curtain wall, a thin strip of water separated the castle from the mainland.

His men would need their rest. They had fought well. He looked out for several minutes, entranced by the flickers of light and occasional bouts of laughter.

He had returned from the damp, muddy recesses of the battle field after a fortnight's campaign to the familiarity of home, the neighbouring town to the north having been seized with relative ease.

As he began to untie his thick black wolf hide under-padding, he scowled at the speckled blood marks on the tough, leathery surface and tried to rub them off with the back of his hand.

Oddvard belonged to the Onjanaha family of Sorcerers and had been ruler of Ysrir for just over a decade when his father was killed by Witches.

Oddvard had his father's bone structure, although lacked some of his other characteristics. He had long blond hair similar to his father and countless generations before him who had strong golden locks. He did, though, have olive-green eyes bathed in shadow from his overhanging brows where the rest of his ancestors had vivid blue eyes. He took pride in his beard, keeping it much neater than the warriors that fought beside him. All in all, it was said that Oddvard was a good specimen of a man – a fine ruler. He had proved himself many times in battle but had yet to rid his land of Witches and avenge his father's death.

His father had told him before the Great War how the family line of Kings must continue until they were rid of the disease that was Witchecraft. Oddvard hung his head with shame as he remembered his father's words and thought of his own son, Jorgan.

Jorgan was anything but fit to be King. He wasn't even fit to be called a warrior – or a Sorcerer even. He shook his head and looked out over the crashing waves below. He felt refreshed by the cool sea air after his travels.

It was said that the Sorcerers had lived among many races in the past, eliminating them one by one due to their inferiority. They now lived in solitude, as they had been forbidden to leave their own territory for centuries. This angered Oddvard greatly, as his people were sea-faring warriors yet were unable to venture further than a couple of miles from shore.

He stood silent, listening to the crash of waves interspersed with joyous, celebratory sounds from the town below. He longed for battle at sea, the crisp spray of the ocean on his face, the panicked screams of sea men who know they are soon to be defeated. He could picture the enemy now, trying to get past his great line of sea defences: the several thousand wooden stakes driven into the sea bed and the hundreds of logs that had been carefully and laboriously laid out centuries ago by the people who built his village, built his castle. What was the point? He longed to have been born in those times, for he had never felt the real fury of the open sea himself.

'I still rule the land, though,' he said aloud to no one in particular as he thought of the battle he had just won. They had dared to question his decisions as a leader and paid the price for betrayal.

Witches were regarded as a disease to Ysrir, relying on the same power of the land to control their magic. The Sorcerers had discovered over time that the more the Witches called upon the magic, the weaker it became. As the land's magic diluted, it had become harder to control and would eventually, some feared, abandon them.

The destruction of the Witche race was necessary for his own to survive. Without the magic of the land, his people would become weak and, one day when the gods allowed, open to war. Oddvard had mastered his father's technique and could break the age-old barrier at Craggy Peaks, leaving his army free to attack the unprepared Witche village when he felt his army was ready again.

He dropped his scarred padding to the floor and began to dress again in preparation for his meal, thinking of his many strategies to attack his most hated – and secretly feared – enemy. The last attack had left the Witches on the back foot, but the sheer number of fatalities and the fact that they had managed to kill his father, one of the most feared warriors there had been, sowed a seed of doubt and indecision in his mind. It was this indecision that his warriors had obviously begun to pick up on.

Oddvard sat to eat his *náttmál*, or night meal as the younger warriors had begun calling it. An array of delicately crafted bowls and drinking cups were laid out ahead of him and he sighed when a knock came at the door as he reached for his first serving.

"What?" he said in a disgruntled voice.

A boy not far from manhood entered the room dressed in large, baggy brown trousers and a white blouse, his face patchy with acne.

"What is it, boy?" Oddvard sighed, his impatience clear in his body language. The boy must have recognised this and shifted uneasily on the spot.

"Sorry for the intrusion, Your Majesty. I hear good news greets us from your travels?" the boy enquired, clearly attempting to lift the King's mood.

"You hear correct. Hundi is defeated. I have gained control of his village and his weapons are now ours. What is the meaning of this intrusion?" asked Oddvard, playing with a chunk of horsemeat, the white residue from the soap dish it had been boiled in still evident.

"A visitor, Your Highness. He says he has information of the utmost importance."

Oddvard teased himself with the warm, succulent steak, letting it hang inches from his open mouth before dropping it back on his plate. He had gone half a month without proper food, so a moment more wouldn't kill him.

"Very well," he groaned.

After a long, low bow during which his nose seemed to nearly touch the floor, the boy scurried out of the room to fetch the visitor. Several minutes later he returned with a short man who hobbled into view and gave a quick bow of his head, his wrinkled face showing his years.

"Trioso, what brings you here at this hour to disturb my return? I presume it is important to have crossed back over," Oddvard stated, his appearance betraying his true exhaustion.

"I bring news of the Witche Qwein, Your Majesty. Valuable news," the spy said, cracking out a nook in his spine from crouching so much in his disguise and feeling the aches and pains from his journey home.

Oddvard stroked his chin and stared at Trioso, eyes seeming to pierce his very soul. Oddvard had many spies throughout the kingdom, and he seldom liked any of them. It was rare to hear useful information, but with his potential war at a critical stage there could be useful insights to learn.

"Go on," Oddvard demanded, sitting up attentively in his chair.

"I bring news of great power, Your Majesty. A power sought by the Witches. The power of the gods."

With this revelation Oddvard's eyes lit like dry wood to a flame. Since his ancestors came to Ysrir many centuries before, they had sought great power. It was Dhogan, the first recorded King of the Onjanaha blood line, who brought his people here from the north. Not since Dhogan had powers so great been wielded by men.

"Tell me of this power," demanded Oddvard. "How do I obtain it?" His lips now dry with anticipation, he attempted to moisten them with his even drier tongue.

"A necklace, Your Majesty. The tale tells of a necklace that holds the spirit of the Sea God, imprisoned after the great battle."

"And this necklace... do the Witches have it in their possession?" asked Oddvard with an alarmed look on his face.

"No, Your Majesty. They have selected a child to search for it. A child who is the heir to the Witche throne, you may be interested to know."

A wry smile flashed across Trioso's face, and Oddvard knew Trioso was pleased with himself for obtaining this valuable information.

"*Really?*" Oddvard said. "That is interesting. I take it you know the whereabouts of this necklace?"

Trioso shrank, his back arching in an attempt to blend into the background as he so often did in the Witche school. "No, Your Majesty, I do not. I don't believe even they know," he attempted.

"No! How can you tell me of this power and dangle it before me only to snatch it away a moment later? You will find this information for me and send it by raven as soon as you do."

Oddvard crossed the room and opened a small wooden panel in the floor, the old metal bolts squealing as he scraped them back and forth to get the door free.

After a few seconds Trioso heard a small flutter of wings, and an enormous charcoal-coloured bird rose and perched on Oddvard's arm, its black, empty eyes making him feel even smaller.

"This is Kallarar. He is of Royal blood and is bound to

mine. You can take him with you and send him back when you have more news."

"But what if you are at war, Your Highness? What if it is important?"

"Do not worry yourself with trivial matters. He will find me. But do not believe your job is finished with this snippet of information. I need you to give this to the Qwein," Oddvard said as he passed a small object to Trioso.

"He will be watching you," he finished with a nod toward the raven. These last words sent shivers through Trioso's marrow and a harsh shriek from Kallarar heightened the chill.

"As you wish, Your Majesty," said Trioso, bowing his head as far as he could. The raven left Oddvard's arm and swooped to Trioso's lowered shoulder, razor-sharp talons piercing his skin. Trioso flinched at this contact but the bird remained firm.

Trioso looked up to see Oddvard already walking away, flicking his wrist to suggest he had taken enough of his time.

"Thank you, Your Majesty. I will not disappoint you," Trioso offered as he left the room. Kallarar looked back at its master as if awaiting any further instruction.

Oddvard sat before his food, now uninterested in its tepid goodness. His heart's desire for power was far greater than his body's need for nourishment.

He knew that this item could ensure dominance for centuries – millennia, even. He looked up at the figures carved in the ceiling, the mountainous waves towering over battling

Sorcerers and, in the background, a figure of flames brandishing his almighty axe for all to see. His people had always had control over the sea as far as war was concerned. With this new power he would at last feel the freedom of the waves. It was a power he could manipulate to his advantage. No longer would the gods prevent his domination. He would become as powerful as the gods himself.

Oddvard had to know more of this necklace. He had to consult the runes. He didn't know how or why the runes worked, but they always did.

Something good the gods have managed, he thought.

He unhooked a burgundy velvet pouch from a spike on the wall and loosened the golden rope. He placed his hand in the bag and let the small spheres, made of ancient hawthorn trees, roll through his fingers.

Slowly closing his eyes, he let his mind go blank and concentrated on the question burning deep in his heart: "What power will this necklace unleash?"

He opened his eyes and tipped the contents of the pouch onto the cold, grey-stone floor. They bounced in all directions and he occasionally glimpsed the amber glow of Sorcerer rune marks as they spun to a stop with a hollow-sounding clink.

The result was a mass of wooden pebbles forming a perfect circle with three rune stones left face up in the middle – the runes of the three sisters who spun and weaved the fates of the universe: Urðr, Verðandi and Skuld. These runes represented necessity and showed a suggestion of the future.

Oddvard kneeled closer to decipher the meaning and, as the amber glow subdued the colour in his cheeks, he froze with the sudden realisation of what the runes had told him.

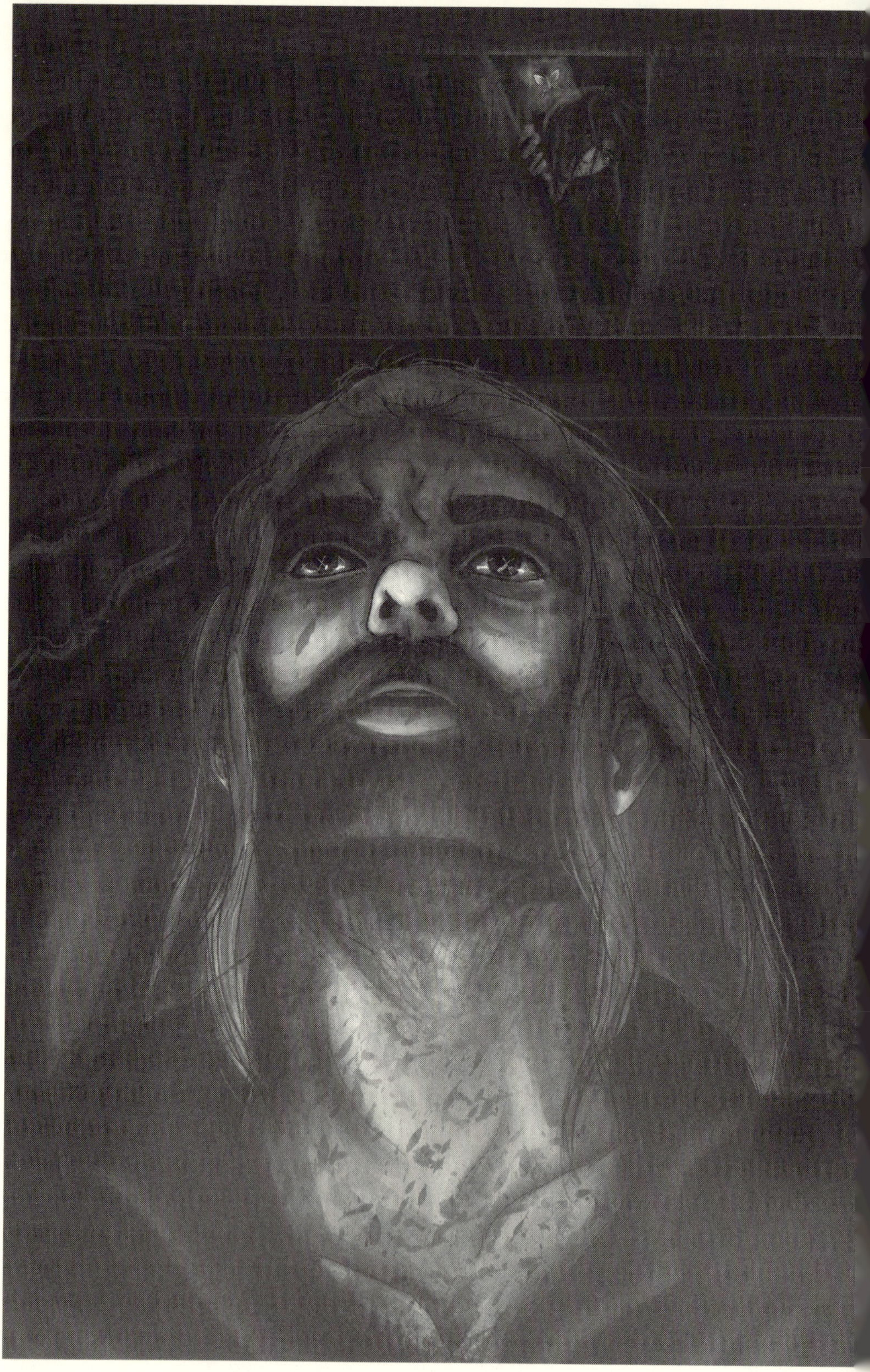

Chapter 5

High in the rafters, through the tiniest of cracks, someone moved suddenly and pressed their back against the cold stone wall. Had he been seen? He was sure for a second his father had noticed the light shift on the floor as he'd moved across the tiny gap he'd been spying through.

Jorgan's heart pummeled the inside of his ribs. He knelt against the rough wooden beams, petrified. His sunken features pulsed in and out of focus in the light of the tiny fluttering butterfly glowing beside his left ear.

He held his hand up to the insect and pinched his thumb and finger over it. It abruptly vanished in a puff of yellow smoke. He sat for a moment longer and decided he needed to know if he'd been spotted.

If his father knew he had been listening in on private meetings, the punishment would be unimaginable. He was obviously already a disappointment to his father, but snooping behind his back would add another level of shame. Jorgan knew he couldn't bear not knowing any more.

He took a deep breath and crawled back over to the gap. As he lay on his front and squinted through into the main hall, he saw his father kneeling, head in hands, over the sacred runes. What could he possibly be doing? The muffled memories of the conversation Jorgan had just overheard with his father and Trioso came flooding back. In the panic of thinking he had been spotted, he had completely forgotten what he had overheard. The story of the necklace certainly intrigued him.

He knew instantly that he couldn't have been spotted or his father would have been storming up the outer stairs to find him and punish him. The last time his father had punished him, he'd been left severely scarred. Jorgan had done as much as he could to restore the skin on his left cheek, but there was still an obvious tightness as his skin stretched over his scrawny skull.

Jorgan knew he was a peculiar-looking boy, and his scarring added an even creepier aspect to his hollow features. He wore dark baggy clothing and his long dark hair had been brown in an attempt to cover his scars. He seemed completely unable to grow hair on the left side of his face now, so tended to shave any facial hair as soon as it grew, making him even less like his father and the typical image of a warrior.

He had recently turned sixteen, a fact that his father had failed to notice. His father was Oddvard, King and ruler of Ysrir. "Some ruler," Jorgan muttered to himself as he climbed out onto the outer staircase and felt a sharp gust of wind lift his scruffy black hair.

He tried to make his way to his tower workshop in the farthest east point of the castle without being spotted. Everyone in the kingdom knew who he was, not for his ancestral bloodline but for his disfigured appearance.

Jorgan had not been a happy child. His mother had died giving birth to him, and his sister had been murdered when he was only a baby.

His father had always blamed him for his mother's tragic death and would constantly remind him on the rare occasions they did speak of what a wonderful woman she had been and what a disappointment Jorgan was to the world.

Jorgan also had an older brother, Hemel, but Jorgan was glad he ruled a neighbouring town and rarely saw him. Whether it was for the same reasons as his father, or simply in an attempt to please his oh-so-great-almighty King, Hemel treated Jorgan in much the same way: with contempt and disgust.

Jorgan made his way through the towering arches leading around the courtyard toward his tower workshop. This was his only retreat in a kingdom of people who pitied him, sniggering behind his back and making cruel jokes just out of earshot. He had no friends and had even taken to staying in his workshop day after day. He knew his father wouldn't notice anyway.

Eventually he reached the tower and climbed the outer spiral staircase three stone steps at a time. His mind raced at what he had overheard. What had the sacred runes told his father that had left him in such a state?

As he reached the large wooden door, he waved his hand past the head of a marble raven protruding from the wall and its mouth fell open. He placed his index finger inside and the door swung open. How he loved his little magic toys!

His father ridiculed him, often in public, about wasting his life. He should be in battle, living up to the reputation his ancestors had paved the way for with their own blood. Jorgan was much happier tinkering in his workshop with his many magical treasures. His knowledge of sorcery reached far beyond most of his father's so-called 'warriors', but his prowess with a weapon, or as a leader, seemed to never have developed.

He sat in his mahogany rocking chair and listened to its mellow creaks and groans as he silently thought about what he had heard. He was already a failure in his father's eyes, so he couldn't possibly make things worse. Anything he could do now to help was bound to work in his favour.

It was settled. Jorgan began hastily packing several of his buzzing toys and gadgets into a satchel. He would find this necklace his father wanted so badly. His father would barely notice him gone and, when he returned, he would be hailed a hero and would finally be seen as the true and rightful heir to the throne.

Jorgan slouched after this brave train of thought and realised that, in all probability, this mission would be a failure too.

Chapter 6

The musty golden light seeped in through the tall, thin windows, causing millions of floating dust motes to jump into action and then disappear again as Magatha stepped in front of the light.

A scrawny shadow grew over Niamh in bed, strangely distorted as it reached the wall. The shift in light caused Niamh to stir after another restless sleep, filled with the recurring nightmares she was now growing used to.

Niamh thrashed her arms as water rushed around her head, white foam bubbling from the power of her splashes.

"No! N...," garbled Niamh as water went up her nose and left her throat raw from coughing. Her head went under again and she kicked out her legs to try and push to the surface. Debris scraped past her sides as she frantically tried to catch a breath. Her lungs were burning and she felt life draining away from her.

"Niamh," she heard. She floated around to see who had spoken and momentarily forgot her shortage of air. She could see no one around and wondered how they had spoken so clearly beneath the icy-cold water.

Light began to dissolve the crystal-clear image like fire eating away at paper as Niamh looked around her room to find her mother stood over her.

"What time is it?" Niamh grunted, rubbing her eyes with the back of her hands.

"Time for breakfast. Are you hungry?" Magatha asked, not waiting for an answer.

What? No argument about getting out of bed? No lecture about the state of her room? She sat up looking puzzled and eyed the figure of her mother as she left her room through the hatch in the floor. Niamh slumped back and looked at the roof. She studied the network of intertwining branches and twigs as her mind raced over her time in the headmistress's office. Had it been a dream? She was sure it had, but a sickly feeling, and her mother's peculiar behavior just now, led her to believe otherwise.

At first, after telling Henry everything, she had thought about what lay ahead. They had all heard stories at school about what lay outside the village walls, and they had definitely all heard the fear in soldiers' voices when speaking of the Sorcerers.

The more she thought about it, the more reluctant she became about going.

When she spoke to Henry she downplayed it as just one of the many duties she was undoubtedly going to face when she would be Qwein anyway, so what was there to worry about? It would be her job.

Despite her blasé front, Niamh was really quite scared. She had spent two hours in the chemics room trying to concoct a solution of braline hermachome 4 to make her ill. She would have gone through with it had she the guts to be throwing up orange mucus and having puffy eyes for five days straight.

In the end she resorted to her initial reaction: excitement. She had asked the old villagers to retell stories of Ysrir the evening before. Whether they were true or not, she cared little. They just added to her anticipation. Now the day had come, she had a fluttery feeling in her stomach.

She swiftly got dressed and brushed her nearly waist-length golden hair before she made her way downstairs. In the kitchen on the large oval table was a satchel, a rolled up sleeping mat and some parchment. On the floor were some other supplies. The room was neither large nor small. It was brightly lit from several windows on all sides and seemed to have too much furniture in it for the space available. Several paintings of Niamh, and a handful of her father, adorned every available space on the walls.

Niamh crossed to the stove in the centre of the room, looked inside, and suddenly turned on her heels.

"Mother?"

"Yes, dear?"

"Is this real? The necklace? The journey?"

Magatha looked down at her feet. "Yes, it is."

"Why can't you come? You're the most powerful Witche there is. Surely it would be better. I mean, I've never even seen the top of Witches Mount!"

"The spirits have spoken, Niamh. You know there is no questioning their predictions. I've seen a lot recently on my visits. There is much trouble with the gods. They selected you for a reason; a reason one day I hope you understand. The gods are angered, Niamh, and I believe this to be the only way."

"But I don't even know where I'm going!" exclaimed Niamh, palming aimlessly through the objects on the table.

"You will, my dear."

My dear? Niamh's head struggled with this new-found affection.

She had never been particularly close to her mother. Things always seemed a struggle. She tried to imagine what things would be like if her father were still alive.

She had never met her father, but always thought of him as her name came from his as tradition stated. Magatha had told her she received news of his death whilst fighting in the Great War. Niamh had often heard her mother crying in the night, but felt it was a private thing that only her mother could understand, so had never disturbed her or asked her about it.

Since the Great War there had been relatively little fighting, with only small forces of Sorcerers being sent through the Craggy Peaks to try and lower the numbers in the Witches Front.

The Witches continued to live in the western corner of Ysrir, the Sorcerers in the east, and several human settlements just north of them – or so her mother told her. Magatha had said she believed the Sorcerers either did not know human settlements still existed or were not interested in them due to their lack of magical abilities.

A welcome stalemate had occurred between the Witches and the Sorcerers as numbers got so low on each side. Activity beyond the great barrier had, however, picked up again over the past few years, and Magatha was extremely worried about how her people would cope.

She had spent many years after the Great War rebuilding her civilisation and gathering her people together in one large stronghold.

Niamh realised that her mother was unravelling the parchment on the table, deep in thought. It was a rough map of Ysrir.

People feared the north. Strange, mysterious things went on up there, and she'd heard many stories. It was rare for anyone to pass much further than the village grounds. It was said that only the most powerful, destined or unlucky could break the great barriers.

"This is where you are heading," a bony finger tapped a point off the map nor'-nor'-east of their home.

"Here, drink this," Magatha said as she handed Niamh a steaming cup from the stove.

"What is it?" Niamh demanded, eyeing the steaming potion suspiciously but holding her nose and drinking it quickly. "It's disgusting! What is it?" she demanded as she coughed and concentrated on trying not to vomit.

"You need it to pass through the great barrier. I have been preparing it for several days now."

"Thanks," Niamh mumbled sarcastically.

"You must pass through the Wooded Realm to get here," Magatha said moving back to the map. "You understand how dangerous this is? The alternative is to travel around but that will add days onto your journey. We cannot waste any time in recovering this object."

"But... but you always told me that place was worse than dangerous. You said all sorts of evil magical creatures lived in there," Niamh stated, her face showing the slightest evidence of concern.

"I know what I told you, Niamh!" Magatha snapped. Although Magatha had lost her temper, Niamh felt more relaxed now, knowing her mother was back to her usual self. Magatha sighed and looked down.

"I'm sorry, I don't want to argue. It has been seen, Niamh. In this world, we choose our own path at our peril. Yours is now laid out before you. You must reach this village before Samhein." Magatha pointed to a small collection of lines and crosses where two diagonal silver lines passed over each other. It is believed this is where the object is. The visions have shown a silver tree, drenched in fog. This tree symbolises the crossed lines of White Witche magic. There is a strong magical force at this point; you must be wary. It is said Witches once ruled this area before they were tortured for their rituals. They were believed to be summoning evil spirits to wreak havoc on the other towns' folk, so I expect they would not react well to magic of any kind. Be careful of your actions around these people. It must be before Samhein as well, remember. This is important, apparently."

Niamh studied the map, her eyes darting from place to place, suddenly aware of the enormous world outside her village walls. She thought of the significance Samhein could have on her destination and why Samhein, a celebration of the dead, would be an important milestone, as her mother clearly thought.

"You must also take the Staff of Light," continued Magatha, holding it outstretched in both palms. Niamh shrank back at the thought of this. The Staff of Light had always been out of bounds. It was meant for the Witche Qwein and the Witche Qwein alone.

She reached out and felt a tingle travel deep into her bones, the surprisingly smooth surface caressing her fingertips.

"I have seen visions that you will need this more than I do. Personally, I've never unlocked its secrets. Some never unlock its secrets. I guess now I am to be one of those people. Hopefully you may have more luck."

"You will still have plenty of time for that. I'm not going to break it, I promise," said Niamh chirpily, missing the fear and anxiety in her mother's voice.

Niamh turned and looked at herself in the mirror. She studied herself holding the staff and thought of the countless fantasies she'd had about showing all the spiteful girls at school. Niamh Retalla, Witche Qwein of Ysrir. The smile on her face faded as she thought of Henry.

Although only of average height for his age, Henry was a surprisingly strong boy. He had fiery ginger hair, a pale face and several freckles on his face.

He had become a great friend as soon as they had caught each other trying to steal humpback mushrooms from Mrs Vlemicks's store cupboard. They had laughed for hours sitting behind the school fence, chewing the humps and spitting out the green shells.

"What about Henry, Mother? Can't I say goodbye?"

Magatha smiled. "You will get plenty of time to talk to Henry. He is waiting for you outside."

Niamh battled with herself for a second, trying to decide whether he was there to wish her farewell or ready to embark on an amazing adventure – this one a lot more real than the stories they had re-enacted in the past.

"Is he... coming as well?" asked Niamh, an erratic butterfly let loose in her stomach.

"Yes, dear. He plays a vital role in this journey and, without him, the fate of our kind is uncertain. You must look out for each other. If something should happen to one of you, I'm afraid the future is uncertain for everyone."

Niamh had already stuffed the items into her satchel and was pulling on her boots, hopping on one foot as she struggled.

Magatha put her hand on her daughter's shoulder as though to calm her. "Niamh, you must get the necklace. Do you understand? Only you can do this. You will know what to do when the time comes."

Niamh's look was now more serious. Her mother was obviously cautious about sending her out of the village.

"Don't worry, Mother. We'll be careful." She reached up and gave her a kiss on the forehead, turned, and walked out of the door, letting it fall shut behind her. Both mother and daughter stood frozen for a second, looking thoughtful, both thinking of the things they wanted to say but couldn't – or wouldn't.

A flicker of guilt was building up inside Niamh. They had never got on, and she knew it wasn't just down to her mother. However, the long spells of time Magatha spent away attending to her kingdom meant Niamh was left to her own devices and found herself lonely, with only Henry to keep her sanity intact.

"I... I love you, Mother," she whispered at the door and headed down the garden path to meet Henry.

He was sitting, legs dangling, on the stone wall beside the gate. Henry was a fairly muscly boy, much stronger than Niamh, and was wearing a fashionable green top with long brown leather gloves. His black cape fell loosely behind him and Niamh couldn't think of a time that she hadn't seen him wearing that very same cape.

Just outside the gate, stood looking away from them, was one of Niamh's mothers' bodyguards.

"Oh no! You're not coming with us are you Abdon?" asked Niamh in a playful tone. Abdon turned his head slightly to acknowledge her without ever taking his eyes away from the town below them and laughed a friendly laugh.

"Only to the outer gates young miss. After that you are on your own," he said.

Niamh suddenly noticed Henry had a silver blade sheathed by his side in a brown leather covering. Weapons such as these had always been banned for students, but they'd got plenty of practice by sneaking into the swashbuckling courts after hours and watching the Witches Front training over the military ground walls.

"Where did you get that?" Niamh gasped.

"Your mother gave it to me. I think she put a cool spell on it as well, because it keeps pulsating. Look, touch it," offered Henry.

Niamh reached out and felt the same tingle that she'd felt from the Staff of Light – the tingle of raw magic. The handle was intricately crafted with bronze and silver intertwining streaks that seemed to slither as though they were liquid.

"She thinks we'll need it?" enquired Niamh, realisation of what dangers may lay ahead flitting through her mind.

"I don't know. She just said 'This is Ghild. It will direct you in times of grave danger. Trust it. It will not let you down'," Henry said in a voice supposedly intended to be Magatha's.

"What do you think that means?" asked Niamh.

Henry studied the length of the blade in the morning light, like a craftsman might study a final piece, and said, "No idea. Looks great, though, doesn't it?"

He leapt from the wall, swung the blade a few times and spun to face Niamh in a playful way. As he turned he felt the blade meet a slight resistance. A shocked Niamh and Henry looked in disbelief as a steaming line, a few inches deep, hissed in the dry stonewall.

"Yikes! It's a bit sharper than I thought," admitted Henry, taking exaggerated care to re-sheath the blade. Abdon let out a small chuckle and shook his head.

After a few seconds spent inspecting the gouge, they turned, Niamh jumping the wall beside the gate as she always did. Henry opened the gate and carefully slid through the gap, his leg now arching slightly away from his sheathed sword.

They headed over the meadow and down the grassy hill into town with Abdon always ahead of them. Out of all the royal bodyguards, Niamh liked Abdon the most. He was friendly but in a distracted, no-nonsense kind of way. She always felt safe around him despite his enormous size and tough image. They crossed the marshes by jumping over the hidden grassy stones. Rusalimum was the capital of Ysrir – at least, capital in the Witches' eyes. The Sorcerers from the east had their own capital, Adiabene.

On nearing the town, they wove in and out of the houses and headed for the town centre and then from there they would head north toward the main village gates and the outer trade circle. The large houses and narrow streets cast gloomy shadows at abstract angles.

They passed through the larger buildings and on past the grande council chambers and then through the inner circle wall out into the outer circle where many men were bustling and trading. Niamh's nose twitched as she inhaled the different spices floating on the air. The streets were crowded but people quickly cleared the way for Abdon and his huge stride allowing Niamh and Henry to follow easily behind him. With some haste they passed through the peasant area, full of small houses constructed from sticks, straw and mud and Niamh felt pity for the poorer people of their town. She knew her mother tried to do a lot for the poorer tradesmen, but they did not seem to approve of her mother and her actions so it sounded like difficult times for them all.

They eventually reached the main village gates and looked back at the safety and comforts of Rusalimum and then out across the void between this gate and the outer gate in the distance, scores of wooden spikes between the two barriers. In the far distance, the Wooded Realm could just be seen as a faint patch of dark green.

"This is as far as I go, young miss," said Abdon, bowing his head and offering an encouraging smile. "I know little of your journey but for you to be being sent outside the safety of the village there must be good cause."

"Well, let's go, then," said Niamh. "I don't like the look of the clouds out there." On the horizon, scores of dense purple-black clouds hung, taunting the clear blue sky stretched out before them.

"Wait," said Henry. "How do we pass the village boundary? I thought people couldn't pass this point." Henry searched the village gates for a hint of magic.

"No, it's further out than that. It's between the hills at Craggy Peaks, I think to the east. I'm not sure where exactly it is to the north. I don't suppose my mother gave you a horrible drink this morning, did she?"

"Yes. How did you know?" asked Henry.

"That is what gets us through the barrier. Some kind of magic potion she has been working on for days."

"Ah, that makes sense," said Henry. "I thought it was just some horrible concoction she had made so I did the polite thing: drank it, smiled, and got out of there quick before she offered me anymore!"

They stood looking into the distance for a while, trying to see what their minds knew was there: a barrier put in place by the gods to stop war and said goodbye to Abdon then made their way through the no-mans-land to the outer wall and gate.

Niamh looked up at the guards manning the towers on each side of the gate. They nodded to her and ordered the men below to open the large wooden gates. *They've obviously received orders from my mother,* she thought. The gate took four men to open by using a series of large wheels connected to chains that Niamh saw passing into the insides of the walls. She didn't pretend to understand how it worked.

After a few seconds of uncertainty, Niamh pulled her

satchel higher up her shoulders as an indication of readiness and crossed the large wooden gates with a skip. Henry jumped between rocks beside her, talking of the adventures they'd enacted in the past.

As much as Niamh longed for adventure, she had a sad, sinking feeling. She leapt onto a rock and looked back at the gate, the rows of spiked defences and the inner wall. She saw smoke rising beyond and imagined what tedious things the people within may be doing, oblivious to the fact she was even outside the village walls. Much uncertainty lay ahead of her but, in a way, she liked it.

Chapter 7

A few hours into the journey, Niamh and Henry could feel the piercing heat from the sun beating down on them. Their clothes stuck to their backs with sweat and their tongues felt glued to the tops of their mouths with dehydration, and they hadn't even got as far as the Wooden Realm yet. The village was just visible in the distance behind them, a snaking path of crumpled grass where they had walked.

"We should rest, Henry," Niamh said, intending it as more of an instruction than a request.

"OK," Henry conceded, shielding his eyes from the sun as he took a sweeping look around. "It is a bit deceptive, really. I thought we'd have reached the woods by now, but we don't look much closer," he said.

Judging by the position of the sun, Henry guessed it to be just after midday. They'd already been travelling for what seemed like an eternity in the sweltering heat. Neither had ever felt so exhausted, the air seeming to thin as they moved further and further away from the safety of their village.

Niamh slumped down in the grass, the shorter blades pricking the back of her calves. She pulled the parchment from her satchel and began to study it, the lines momentarily seeming to shift and move like liquid in the light.

As there was no way of seeing what was above the northern line, it was impossible to know how far they had left to travel.

"Niamh," whispered Henry, slowly shrinking into the ineffective cover of the grass. "Niamh, look," Henry said as he pointed ahead of them.

Niamh looked up toward the trees in the distance, her legs burning with fatigue. All she could see was the towering expanse of trees, the top canopy of leaves looking like dark green clouds suspended by a mass of darkness.

Niamh studied the horizon for a while, baffled at Henry's alarm. As she continued to stare, her eyes focused on something much nearer. Just a few feet ahead of them was what seemed like a huge stretch of water falling from the sky like a waterfall. She could only see it by crossing her eyes slightly and trying not to look at it directly. The line of water continued as far as they could see to either side of them.

As Niamh studied it further, she saw rainbows springing to life all along the horizon as the midday sun shattered the near-invisible waterfall from the sky.

Niamh got to her feet and edged slowly toward it, Henry following behind her. A chilling breeze hit them as they reached it. Niamh felt her arteries begin to freeze shut, a bleak few seconds of death before the chill passed and they both fell to their hands and knees, coughing and wheezing.

"What... what was that?" gasped Niamh, face still pale from the chill.

She grasped at her staff and pushed herself upright, frantically looking around. Henry, who was already on his feet, blade outstretched, muttered, "I don't know. I felt frozen to the spot."

"Like all hope was lost," Niamh added.

Henry didn't reply, but stood there clutching at his chest as though to warm his heart with his hand. A few seconds passed before Niamh realised the water ahead of them had disappeared.

"Where is...?" She began to ask when she turned to look back toward the village. "Look," she whispered as though noise might reverse what had happened.

Henry turned to see that they had passed through the water, yet he was completely dry. He took a step toward it again.

"No! Henry, we've got through once. We don't know what that did to us. I don't want to risk it again. Maybe this is the great barrier," she mused, an inquisitive look on her face. It suddenly seemed so obvious: of course it was the great barrier. What else could generate magic at such scale?

It was said that your soul was a spiritual component of your overall being, and the barrier was supposed to separate your soul from your physical form. She definitely felt like something had tried.

"I think you're right," said Henry. "My grandmother always warned of leaving the walls." Henry always took what his grandmother said as truth. She had raised him after he lost his parents in the Great War – a fact he rarely spoke of.

The sun seemed to have shifted quickly, and the two of them reluctantly set off again toward the eerie shade of the Wooded Realm.

It was almost sunset when they reached the edge of the Wooden Realm, a sickly orange-pink glow just visible over to the left above the tree tops, creating a new, daunting interior of dancing black shapes within.

"My mother said this is the only way," Niamh added to reassure herself. Then she whispered, "I don't like this, Henry," her eyes seeming much larger than before in front of the great expanse.

Henry was slightly shocked at this revelation. He'd always looked up to Niamh. She wasn't scared of anyone or anything except, maybe, her mother.

"We can do this, no problem. I've seen scarier things in Mrs Tollouse's history of magic class. We'll take a look around then set up camp somewhere nearby. I'm hungry now as well," said Henry, suddenly realising he'd not eaten yet today.

"Oh, I know we can do it," said Niamh. "It was you I was worried about. You get lost in my bedroom, so you've no chance in here," she added, giving Henry a cheeky smile. Her smile soon faded as she crossed from the relatively warm plain into the murky darkness of the forest. The sunlight behind seemed unreachable, a place of safety and happiness just out of arm's reach. They also noticed a sudden humming – a constant droning noise that they quickly realised was the tapping of rain on the canopy above.

As they looked back, they realised there was no rain outside and the first signs of dusk were setting in. *She said it was a strange place*, Niamh thought, considering the tales her mother had told her.

They were now confronted by a musky, almost black mass of dead space. The only things the eye could differentiate between were the even darker shapes where trees extended from the ground. Trails of thick roots spread for several feet before ducking underground to suck more life from the soil below.

Niamh felt the hairs on the back of her neck stand up. She might have whimpered with fear had she been on her own.

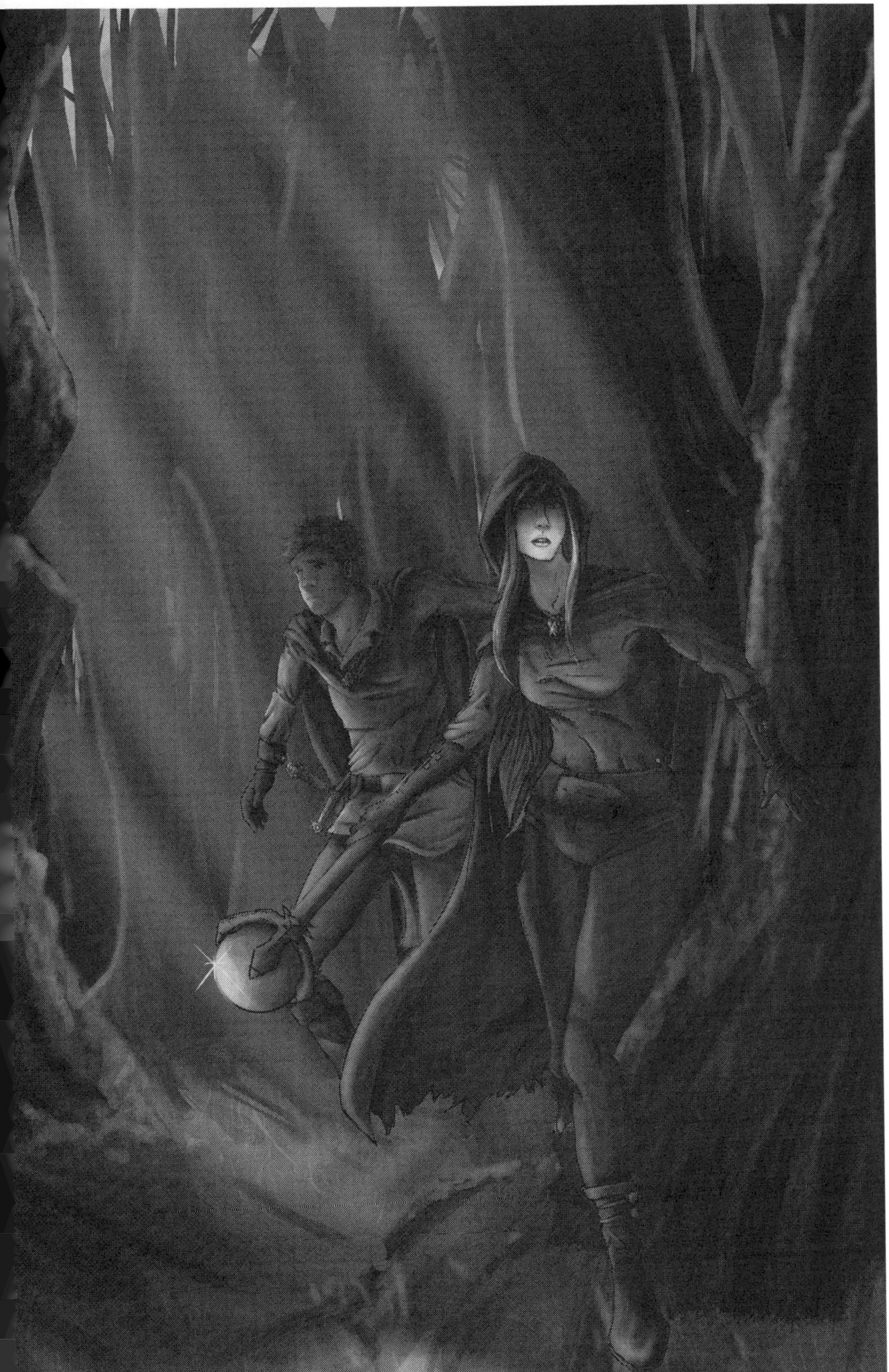

"We'll make camp here, I think," Henry said, selecting an alcove within the base of a tree. It seemed to offer shelter from the occasional drip making it through the thick protection above. "Maybe we'll see more at first light," he offered, spotting the look of concern on Niamh's face even in this dim light.

Henry carefully removed his blade and placed it against the tree trunk, kicking together some dead branches and stones as he did. He began to picture the symbols he needed for a flame spell, but got only sparks due to his exhaustion.

Most children could only muster a few spells and, even by adulthood, the power of the land was often weak in most people. Magic was definitely not a skill to be relied on, but it was a skill nonetheless.

After a few goes, he moodily turned to Niamh for help. He found her slumped between two roots, sound asleep. Accepting defeat, Henry laid his head on his satchel and counted to eight.

Niamh woke with a start, panting and sweating, her vision blurred from the salty beads of sweat stinging her eyes. For a brief moment she waited for the frantic yells of her mother: *'Niamh! Get out of that pit right now and get to school! Don't make me come up there, young lady!'*

After a few seconds she laid her head back down and looked up. Instead of the slanting roof of her attic room, she saw an almost endless expanse of grey. A sudden realisation washed over her, and she sat bolt upright to look for Henry, her head still swimming with images from her nightmare.

It was a nightmare she'd had many times before, from which she'd wake, trying to decipher what was real and what came from the dark recesses of her mind – a mind in which she was drowning, tepid water seeping into her lungs as she fought desperately for a second's more breath, an extra moment of life as her lungs cried for air.

Wiping her brow, she scanned her surroundings, the sleep in her eyes occasionally blurring her view. Light speared randomly around her, dissecting the cold monochrome surroundings. She soon realised that Henry was gone. The blade and his things had also vanished. She was suddenly aware of the fact that she was alone, with unknown dangers all around her – dangers that may have taken Henry already.

She grabbed her things and headed for the edge of the wood, fearful that her companion had set off home, scared of what lay ahead. After a few steps, she heard shouting from behind her.

"Niamh! NIAMH! Over here!" the voice called. She soon felt comforted, as she recognised Henry's voice.

She darted around, trying to focus in the indistinct dullness. "Henry!" she yelled, suddenly spotting his shirtless physique heading toward her. She felt colour rushing to her cheeks, and was unsure whether it was due to his semi-naked figure or the guilt felt from thinking her lifelong friend would have deserted her.

"I've found a stream," Henry revealed as he headed toward her, pulling his green shirt over his head. "It's freezing but drinkable. I think." Henry struggled with his shirt and gave Niamh a reassuring hug. "I thought I'd take a look around before you woke. We must have needed the sleep, it's nearly midday, I think. Why don't you go for a wash and wake yourself up? I'll sort out some food."

"OK. Is it far?" she asked.

"Just over that mound. Don't worry, I'll wait here and won't look," Henry laughed.

Niamh hid her face as she blushed again and headed through the trees, the smell of pine tickling her senses. As she reached the mound the sound of running water soon took her thoughts back to her nightmare: the feeling of freezing water rushing up her nose, the frantic panicking while her fingers desperately clutched for air.

She struggled to put it out of her mind. Since she began at St Guinevere's, she'd been having the same nightmare. She recalled how Henry had wailed with laughter when she thought everyone had the same dream as a result of the Witche initiation.

As she dropped down the mound, she noticed the stream running across her path. Although only a few feet wide, the water seemed unrealistically deep. It was as though the stream was a giant gash in the ground, a wound running right to the land's core with dark blood coursing through it.

Niamh approached it with caution. The water was as black as the night to look at, the insipid wooded light adding to the effect.

Niamh was startled at first, as her look wasn't met by a diffused reflection. She put this down to the light, although she knew it was likely more sinister than that, and began to wash. Her skin tightened at the touch of the ice-cold water, and her thoughts rushed to her fading nightmare.

"Hey, Niamh, you decent?" yelled Henry. She quickly attempted to flatten her hair, quietly cursing her lack of reflection.

"Erm, yeah."

Henry made his way over the mound and glanced at Niamh, who stood there fully clothed, hair wet and ruffled like she'd been dragged through a hedge.

"I think we should make a move. It's already noon and I want to be out of here before dark."

"What about food?" Niamh enquired, a hungry look in her eye.

"We can eat on the move. I got some *wicci* bread from your pack." He threw a piece to her, which she caught and studied before devouring it like a ravenous dog.

"OK, which way?" she enquired with a mouth full of food.

"Well, I noticed the path of the sun through a few of the cracks," he pointed up whilst still studying Niamh. "We should go that way. According to your map it is about twenty miles, give or take."

"You think we can do it before nightfall?" asked Niamh.

Henry looked up and shivered from the haunting feeling the trees gave off. It was a feeling of raw magic; of unchartered evil that tingled up your spine and caused acid to burn in your throat.

"I hope to Seirim we can!" exclaimed Henry.

After what seemed like several lifetimes of walking, the pair came across the stream again, its snaking form seeming to follow them for miles.

"This looks like the mound from earlier, Henry,"

Niamh stated, a puzzled look crossing her face.

Henry knelt down as though studying the soil. "I think it is. Look," he pointed at a small pile of ash by his feet. "I managed to get a fire charm to heat the water. Look, here's the residue it left."

"How can that be? We've walked for hours since we jumped the stream!" She shook her head, dismay obvious on her face. "We have to get out of here. If we don't reach the village by Samhein... well, I don't know what will happen, but my mother said it is important not to hang around."

She picked up a handful of ash and let it slowly fall from her grip as sand drains from an hourglass, hoping it wasn't a reflection of the time they had remaining dripping away. In the dull, empty light something seemed to move: a quick darting movement in a dead landscape. Then she heard the faint whispers of an enchanting sound lingering just out of earshot.

The movement seemed to be in the trees near a bridge that neither of them had noticed before.

"Look," Henry nodded toward the bridge.

Niamh squinted to see better in the dim light. As they watched they saw more playful movement and dancing around the small white arch.

"They look like twigs. Are they cumbersticks?" Niamh asked, already knowing the answer but suggesting it to break the silent trance they had both fallen into.

"Not sure." Henry stood up straight and headed cautiously toward the noise, suddenly realising how devoid of life the woods had been until now. There had been no chirping of birds, no creepy crawlies rummaging in the undergrowth, and even the trees seemed dead, the leaves too high to discern their colour from this distance.

"Let's find out," Henry said, his right hand fingering the handle of his sword. As they approached they saw many more creatures darting from tree to tree. The music was captivating, and they found it hard to resist humming along as they were drawn closer.

As they neared the bridge, they heard small yells and screams as more of the wooden creatures rushed about, holding small daggers.

"Look," Henry said, startled as more flew above them like a swarm of bees, their wings buzzing lightly as they passed overhead firing scores of arrows into the distance.

"They must be some sort of fayerye, I think," said Niamh. "Mother used to recite old myths about them when I was younger." As the pair got closer to the bridge, they noticed how the white marble stonework shimmered with life and beauty.

The whole area around the fayerye bridge seemed to be a hive of activity. By contrast, it was clear by the littered floor that they had entered some kind of a war zone. The leaves and twigs on the ground were actually bodies, white sap oozing from their wooden limbs.

They approached the bridge with caution and crouched behind a huge, black root, undecided about what to do. Suddenly a blinding light shot from a hole in a tree beside them and another stick creature emerged, wings flapping, a two-bladed spear held high. The fayerye was obviously startled by their appearance and began to grow a little in size.

"HALT! You there. State your business!" yelled the fayerye, its skin now pulsating with a fiery red glow. The small creature looked to be made completely of wood. Its skin was a mossy bark, flaking in places, and its limbs seemed to be knotted twigs and branches.

"We are trying to get out. We are searching for a human village to the north of here somewhere. Can you help us?" asked Niamh.

The fayerye straightened to its full height, which was little bigger than Niamh's hand. "Help you?" the fayerye asked. "I do not help people. I am a servant to the Elm and no one else. You are coming with me. I think my lord will definitely be interested to hear of this little trick."

"Trick? No, we just need directions to the edge of the wood," Henry said.

"Did you misunderstand me, or are you plain stupid? I help only the Elm. GUARDS! GUARDS!" he shouted as he fluttered into the air. The fayerye was only about six inches tall, but his body was proportionately well built. He had four paper-thin wings coming from his shoulder blades. His appearance was obviously intended for camouflage and Niamh and Henry struggled to discern him amid the murky surroundings.

Several fayeryes fluttered from under the bridge in their direction, small spears in hand. "Seize them under the power of the Elm!" he shouted. The fayeryes swooped down and began pricking Niamh and Henry in the arm.

"Ow! Get off me, you little swines!" Niamh yelled, her arm beginning to sting and swell. Her surroundings began to blur and her head became warm and clammy.

"Henry, what's happeni... " Niamh asked as black approached like the veil of death to diffuse her surroundings and lull her to sleep.

She fell to the ground with a thud, thick, red-black blood oozing from her skull as she banged it on a tree root.

Henry fought to stay upright for longer, but eventually had to give into the fayerye poison. He clutched at his dagger as he fell heavily on the forest floor, the rush of fayeryes barely visible through his heavy eyelids as the glowing lights began to form shifting, snowflake-like images all around him.

Chapter 8

A fog clung to the air – a close fog, hugging the buildings like a damp, murky blanket. The inhabitants of Teare Gro had grown used to the random weather. The sun forced itself over the horizon as orange beams cut through the cloudy haze creating a strange, pulsing glow within the walls of the village.

Trialla unblocked the door to her hut with great apprehension, moving branches and lengths of timber to clear a path. After several minutes' struggle, she heaved the three-foot-thick horizontal plank and rested it in the corner of her shabby hut, leaves and moss creeping in through the gaps below the roof. It was small and damp, but it was home.

She stood at the door, hand on the rough wooden handle, and took a long, deep breath.

"Come on, Trialla. There's nothing there," she said to herself, thinking, *How many times have you been out at this time and everything has been fine?'* She looked up, puffed out her chest and opened the door, fiddling with her necklace in her left hand. Her right hand was always ready to unleash her handy mining pick.

As her eyes became accustomed to the morning light, a familiar sight came into focus. Carts had been upturned and the headless carcasses of horses and local wildlife lay strewn across the floor, which was now black with dried blood.

As Trialla hesitantly edged further away from safety, the true horror of the scene became clear. Scores of bodies lay scattered across the churned mud.

The bodies were of people Trialla knew well. She

rummaged around, turning over the pale, blood-soaked figures. She hoped the need for her pick would not arise, for she knew the bodies she inspected were her friends, her family.

Passing the great oak tree near the edge of the village, she recognised a brilliant yellow headscarf. She flew at the body and fell to her knees, cradling the victim's head in her hands. The woman's taut skin became more pliable as Trialla stroked her cheek, pushing the locks of deep black hair behind the woman's purple, bruised ear.

"Trialla, darling, is that you?" the woman asked, squinting to see in the harshness of the blinding morning light.

Trialla paused for a moment, trying to fight back the tears in their battle for freedom – tears that she would hold back until nightfall came and she could retreat to the solitude of her hut to reflect on the day.

"Yes, Ma, it is I. Come, you are weak. I will find Pa and fetch you some water."

As she gently laid her mother's head back on the ground, Trialla noticed several of the bodies rising to their feet. *Corpses returning from the grave,* she thought to herself. People were stumbling into huts, dazed and confused, the shock of blood on their clothes and, in some cases, their hands immediately apparent across their sleepless faces.

"What is this atrocity?" she heard one man speak. On closer inspection she recognised him to be Alonso, the local sword merchant. Trialla had spent many days learning the skills of Alonso's family.

Trialla didn't attend school as such; Teare Gro relied

solely on the skills of life. Children would begin work as soon as they were able, often switching from family to family to learn new skills. When the time came for them to become an adult, they would select a trade they excelled in and begin proper training.

Trialla was nearly at that age. Teare Gro insisted girls became women at sixteen and boys became men at fourteen – a fact Trialla often disputed with the local boys. As well as being strong, Trialla was considered very beautiful. She had thick black hair that she wore in a bun, piercing blue eyes and brown-black skin. She wore a long green silk and cotton dress with red and green triangle patterns around the neck and wrists.

"Trialla?" she heard in the muffled surroundings. She quickly turned on her heels and spotted her father, his large, muscular build setting him apart from the crowd of massing villagers. Trialla ran to her father and attempted to wrap her arms around him, her fingers barely reaching his sides. Jonna was well known in the village and extremely useful. The work of three lumberjacks could be done by this one beast.

"Pa!" she rejoiced, his big sweaty palm plummeting down to reach her head. He knelt down, still a foot taller than Trialla, and grabbed her by the shoulders.

"What happened here, Trialla? I had the most hellish nightmares. And this..." He aimlessly pointed around, destruction evident in every direction. "...This blood. How do I know nothing of this? Where is your mother? Your brother?"

"I left her by the outskirts. She is fine. I haven't seen Anag yet, but I'm sure he will be fine. Please, go see to Ma and I will find Anag. I will explain all when I return."

Under normal circumstances, Jonna would have

argued this. However, these were far from normal circumstances, and it was clear Trialla had some understanding of the situation, some grip on the recent confusion.

"Very well, Trialla. You be careful." Jonna headed toward their hut, still obviously bewildered by the incident, his mammoth limbs meandering carefully between the rickety huts.

After nearly an hour looking for her brother, Trialla set off back to the hut. The scene as she neared the village seemed back to normal bar the occasional bloodstain. She took a long, deep breath, held it for a few seconds, and sighed. She had survived another treacherous night. She knew there must be safer places, and had contemplated leaving in the past, but her family was here. Who could tell what would happen if she left? Only last month she had found her brother half-starved and surrounded by forest wolves. His day-old blood had obviously tempted their well-honed senses.

Back at the hut she was met by a look of eager concern. Her mother sat by the table; her father stood behind her, boulder-like hands resting on the back of her chair.

"Trialla. We were so worried," her mother said, her face looking more human now.

"I'm fine. I haven't found Anag yet, though." As she said this, Anag appeared, the bulk of her father had been shielding him from view until Anag stepped out from behind him.

A brief look of appreciation for the concern Trialla had shown crossed Anag's face. All eyes were now focused on Trialla, and she felt a sickening fear rise in her chest, words obviously struggling to escape.

She crossed to the stove, moving pieces of barricade from her path, and sat by it. She felt the sudden white-hot glow of the embers beneath brightening her cheeks and her skin began to tingle from the heat.

"This will sound strange at first, I am sure. What I am about to tell you I have told you many times before, strange evil allowing the information to escape you like dust in the wind." She knew she had said the very same thing before but no one would know.

"At night the people of this village change. It isn't every night. There appears to be no one other than myself who escapes the transformation. I believe this to be the work of a far-off magic; or a curse or punishment for something." Trialla looked around and saw a familiar expression crossing the faces of each member of her family. She knew exactly how they would react.

"I know you must be wondering many things. Why I am not affected? Why does this happen?" she added. "I cannot answer these questions. I don't know of a reason why I seem unaffected, or why it happens. Maybe we are destined to live this way."

She looked up at her parents, petrified of what they had been only hours before – of what they had done. She fought these emotions, knowing they knew nothing of their horrific metamorphosis. But their faces... She could still picture them hours earlier, rotten flesh clinging to their tendons, blood-smeared from a recent kill.

"But what is it, this curse? The village looked like we had been at war. What evil walks us in our sleep?" Jonna asked.

"I do not know. I have seen you change many times,

the love and hope of your eyes replaced with black fire, the beauty of your skin replaced with decay. I see it in my dreams when I sleep. I see many things, but all is distorted. Even my waking hours are hindered by a thick haze. I see a spirit inside you taking over: a demon that wants to be set free. He says we must pay. We must all pay – living and dead. He says you are alive by day, spirits of the dead by night. Our time will come to pay, and it is our ancestors, the foundations, who are as much to blame as us. They can never be allowed to rest, lingering just beyond reach of the black gates of death by dark and forced back to the misery of this by light."

The mood in the room had changed as quickly as her people changed at sun-down, her mother darting frantic looks at each of her family members.

"What do we do?" her mother asked. "I mean, all the blood... " An almost unknowing shame was clear in her eyes. *At least they're her eyes,* Trialla thought to herself.

"I don't really know. When the sun vanishes, people go limp, their muscles seeming to give up hope of movement. People are drawn toward the centre of the village, and then the screams start – the most excruciating, mind-numbing shrieks imaginable. Eyes roll back; pierced tongues hang as blood oozes to the ground. It is clear in your eyes what you seek: life. Cattle, birds... humans. It makes no difference. By morning, you have no recollection."

Trialla looked at her feet ashamedly. "I have attempted to leave many times, but I cannot. The pain of leaving you is too great. The actual physical pain to my heart is unbearable. Some force does not allow me to leave. We are stuck with this curse and it appears there is no immediate answer. We must pay for our sins, whatever they may be."

An eerie silence met her words. As long as Trialla could

remember, this had been the case for her small village of fellow humans: the fog descending with the coming of a new moon, people disappearing into the night, and dreadful scenes in the morning. It had affected her deeply as a child, mentally and physically, but it had also hardened her.

Trialla had become proficient with many weapons, and her strength and agility were outstanding – even compared to the local boys, who would taunt her during the day.

"I know nothing more than I have told you. You will spend time discussing with the other town folk what can be done to find more information but, in the end, it will fall upon you again and erase any recollection."

Trialla's father scratched his head with an ogre-like claw. Obviously this was not the kind of information anyone could take in and accept easily. He motioned for Trialla to come closer and embraced all his family in one giant grasp.

"Don't worry, Trialla. I will help you build defences for the future. That should help your mind be at ease. I love you all. You have never let us down. I'm sure you will find the reasoning behind this madness," he boomed, his arms trembling with every word bellowed from his gigantic chest.

Trialla looked up. "I hope so," she managed, the lump in her throat making it hard to swallow. As much as she wanted things to be normal, she doubted it would happen any time soon.

Chapter 9

Niamh felt her eyes crunch as she fought to open them, a yellow crust having sealed them shut. Her head felt fuzzy and light, and a terrible headache pulsed behind her eyes and ears.

"Henry?" she mumbled, her tongue stuck to the roof of her mouth. "Henry. You there?"

As her eyes opened and the wash of colours began to come into focus, she noticed she was in a small, circular garden with giant lilies bending over where she lay. These were bigger than any flower she had ever seen. There were occasional piles of orange powder around her where the pollen had fallen and partially dyed the ground. Niamh sat there for a few seconds, hoping the bees wouldn't be in proportion to the plant life.

She could see an array of dancing colour all around her, and a pale blue sky that looked oddly like water. She moved to get up, but found her hands and legs had been bound with some kind of thick twine.

"Well, well. Won't you look who's awake?" said a fayerye, a curious smile twisting his lips. He seemed to study her for a while, then drop from the sky onto the bent stem of a gladiolus, its neck swaying slightly with the minuscule weight.

The creature looked completely different now, but she instantly recognised his voice as the fayerye who attached them. He now had a striking white glow, his wings pure and clean. He wore a knee-length silver tunic as opposed to the bark-like outfit he wore before and he now seemed to pulsate with a red or maybe deep orange glow.

"What do you want? And where's Henry?" asked Niamh, rubbing her head. Her hair was stuck together in a solid knot. "If you've hurt him...!" she said as she studied her bloody hand and winced at the pain.

"If you must know, you banged your head when you fell. Are you ready for your interrogation?"

"Interrogation? But why? What have we done to you? We only wanted to get through the wood," Niamh pleaded. "Where is Henry? Tell me!"

"The one you call 'Henry' is fine. He has been awake for a while. He is restrained by the Shimmery Falls, being interrogated," said the winged creature as he looked over toward a distant crashing of water. Niamh did not like the way he emphasised the word 'interrogated'.

"I am Grannah, Imperial Guard 4th Regiment of the Croishees. I know who you are, but I expect I won't have the pleasure for long." The last words sent shivers down Niamh's spine. Who were these people? What did they want?

She heard the crashing of water on rocks, and thought of how she had struggled for air in her nightmare. Even when unconscious she still could not escape her nightly torture.

"Why are you interrogating him? We haven't done anything."

"No? You try to infiltrate our camp, force us to change our ways. You expect us to accept this trickery? The Sidhe have waffled on about you for long enough now, so we should have seen this coming."

Niamh could detect a strong disgust at whoever the 'Sidhe' were. Her head swam, and she sat back down on the grass. Grannah was only small, but his body language was obviously aggressive and he appeared a little unstable.

"What do you mean?" asked Niamh, clearly confused by his offered explanation and the situation.

"You are the chosen ones, are you not? The saviours? Please!" he snorted, his small face crumpling with derision. "We know what you are up to, Sidhe. Do you think we are stupid?"

"Really," Niamh pleaded. "I have no idea what you are talking about."

"DO NOT LIE TO ME!" Grannah roared, flaring an insanely bright shade of red and fluttering to within inches of her nose. "YOU WERE SENT TO SPY, TO INTERFERE."

"Please, we just wanted to leave the wood but couldn't find our way."

"Please, please, we just wanted to leave... " sniggered Grannah in a sarcastic imitation of Niamh. "You know full well that is not the truth. You have been sent to stir up doubt.

"The Sidhe have always waffled on about your coming. A girl and an orphan Witche boy who would save our race from turmoil and destruction. These are the dangerous, fictitious ideas that have split our people. There is only one God who we worship. The worship of this friend of yours is not acceptable. And worship our one God you will. 'One God. One leader. One who will deliver you from evil and hatred.' They are the words of the Shieran and this attempt to dissuade us will not work."

"Wait, you think Henry is the chosen one?" Niamh asked, finding it hard not to chuckle.

"Do you not listen, you stupid girl? Of course he isn't. You have obviously been sent here by the Sidhe to cast doubt on our beliefs, and to cause instability between our people. Well, it won't work. I don't know where they have dragged you from but we'll be sure you are disposed of before anyone can see you. How can he be the Saviour if he's DEAD? Hmmm?"

There was something about Grannah that made Niamh feel extremely uneasy. He seemed deranged. She had to find Henry and find a way out of here. Wherever here was.

Grannah jumped, spun around a few times in the air and held his left finger in his ear. Niamh went to speak and he waved with his hand indicating that she should be quiet.

"Yes, yes, very well. I will bring her, my lord," Grannah said to no one in particular. Niamh was convinced that talking to yourself while rubbing your ear was definitely a sign that backed up her earlier diagnosis: crazy.

"You will follow me now. This way."

He snapped his fingers and the twine around Niamh's legs slackened and began to disappear beneath the soil. Her hands remained tightly fastened and she could feel the thorns from the twine cutting into her wrists.

They walked a short way under the shade of enormous plants and flowers and approached the huge towering waterfall Grannah had called 'Shimmery Falls', but there was no sign of Henry. She looked up and noticed the water seemed to be coming over nothing – there was no cliff face. She could, in fact, see the underside of the river. The water seemed to float on nothing until it reached the edge and plummeted to a small pool near their feet.

"This way," Grannah said as he prodded Niamh in the back of her neck with the side of his spear, obviously tired of her studying the surroundings. *If he thinks I am a spy, I wonder what hope there is of getting out of here alive if I see too much of their hideout,* she thought.

As they reached the waterfall, Niamh stopped. "Where to?" she asked.

"Get in there, you fool!" Grannah snapped as he pushed her through the water. "Don't play games with me."

To her amazement, Niamh found that she was not wet at all. In fact, her clothes smelt strangely of fresh morning dew. She looked ahead of her to see a dark, damp corridor, with walls that appeared to be made of wet mud. Dirty puddles shimmered on the floor from the light cast by occasional floating orbs.

"What... what is this place?" Niamh asked, stumbling down a couple of stone steps she hadn't seen.

Grannah chuckled to himself. "It's your home. Your new home, until we can find out what is going on. I hope you like the view."

Grannah pushed and shoved Niamh down the corridor toward a small, circular hole at the rear.

"In there?" asked Niamh, the horror clear on her face.

Grannah just nodded, casting a quick look behind. Niamh climbed through the hole and found she was in a barred cell no larger than five feet square. She looked back to see Grannah smirking through the hole.

"Sleep tight," he said, the amusement of the situation

obvious on his face. As he turned, Niamh moved toward the hole to plead with him, but found it was shrinking in size, the dripping mud closing in. By the time she had even moved, the hole was gone and she was staring at a solid brown wall of mud and dirt.

As she looked around, all the other walls were made of strong metal horizontal bars about an inch apart. Beyond them Niamh could see only blackness.

She squinted to try and see more, but found it impossible. She couldn't decide whether it was too dark to see or whether there really wasn't anything out there.

She sat down in the corner and wrapped her arms around her knees. She felt a huge blast of exhaustion catch up with her, and began to sob. She sobbed for the situation, she sobbed for Henry, she sobbed for her mother but, most of all and for the first time, she sobbed because she wished her father had been there to help her.

A rumble came from the wall she had just entered through and she looked up, teary-eyed. She heard a thud and by the time she could register what had happened, she saw a body crumpled up beside her. She knelt over to see if she could help. As she rolled the body over she jumped back, her arms clanging against the metal bars.

"Henry!" she gasped.

Chapter 10

'Finally,' Jorgan thought as he approached the shimmering barrier of the gods and gazed at what lay ahead on the other side. He placed his pack on the ground and began removing small metal objects wrapped in deep purple and black velvet. The material was soft to touch and reminded Jorgan of his mother's wedding gown, which his father still kept locked away.

Jorgan had never had trouble getting into places he wasn't supposed to. From an early age he had shown a distinct skill in not only using the power of the land but channelling it through objects – a skill rarely seen as far as he could tell, except for weapon enchantments in battle.

He would spend day and night working on his small toys in his workshop. Nobody missed him anyway. His father only told him to stop wasting his time on the occasions when he'd plucked up the courage to show him the fruits of his labours.

"Father, look," he would demand, which would be received with a grunt, a sharp glare and, "Get out of my sight, boy, with your little trinkets. You're a disgrace. You should be riding alongside me in battle now. Even the other chiefs think you a coward. A coward! Never in all my life has anyone dared to call a member of the Onjanaha bloodline a coward and lived, but, do you know what I said? Do you? That coward is no son of mine. Maybe someday you'll have to prove yourself a man and when that day comes I hope you stand and fight, boy."

Jorgan realised he had been standing motionless for several minutes now, his brow wrinkled in frustrated concentration.

He often found he would talk and argue with himself, acting out things he wished he had the courage to say to his father but couldn't.

He thought back to the fly he had made. Jorgan hadn't known what he was agreeing to when he made it. He actually thought his father had become interested in what he did when he asked if it was possible. Only too eager to please, Jorgan had worked for three days solid perfecting it. When the time came to reveal it to his father, he discovered it was gone. It was already half way to Rusalimum with a reckless soldier who knew little, if anything, of the power he possessed.

Jorgan shook his head and, with the precision of a soldier assembling a weapon before battle, he had already constructed the pyramid-shaped metal object housing a cylindrical glass container filled with a viscous crimson liquid. He could not remember even getting the objects out of his bag, but there he stood, a man in front of gods, ready to see just how powerful his so-called 'trinkets' really were.

Wiping the sweat from his forehead, he stepped forward, clenched the object tightly in his hand and plunged his fist through the wall of water with a quick jab. His wrist moved so quickly that it was like an adder striking its prey dead. Jorgan had expected his hand to return as quickly as it had entered, but he found himself suspended there. He tried to move his hand, but couldn't. He stood, horrified, as he watched ice climb the length of his arm and a thick layer crack and reform as he struggled against it. He felt a pull at his chest like he'd swallowed a lead weight, and he instinctively angled his head as far away from his arm as possible. It wasn't supposed to happen like this.

With the approach of imminent death, Jorgan thought *at least my father isn't here to mock me.* He closed his eyes and prayed he would find a safe journey to the other side, when he felt a sudden rush of air and a sinking sensation. He opened his eyes with just enough time to spare and launched his hands out in front of him.

As he fell forward to the ground, he rolled over instinctively and came to a crashing stop against the stump of a tree. The scent of grass and woodlands rushed back through his airways.

He slowly got to his hands and knees and shook his head comically. As he steadied himself and began to stand, he looked up at the wall of water he had just passed through. The pyramid vial of virgin blood floated in mid-air as veins of red shot off in every direction creating a gaping hole in the wall. The effect was one of a mist clearing after a muggy night. Red lines flowed outwards and actively searched for the strengths in the barrier, destroying them.

He turned and carried on his journey, shaking his head and occasionally glancing back to look as his work faded and the wall returned to its original state.

Chapter 11

"Wake up! Henry, wake up!" Niamh yelled. Henry's limp body lolled in her arms as she fought to sit him up. She felt the walls of the tiny, cramped cage closing in on her and could feel a throbbing in her ears. *Come on, think!*

She knelt down beside him and thought of the string of symbols she would need to form a healing charm. She tried making the symbols with her right hand as she held him upright with her left, but she couldn't concentrate. *Come on! COME ON,* she thought.

"You're not going to die on me, Henry Keala. You're not!"

She shook him violently as she shouted, and heard a tiny splutter. He was alive. Henry coughed and keeled over onto his side, as far as the space would allow, spluttering and wheezing.

"Niamh," he said weakly, his voice hoarse and distant. "I need water," he managed.

Of course, water, she thought suddenly. She produced the basic symbol for water. This was one of the land's main nourishments. It was also something easily called upon if the need was great enough. A floating ball of liquid appeared above Henry's head. Niamh cupped her hands and held them beneath the floating globule and brought them up to touch the bottom of it. It splashed into her palms, spilling the majority to the ground. She held what remained to Henry's lips and he seemed to inhale it into his body. He sat there motionless for several minutes, gasping, then began to calm down.

His face was black with bruises and dried blood, and

his clothes were torn and scratched.

"You... OK?" Henry asked, managing to lift his head to look Niamh in the eyes.

She shifted for a few seconds, feeling a little guilty at the fact that she was relatively unharmed. She saw Henry's face tighten in shock as he saw the blood on her hand. She put her hand to her head.

"Oh no, that's fine. I did it when they stunned us. I fell over and banged my head, I think."

"So they say, little beggars!" Henry spat. "Some of the rubbish they've been coming out with is unbelievable. They think I'm some god," he paused. "Or... or... don't. I don't even know anymore. What I do know is we have to get out of here."

"Not a god, no," came a tingly voice from above. "A saviour. There is a distinct difference."

From above the cage fluttered a small golden light, growing in size as it neared them. It stopped on the roof bars and struggled to squeeze through the gaps.

Like the other fayeryes, this one was about six inches high, brilliantly clean and sparkly, but this one pulsed with a light blue and silver colour. It also wore a long blue tunic with a silver tree engraved into the front. He had long blond hair tied in a string at the end and sharp, pointed ears. It popped through the bars and fluttered to a stop on Niamh's head.

"Get off me!" she cried as she began violently flapping her arms above her head as though trying to swat a fly. "Get off me!"

"Whoa now, missy. Whoa... I said WHOA!" he shouted.

Niamh found herself submitting to his order due to the sheer volume of it.

"Now that's better. I think introductions are in order first," the fayerye said keeping his gaze firmly fixed on Henry.

"I'm Patch, a royal servant of King Misa of the Sidhe. If there is anything I can do to assist, please do not hesitate to ask. Now, I already know the answer but, fair's fair, I had my go, so... who are you two, then?" he added in a playful tone.

"Erm... I'm Niamh and this is He—"

"Henry, yes, we know, we know. Now, unless you want to leave here in a stone box you'll come with me. That is unless you want to find yourself dead? No, that's what I thought."

"Great," Niamh said. There was a long silence as Patch hovered, studying them inquiringly. "Well, then?" said Niamh.

"Are you kidding me? You're the chosen one," he fired at Henry. "You can do anything. I thought you would get us out of here."

"What?" roared Henry. "You don't know how to get out? Can't we just go the way you came, through there somehow?"

Patch spun round twice in the air, throwing his arms about. "No, silly, we can't go that way. Can you fit through that gap? Can you fly? Can you exist in a void between your world and ours where, without the right connection, you could float forever into oblivion? Eh? Well? Can you?"

Henry sat there, mouth open, and stared. He had no idea what to say. He tried, but nothing came out.

"Well, we're stuck here then," added Niamh. "Perfect!"

"No, no, no. I know a way out, that's easy. I just thought you'd know, being the Saviour and all. Just thought I'd test you a bit. I thought you'd know everything really, but I guess not. Come on." Patch shot through the air to the mud wall they had entered through. He plunged his hand into the soil and rummaged around for what felt like hours, humming the tune they'd heard earlier with his tongue sticking out between his teeth in concentration.

"Tricky devils, these new ones," he said as they heard a loud click.

"Got it!" he cheered. From the depths of the mud wall Patch pulled a piece of long golden thread and tied it around Niamh's feet and then Henry's.

"What is this trickery?" Henry demanded as he tried to wriggle free, his face turning a dark shade of pink in frustration. Niamh simply turned to Patch and gave him a look that said 'explain this minute or suffer the consequences'. Henry instinctively reached for his blade before remembering it had been missing since he awoke in this strange land.

"OK, OK. Don't over-react. I'm taking you to the Great Hall. There will be food and drink and shelter there. Trust me," said Patch. Henry continued to fight for several seconds with his hand, not wanting to risk cutting himself on the fine thread, then settled down.

"Good, now close your eyes and mouth. I've never

done this with such big folk before."

Before Henry could argue he was whisked across the floor and dragged towards the solid muddy wall by the thread. He heard Niamh's cry from ahead of him as they were sucked into the hole Patch had made feet first, the cold damp soil brushing past their faces like thick, soft putty. Henry didn't dare open his eyes and thoughts rushed through his mind of being buried alive as he felt the top of his head get swallowed up by the hole they had just entered.

Henry felt himself stop and began to panic as he realised he hadn't taken a breath for about a minute. He began to thrash his cramped body around as he felt something tugging at his feet. He wriggled frantically until he felt warm air caress his legs. As he fell to the ground he gasped for air on all fours, and looked up to see Patch panting on the floor.

"How much do you weigh?" puffed Patch, his body glowing green tinged with specks of red and blue light. Despite the need for air, Henry couldn't help but notice the strange network of internal organs glowing erratically in Patch's body through his clothing. It was strangely beautiful.

"What are you trying to do? Kill us?" yelled Henry, getting to his feet worrying that he'd been pricked by the poisoned needles again as the blood rushed to his head and white shapes danced in front of his eyes.

"No, no, of course not," said Patch apologetically. "It is usually only me using that route. It is the first time Witche folk have entered my kingdom and it is somewhat unorthodox to try and get someone of your... erm, girth through a thread route." Patch turned to walk toward Niamh, satisfied that his explanation was good enough. Henry puffed out his chest and pointed a finger at Patch, but before he could speak he looked out at the room they now occupied.

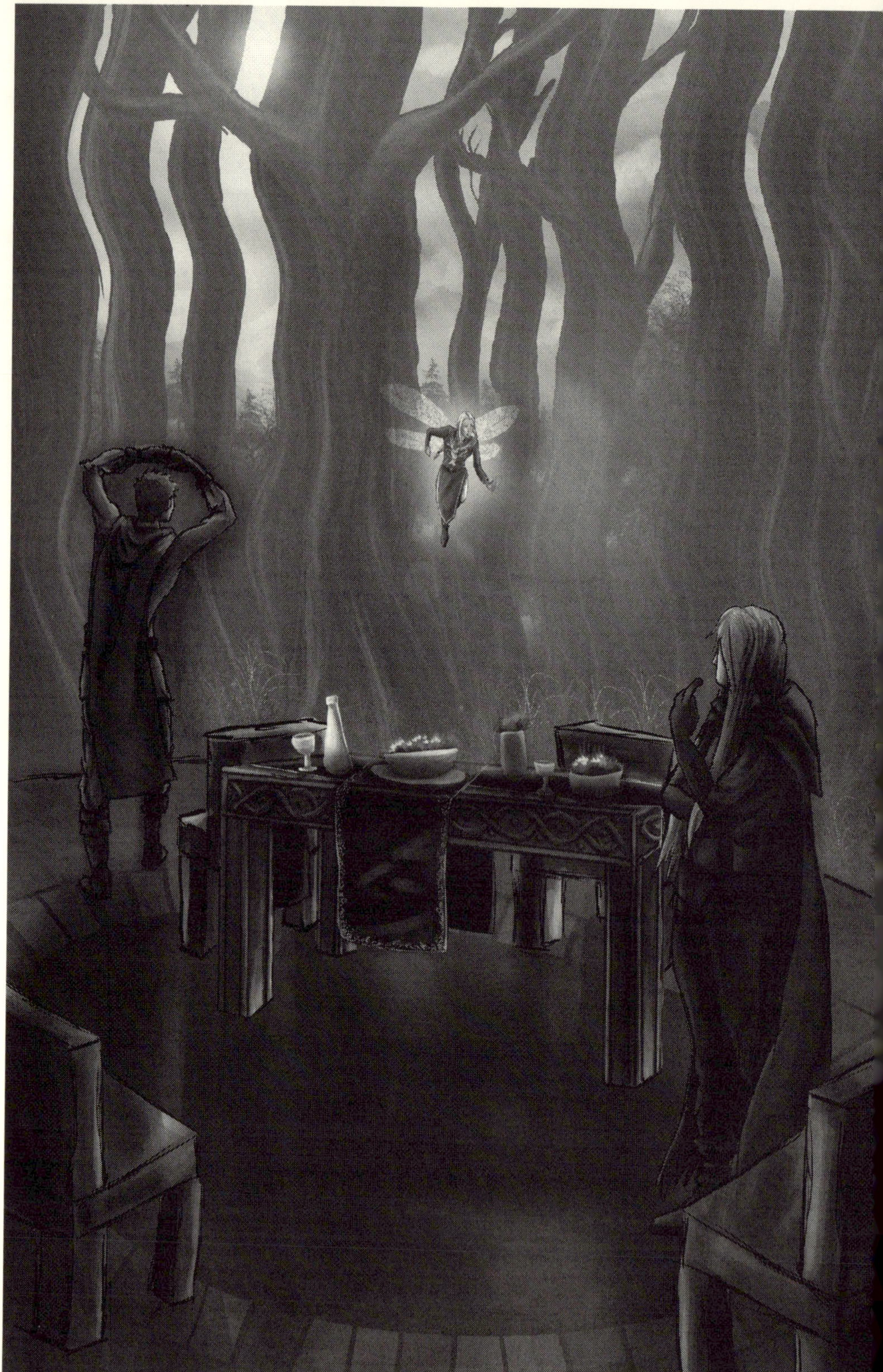

They seemed to be encased in large, circular glass room. The view through the glass seemed distorted as though they were looking through glass that had water running down it.

"Where are we?" Henry asked as he passed over to a wall to look closer. He placed his open palm on the wall and felt the moisture within it as though they were inside a giant icicle. He cupped his hands to the glass and looked through.

"Hey, I recognise those hills. That's just outside Rusalimum. Niamh, he's taken us miles further back!" Henry gasped.

Patch hung his head and shook it as he flew over to an intricately decorated stone table. "Have you learned nothing during your time here? Things are not always as they appear. What you are looking at is the world before the wars started many millennia ago."

"It's... beautiful," Henry said, looking away to hide his embarrassment.

"Why did the wars have to happen?" Henry said rhetorically. Niamh was not sure what to say. The Great War had not been the only conflict Ysrir had seen, and although she'd lost her father in battle she still had one parent left, even if she was rarely around.

Patch rubbed his chin with the bottom of his curled wing as though he was carefully thinking what to say next. "We are the only race who can still travel the land, and far-off lands as well, and have seen the devastation that people cause. However, we retreated to the solitude of the Wooden Realm. Only there could we be free from the evil that roams our once beautiful pastures.

"We have also managed to source a great pool of magic from the land here. The Elm make great homes as well as being a highly conductive magical material. We believe it is because, in here, no one can distort the power with their selfishness and their fighting," explained Patch.

Niamh sympathised with Patch and also wished her people could escape like his people. "So now you just live in the wood? Where are we now? This doesn't look like the wood we were in earlier."

"You are still in the wood, but now you are in the heart of the wood. We are inside the Elm trees. We have channelled the magic from these woods and created somewhere we can live in safety. It is not affected by the outside world as such. As long as the trees are healthy then our home is safe. We have no need for our camouflage in here. We can be ourselves."

"It seems to me that your people are in just as much trouble as ours from what we have seen so far," Niamh said.

Patch hung his head and began to sob. "It is true. For centuries we have travelled and condemned such acts of violence and hatred. Different races fighting, believing one is better than the other. Believing one has the right to summon the lands magic more than the next. Believing one god is better than another. We pitied you but we couldn't help you.

"Then, nearly five hundred years ago Oiseena, the Qwein of the fayeryes, had a vision in the Shimmery Falls. She saw you, Henry; the Chosen One. You would ensure our race survived in a world of war. You became a hope in times of darkness. We found that the more this hope was preached the more we became divided as a society. Some just wouldn't accept what was obviously the fate of our kind, that we would be saved by a young witche boy. They called us blasphemers for worshipping someone other than our true God. It seemed the conflict that had devastated the land around us for so long had managed to worm its way into our sacred home. Our people became divided between those who believed in the Saviour and those who did not. When we got word from one of our spies that you had finally arrived, we knew they would try to kill you. They cannot afford to let all they have built up over centuries be destroyed by your sudden appearance."

The seriousness of the moment was lost when Patch leaped across the room to catch a fly, forcing it to the ground. The fly, nearly as big as Patch's arm, put up a good fight but ended up wingless on its back. Patch took a big bite from its torso before looking up ashamedly. "Sorry, how rude. Do you want some?"

"Erm, no thank you," replied Niamh with a look of disgust.

Henry was feeling a lot stronger now, but his face still stung and he felt weak and hungry. He turned away from the glass and its mesmerising view and said, "But why? Why am I the Chosen One? What do I need to do to save your people? Talk to both your leaders? We don't have much time; we have things of our own to do."

"Well, we have travelled far and wide in search of solitude. We have visited the place you seek; we have seen the place where Ysrir was severed when the gods fought. We know more than you can imagine about your voyage and its purpose.

"Before the northern folk came to conquer, our land was lush and green with crops, and people lived in harmony. Many different races mixed and grew as one. With the Norsemen came war and treachery. If we help you, you must grant us one favour," Patch said.

"OK, but how do we know we can trust you? There are bound to be people who want what we're after for evil."

"You can only follow your heart at times like these. We, too, have to trust you in what we ask. Will you help us?"

Niamh cast a sideways look at Henry and caught his obvious uncertainty. While this fayerye appeared trustworthy, it was clear they were already powerful creatures. If they were after the necklace, who knew what power they could unleash?

"We will help you," said Niamh, getting to her feet. "As long as it is within our power to and we agree with what you want. In exchange we need your help to find the island. We also need food and shelter for tonight. I think we should rest." Although Niamh was now wide awake, she still felt the after-effects of the sedative passing through her body.

"Very well, we will grant you these requests. It may also please you to know that time within my kingdom does not run parallel to your own. You can stay and rest the night and you will have lost simply minutes back in your own time."

Niamh contemplated this for a second and then smiled at Henry, "That's great. We can eat and rest now and we'll still be on course to leave the woods by nightfall."

"Wait, wait," Henry said holding his tired hand in the air to get their attention. "You said 'my kingdom' with a strange twang. Who are you?" he asked whilst carefully studying the intricate detail in Patch's wings compared to the plain covered ones of the other fayeryes they had seen.

"My name is Patch. I have no real birth name as your people do. We are called by title alone. Patch translates to 'King' in your language. I am Patch of the Elm world and protector of all the Wooded Realm."

"So why were you the one that saved us? Surely you would have sent the guards to rescue us?" suggested Niamh.

"This would usually be true, but I do not reveal my true identity, even to my own people. King Misa is simply a decoy. I do my ruling through him disguised as a servant. It has been foretold this way. Do you really think I would have got out of my castle without a score of armed guards to come and rescue you if they thought I was the King?"

"I guess not," mumbled Henry. "When you say 'foretold', what else have you seen?"

"Many races on Ysrir have ways and means of telling the future. Your mother, for example, I expect consults with Seirim – a lesser apparition of the gods. The Sorcerers rely solely on the scattering of their sacred runes, whilst certain humans simply dream of what is to come. Fayeryes can see things in the pool of the Shimmery Falls and it was seen that I would meet and rescue the Chosen One. Therefore, it is I who wanders the Wooded Realm in the hope you may one day approach."

Patch circled above their heads and pointed at the ceiling with a look of extreme concentration. Niamh noticed it shimmer from glass to sky and back again. In this brief flicker she saw a glimpse of Henry and Patch sitting side by side on a rock surrounded by the ocean.

"How people use the information they receive depends on their nature and beliefs," he continued, studying Niamh. "However, not all that is foretold necessarily happens. They should be used as guidelines. It is the bearer of these guidelines who must put things into action as they see best for the good of the land."

"So why does our journey benefit the land?" asked Niamh.

Patch swooped down to hover a foot in front of Niamh's face, his wings glittering as they hummed at great speed.

"It is not my responsibility to tell you," he said after what seemed like much internal conflict. "If your mother knew and did not tell you then it is in the interest of the land she did this. Everything happens for a reason, and your journey is of great importance to all that will walk the land for centuries to come. Future generations will be greatly indebted to you if you complete this task. Now, come, let us eat," Patch gestured toward the table as he landed on it next to a plate of bluebottles that appeared in a cloud of silver dust. Several other plates of breads and meats appeared beside Niamh and Henry. "Please, you must be hungry. Eat what you want."

Niamh looked over at Henry and then dived at the table as plates of food fuller than they had ever seen before continued to materialise. They had gone longer than this before without food, but had never felt hungrier. They devoured three chicken legs, a pig's head, six lamb chops and what felt like enough vegetables to feed their class at St Guinevere's.

Niamh struggled to lick her lips as she sat back in her uncomfortable stone chair. She was sure her belly had grown to double the size already.

"Thvhat as gwhret," Henry spluttered, his mouth still full of potato.

"Come, you should rest. I will wake you when the time is right." Patch fluttered up into the air and over to the wall they had entered through.

"Oh no, you don't. I'm not going through there again," Henry stated with a determined look on his face.

Patch picked up the thread and made a square with it on the wall.

"We are not leaving the room, just changing it a bit." The thread sank through the glass wall and a small doorway appeared. Through it they found two straw beds that they settled down onto with great appreciation. They fought to stay awake, wanting to talk of what had happened and what they should do next, but it was a battle they could not overcome. Talk would have to wait until morning.

Niamh looked up for Patch but he had already gone, a faint flicker of silver dust where he had been.

***

"Is it him?" asked Guard 412 with a hopeful glint in his eye.

Patch swooped to stand on the rock beside him, obviously overwhelmed with happiness.

"It is him, the Chosen One. I have waited so long for this moment. Even I have had my doubts over the years if I am honest, but it is really him." A silver tear as shiny as mercury rolled down his cheek and he wiped it away with the bottom of his wing. The two fayeryes embraced then moved apart again. "Anything to report?" Patch asked, a more serious look on his wet face.

"No, all is well. Oh, Guard 016 has gone AWOL again. We have D-unit looking for him as we speak. He'll show up again. He always does."

Patch looked up at the light glistening through the

patchwork of leaves and sighed. "I hope so. His disappearances trouble me, especially now."

Chapter 12

The courtyard of the Sorcerer king was eerily quiet. In the distance the light of camp fires could be seen flickering in the cool night breeze.

"Blasted night duty," a soldier in all black clothing and a red hood declared to himself. He had been put on the night duty after failing to bring back enough loot from a recent scavenge to a neighbouring village. He knew this was a light punishment compared to the fate suffered by his men, but this thought didn't make it go any quicker. He took a container of *bjórr* from his pocket, carefully checked for anyone watching and took a long swig, wiping his mouth afterwards with his sleeve and checking his breath. The sweet scent of honey was strong but he could do nothing about it now.

He made his way down the stone steps from his post in the curtain wall and headed toward the kitchens for a refill.

As he stumbled past the Great Hall, a light caught his attention – not the amber glow of fire but the silvery sparkle of a star. He watched as a glowing orb appeared in the centre of the courtyard. The shape grew to be a few inches tall then, with a scattering of dust, landed at speed, rolled a few times and uncurled its miniature body.

The soldier looked in amazement as he saw a winged creature lying on the floor coughing and swearing. After resting for a while it pushed itself to its feet and looked around.

The castle grounds were deadly silent, but Guard 016 was fully aware of his own eye-catching appearance, especially among folk who had never seen his kind. Guard 016 studied his surroundings and found a large man stood staring, open-mouthed, at him.

"What's your problem?" Guard 016 asked as he took flight and headed toward the forebuilding, appearing to grow a bark-like appearance as he flew.

"Erm...?"

The soldier was obviously struggling to comprehend the creature. The fact that it spoke to him didn't help his grip on the situation, or reality. He looked at his bottle and then back at the creature flying away from him in a cloud of sparkling dust. He attempted to speak again, "!"

He rubbed his eyes, threw his bottle to the ground and went inside to try and bribe someone to cover his shift.

Guard 016 headed straight for the wall of the Great Hall and spotted a stone missing near the base. He slid through the hole, scrunching his wings up behind his head to prevent damaging the delicate membrane. He found himself sliding down a rectangular passage. As he dropped from the hole at the bottom he flexed his wings and let out a small yelp of fright. He hadn't expected the ground to come up on him so quickly.

He hovered an inch from the floor and wiped his brow. Concentrating hard, he managed to increase his glow, momentarily illuminating the majority of the room. The corners stayed bathed in shadow but he suspected even the strongest of lights would not help in a place like this.

He didn't like this castle. He could sense evil goings-on and it sickened him to the core to feel magic being used for such meaningless tasks. He knew the land's magic had decreased, but he struggled to even sense it in the dark pit beneath the Keep.

"Guard 016?" came a voice from the stone stairs. "I have been waiting for you. I hope you bring me good news," Oddvard said. Guard 016 cowered at the sight of the Sorcerer.

"I bring news of the Witche, my lord," Guard 016 muttered.

Oddvard's eye lit with a flicker of power. Guard 016 recognised this and immediately realised his mistake. His people had seen this look many times before and it had cost the land dearly. However, he was under the command of the Great Sorcerer now; power and riches his reward.

Oddvard walked over to a large opening in the wall, muttered something under his breath and flicked his wrist. A bolt of orange fire shot from his hand to ignite several old, dry logs in the hearth.

Guard 016 jumped back aghast at his master's blatant disregard for the tree-souls, their screeches clearly only evident to his well attuned ears. Oddvard crossed the room again toward the fayerye with a nasty smile on his lips and beckoned for him to approach with a wave of his hand. Guard 016 tried to block the screeches out and fluttered slowly forward.

"Come, tell me. What have you learned, man of the woods?"

"We found the boy," he explained.

"What boy? I am in search of a female Witche. Have you found her?" Oddvard demanded.

"Yes, it is true. There is also a female Witche travelling with him. They are in search of the necklace of the gods, as you thought. They will be heading for Teare Gro by morning."

"Good, and Patch?" asked Oddvard.

"Patch is going to help them. He knows of their destination. It is a place visited by my people long before I was born. It is not an easy journey, though, and there are strange happenings in Teare Gro. Patch puts far too much faith in the prophecies. He would risk everything to fulfill his part."

"Maybe," said Oddvard, deep in thought.

"What do you intend to do, master?" asked Guard 016.

"I will find the necklace. I have people out searching for it now. If the Witche finds it first, then we will track her down and do whatever it takes to stop her. She must not be allowed to return the necklace."

"Kill her?" asked Guard 016 with a look of shock on his face. He knew the Sorcerer had killed many times before, both in and out of battle, but these were children. It went against the will of the gods to wage war and fight, but to harm children was the worst of the fourteen sins.

"Whatever it takes," said Oddvard distantly.

Guard 016 stared at Oddvard, appalled. "What do you wish me to do, master?" he asked reluctantly.

Oddvard seemed to think for several minutes before finally opening his tight lips. "Your part is done now, little man," Oddvard said. "You have been very... helpful."

"I will go, then?" the fayerye asked timidly, as though unsure whether this was what his master intended.

"No, I think not," Oddvard replied, his face even more

solemn-looking now as he turned to face the flickering orange fire. He spun and raised his hands towards the cowering fayerye, who spotted the movement far too late, taking a blow of fierce white light to his minuscule body. The spell engulfed him in a white ice-like mist.

As Oddvard slowly walked toward the writhing figure on the ground, his skin red and wings curled flat against his back, he began reciting complicated strings of ancient spells that he would need to get exactly right if he stood a chance of getting the necklace before the Witche heir did.

"Wait," pleaded Guard 016. "What are you doing?" The crumpled figure began crawling away from the approaching Sorcerer but couldn't muster the energy to lift his tiny body from the ground. Terror and realisation of the situation were now clear on his tiny face.

Oddvard towered over the fayerye. He cast no shadow as the dungeon room had already sucked all the light and life from the air. Accepting his fate, Guard 016 managed to topple over and raise himself onto his knees.

"There is no other way," Oddvard spoke softly. "It is for the greater good." As Guard 016 lowered his gaze, Oddvard completed the spell, causing the fayerye's chest to rise violently into the air. His limp arms and legs seemed to hang backwards below his upper torso. His chest began to glow a vicious white, streams flowing in all directions. Guard 016 had never left his home planet, but he imagined that in these last few moments of his life he experienced what it must be like to see a star explode

As his glow began to lessen, small glittering particles of light began to float across toward Oddvard. The fayerye began to droop and his skin became wrinkled and aged rapidly. Oddvard received an ever-growing stream of light, which lit deep corners of his insides.

As the power and life drained from Guard 016, Oddvard became temporarily empowered with the knowledge that he would need to capture the necklace before the Witches. He knew of the fayeryes' ability to travel between the real world and the fayerye world, and it was this that would allow him to retrieve the necklace and, if luck was on his side, retrieve a certain Witche girl in the process – an added incentive for the remaining Witches to surrender without any more resistance.

As Guard 016 finally fell to the ground with a small thud, his body disappeared into a pile of yellow dust. Oddvard studied his now pulsating skin in awe. He had heard many powerful Sorcerers in the past speak of this complicated spell, but had never heard of it being achieved in his lifetime. He felt strangely warm and tingly, his palms sweaty and throbbing.

He left the dungeon and climbed the damp spiral staircase out into the open courtyard and studied the waves on the horizon. He concentrated on reaching his destination and had an excruciating tightening sensation. His surroundings began to grow in a hazy blur. He bent over double and screamed in agony as he felt the flesh above his shoulder blades tear as four jet-black, spiked wings sprouted out.

He threw himself to his knees and vomited. When he stood he found he was looking at the world from a surreally different perspective. He had never imagined the effects to be so quick. He didn't, however, know how long the effects would last, so he hurried to his task.

As he crossed the courtyard, heading for the postern, he spotted a soldier sitting against a wall, head in hands.

Oddvard flew past him and said, "Get back to work, soldier," as he headed through an opening in the wall and out of sight, searching for a suitable place to connect with the fayerye world.

The soldier looked up to catch a glimpse of the fayerye disappearing, and shot up after it. As he looked out over the boundaries and the crashing waves, he encountered nothing but the dead silence of the night. He shook his head and headed inside for another new bottle.

Chapter 13

"Wake, you must wake!" shouted Patch. Niamh felt freezing cold water hit her face, and she was immediately awake, her nightmare feeling real, until she realised where she was.

"And you!" Patch yelled at Henry. Niamh looked around and saw Henry fighting with the water as it splashed in his eyes. Patch was at the entrance with a hand piercing the outer wall and water flying in which Patch was aiming directly toward them.

"Stop that! What is it? You could have just shouted, you stupid insect," Niamh said grumpily. She stood and realised that she was, in fact, completely dry and her clothes seemed to be clean and smelt of pine cones.

"Please, you must hurry," demanded Patch, appearing to have missed the insult thrown at him. "You have little time."

"What's wrong?" asked Henry, looking confused and scratching the sleep from his eyes. Although they had been woken up so harshly, they both felt more awake than they had in days. They had no idea how long had passed since falling asleep. Henry grabbed his sword and sheathed it carefully, paying little attention to why it had appeared by his side again. He then noticed his other belongings in a pile and looked at Patch enquiringly.

"We have our ways," he said.

Henry found comfort in the fact that he hadn't really had to use Ghild yet. Maybe this was going to be easier than they thought. He soon regretted thinking this when Patch began to speak.

"You are in great danger!" he exclaimed. "One of our guards went missing last night. He has done this before and we have had our suspicions in the past. One of my sergeants got wind of where he was and sent a unit to follow him this time, and his portal led to the Sorcerers. To their leader's castle."

Niamh gasped as Henry rushed forward to Patch, who was now floating by the exit, eager to leave.

"What? I thought we were safe here? How much does he know?" asked Henry.

"He knows of the village, the necklace, its power and your destination," said Patch, backing away a little but increasing in radiance.

"So, everything then?" Niamh said, but hoping Patch was mistaken.

"All is not lost. I expect he is too young to remember the exact location of the island you seek. My people rarely speak of times before the Great War of your people. It can do no good to dwell on what we can no longer have, so it is unlikely he knows where this place is. Quick, you must hurry. Little time has passed here but you should return to your own time if you hope to outrun the Sorcerer and his allies."

Niamh went to speak but was hurried through the door into the glass chamber. It was a lot darker than it had been last time, but Niamh realised it was not night time, as she had first suspected, but sheltered. The glass room was in the Wooded Realm. Light splintered in an array of beams across the room as it hit the top of the glass.

"But how far away is the Sorcerer's castle? Surely we are far enough away to be safe. How could they catch us here anyway?"

Patch seemed to consider this for a few moments, but fought his disbelief at the situation. "There appear to be ways. The Sorcerer is here. He has somehow taken the shape and size of my people. I do not know of this misuse of our land's magic, but I know you must go. You must not fail in your task. Everything you will ever know will be altered by your success or failure. Everything depends on you.

"Our encounter is nearly complete. Now, I must give you what we ask of you in return." Patch flew over to the stone table and landed running, waving his arms in circles to stop himself falling from the far end. He obviously feared the Sorcerers as Niamh's mother did. On the table were two golden stands in the shape of open hands. Resting in each of them was a small glowing caster.

On closer inspection they saw the casters were pulsating and glowing. One was silver and green, the other gold and pink. When the light rose to its greatest point, it was possible to see something moving inside.

"What are they?" asked Niamh. "They're beautiful."

Henry seemed fixed in a daze as he moved closer and pressed his nose up to one, a warm glow ebbing from its core.

"They are Elmites. I believe your translation for them is 'heirs'. They are not safe here at this time of war. It is only a matter of time before the destruction reaches our woods. Trees should be used to preserve the land's magic and life, yet they are still thought of as unnecessary to our world's survival. Used for tools, furnishings, boats."

Both Niamh and Henry bowed their heads in shame. They knew the stools they used at school were wooden – the desks, the doors... the list was endless. Niamh suddenly understood the uncomfortable stone chair and table in the glass chamber.

"We will take them and look after them. We will return them safely when the time is right and the gods are happy."

"Thank you, Chosen One," Patch said, looking at Henry. He fluttered his wings a few times then lifted the spheres from each stand into Henry's hand. Henry was amazed at the size of the eggs being nearly as big as Patch.

"And thank you, Witche. You will make a good leader for your people." Patch bowed his head whilst landing on one knee on the table. Niamh shifted a little uneasily as she felt a glow filtering through her cheeks to reveal her embarrassment. Her blushing reminded her of Henry's bare chest earlier, or yesterday morning. She wasn't sure anymore.

"Now hurry, you must go." Patch went to the glass wall and pulled out a new thread. This one was a dull copper colour and obviously hurt Patch to touch.

"Hurry, I cannot hold the passage open for long going this way."

Niamh and Henry ran at the new doorway with Henry placing the Elmites in his cloth sack as carefully as possible.

"Farewell, Chosen One. Travel well and good luck."

Niamh felt herself crash to the ground and roll into a tree as they were sucked through the opening. Henry came tumbling behind her and landed face-down in the mud. They had both forgotten the dullness of the Wooden Realm and sat for a few seconds looking into the dreariness. It seemed a little lighter than last time but it was still a horrible shade of grey.

Niamh stood first and helped Henry up.

"We should go," said Niamh.

"Go where?" asked Henry suddenly. "He didn't tell us where to go."

As though he had heard them, Patch popped his head through the disappearing glass wall and threw a small glass tube containing a rolled piece of parchment towards them. As he did he was thrown out onto the earthy floor, rolling and tangling with another fayerye as they ricocheted off a tree root and tumbled to a stop.

Henry saw the attacking fayerye was much harder to see in the light. His skin seemed black and covered in tiny red horns and spikes. It was obvious that this fayerye meant harm, and Henry moved toward Patch to help him.

"Now go!" Patch yelled. "You mustn't fall into his hands."

Niamh suddenly realised she was watching the greatest threat to their task, and her people, without even realising it. The Sorcerer fired spell after spell at Patch, who was obviously struggling to protect himself. Patch took a sharp red flash to his chest and rolled backwards, landing face down in a small, mossy ditch.

Oddvard fluttered over to him and prodded the fayerye's head with the ball of his foot. Satisfied that he no longer posed a threat, he turned to Niamh and Henry and started towards them.

Henry looked at Niamh and picked up the glass tube. As they ran they realised they were on the other side of the Fayerye Bridge — the edge of the forest having magically appeared just several hundred feet away from them.

As Oddvard moved toward them, a triumphant grin spread across his lips. His expression soon faded as he received a hard blow to his lower back and was rammed back into the glass room by a battered Patch. Henry watched as the distorted figures battled fiercely inside the room and Patch fought the Sorcerer back toward the far end of the chamber.

Henry and Niamh ran until their limbs ached with pain. They crossed the outer edge of trees and stopped, panting, with their hands on their knees in doubled-over exhaustion.

Henry pulled the piece of cloth from the tube and it began to glow. Glittery dust fell from the glass funnel. It unravelled itself in his hands and Henry and Niamh began to study it. It was the map Niamh's mother had given them, but it looked different.

Silver lines began to throb, like veins showing their current location with a circle and a long snaking line to a point on the far north coast line. They noticed how vast Ysrir actually was. Several new landmarks they didn't recognise shimmered above the surface of the yellow-bleached cloth.

"Look, that is the town we're heading for," Henry panted. "We should be able to make it there fairly quickly. We should go."

"Do you think Patch will be OK?" Niamh asked, looking worried.

"I think Patch probably knows how to look after

himself better than we do. We should go now," Henry stated as he began a slow run, the pains in his chest from the interrogation now easing slightly. He pressed on, not wanting to think about what he had been through.

Henry rolled the cloth back into the glass tube and slid it inside his belt. It was nearing dusk, the orange-purple sky a perfect backdrop for the beautiful landscape below them. As they peered out over the valley they truly understood what Patch had spoken of. They had never seen Ysrir looking so beautiful. The grass seemed greener, the birds chirpier. It seemed so perfect compared to the misery of the shaded trees they had just left.

In the far distance they saw several lines of smoke rising from behind a hilltop.

"Guess we're going that way," Niamh said, trying to keep up.

"Yeah, but it's nearly nightfall. Samhein can only be a few hours away now, I guess."

After some time running Niamh noticed they hadn't spoken much and felt the silence eating away at her thoughts.

"You... OK?" she asked Henry.

"Yeah, I think so. I felt awful before but I think Patch must have done something because I felt a lot better once he turned up. I feel great now, actually. How are you doing? You banged your head, didn't you?"

Niamh put her hand to her head and winced at the sharp stabbing pain she got. When she studied her hand, she noticed the dark stains of dried blood. In all the panic and excitement she had forgotten her knock to the head.

Obviously Patch hadn't thought it necessary to do anything for *her* pain, she thought grumpily.

Chapter 14

Magatha's heart pummelled the interior of her rib cage as she sped down the hill from her house. The distant shrill of war horns echoed through the village. She knew the third and fourth regiment of the Witches Front were on duty today and would be implementing the first stages of defence.

As Magatha raced through the village, shutters slammed and doors were barred. Everyone who could not fight – or would not – barricaded themselves behind as much clutter as they could lay their trembling hands on. Magatha knew their defences were weak. This feeble attempt at safety could be all that stood between them and death or eternal slavery.

The horn continued to carry from way on the horizon, penetrating the outer wall and creeping around the village to torment all those who heard it. Magatha weaved her way through the throbbing crowd, who were eager to flee, and counted the heartbeats between the war cries.

Stand and fight, you cowards! she felt herself scream inwardly, but she knew few had the power or knowledge to fight in battle – especially against such a great force. Witchecraft involved a series of complicated hand movements to cast an effective power spell. These could be taught, but the true power depended on the blood of the castor. As the generations had passed, she had seen a steep decline in the overall power of the land's magic, and with it a weaker breed of Witches. She knew few would survive what lay ahead now that they had lost many of their best fighters in the earlier encounters.

As she rounded the corner of the armament, she stopped and gawped at the hive of activity bubbling around her. Scores of troops, all dressed head to foot in swirling black and purple outfits, were running in lines of ten, maybe fifteen, out of the main gate. Spotting Colonel Balla on the far side of the gate, she nodded and began to precariously manoeuvre her way between the jogging soldiers.

"Good turnout, Magatha, don't you think?" he said, his ginger moustache tickling his nose as he spoke. Colonel Balla was in charge of the six regiments of the Witches Front. He was a large, jolly-looking man of about fifty years, with a shaven head, the slightest evidence of ginger hair showing in the stubble. This was reinforced by his bushy ginger moustache. A deep purple scar crossed the width of his left cheek. Colonel Balla was a veteran of the Great War and had seen his fair share of action.

"Very good," she replied absently. She watched as row after row of soldiers marched toward certain doom, the look of terror clear on each of their pale faces. The majority of the fourth and fifth guard fell in the last attack, and many of the replacements looked barely old enough to graduate from Niamh's class, never mind fight in combat. The fact that they were there suggested they had at least basic knowledge of Witchecraft, though. *Failing that, they had better be good with a sword*, Magatha thought.

Magatha's thoughts turned briefly to Niamh, and she wondered how far she had got in her quest. She knew many perils lay ahead of her but, for the time being, she had her own worries and focused on the task at hand.

"OK, Colonel, I assume the men have been well briefed? Let us move into place. If this tactic works, we may be able to end this for good, but I fear it may be beyond hope. I had not wanted to see days like these again."

"Magatha, I don't see why we are always on the

defensive. If we could just attack them rather than waiting, trapped like rabbits in a burrow longing for a lucky escape."

"No, Colonel, we are not an aggressive race. I refuse to drop to their level. Anyway, enough damage has been done to our beautiful land without us adding to it."

The Colonel nodded, his eyes searching for his feet. Magatha knew the Colonel understood: it was not the way of a Witche to damage their own land. Magatha had tried many alternatives and was out of ideas. She had even travelled far past the Witches' permitted area to try and reason with their leader, but was lucky to make it back alive.

Colonel Balla must have been able to see Magatha was deep in distressing thought, and placed a hand on her shoulder. "By the Will of Seirim, this mess will be resolved," he said, his eyes looking deep into hers as he reached for his sword. Although the Witches Front relied heavily on the force of magic in combat, especially against such a powerful opponent, their weapons were essential for close combat or when all else failed. Magic weaved about the surface of Colonel Balla's sword, and Magatha noted the presence of defensive charms rather than aggressive. She smiled in acknowledgment that the Colonel's rant about attacking was not supported by his true feelings.

"I will be moving up the left flank with Sergeant Yallaho's unit. If all goes to plan I will see you at the summit alive and well, my friend."

She looked at her feet for a minute in deep thought then looked up, exchanged handshakes and joined the throng of soldiers marching to fulfill their destiny. As she reached the outer gate, a small hunched man crossed her path and knelt before her. Magatha, skidding to a stop, was clearly angered by this interruption. Her mind was now set on what lay ahead.

"Fool!" she blurted. "Out of my way." She made to move around the old man when he stood and bowed his head.

"My greatest wishes at this time of war, ma'am. If I could fight alongside you I would die a happy man, but it is not to be." The man made a gesture toward his back and grimaced. Magatha had noticed a collection of soldiers caught up behind them waiting to get out. Secretly she knew they were glad, but it was only delaying the inevitable.

"Please take this," said the old man. He rummaged in his pocket and pulled out a small golden brooch shaped like a fly. "It has always brought me luck and I hope it will do the same for you."

"Very well, old man. Now please, I must get on," she said, feeling a sense of *déjà vu*, like she had met this old man before. Maybe she had, she thought, and dismissed it as she needed to get moving.

"As you wish, Your Highness." The man moved away through the crowd backwards, head bowed and his dark brown eyes boring into Magatha until he was enveloped by the next wave of soldiers and seemed to disappear.

Magatha jogged out of the town walls trying to keep pace with the younger soldiers. She toyed with the fly between her fingers as she ran, caressing its cool metallic curves, unknowing of the evil coursing through its cold surface.

Chapter 15

The ground began to rise into a series of barren slopes. Trees were burnt, grass singed. Huge craters formed the new pocked surface of Magatha's beautiful land.

The Sorcerers had yet to advance past the many hills of Craggy Range. She began the long stretch up Cribden Hill with her team and looked down into the valley to her right, carefully crouching so as not to be seen.

The pounding of feet could be heard below as the collective march of Sorcerers came into view in the distance. Magatha sensed they were prepared for one final push to rid their land of this unfortunate disease: her people.

Ahead of her, a hundred or so members of the Witches Front jogged, half crouched, swords held so low the blades skimmed where the once-long grass would have grown. They approached the summit of the hill and formed a tight huddle on the ground, awaiting further instruction.

***

Jolla shifted on his horse to obtain a better view. Between his stead and the enemy lay six personal bodyguards on horseback, a line of approximately a hundred archers, several hundred axe-bearers and the front line.

The front line consisted of the youngest soldiers, many with minimal knowledge or control of combat magic, who were intended to scare the enemy and hinder them with their sheer number. They also acted as a human shield, each with a circular wooden board, edged in iron for protection.

They carried a double-edged long sword that had become their weapon of choice. They also carried a *handox*, a small, carefully carved axe that attached to the back of their shields in the event of losing their sword. The shields were riddled with extremely powerful defensive magic and the name *skjaldbord* actually came from the early Sorcerer settlements, when it meant 'shield-fort'.

They were vividly decorated and used mainly yellow and black to denote the clan they belonged to. The shimmering defensive spells reflected playfully on the leather reinforcements that the soldiers had recently added.

When lined up and interlocked, these shields formed an effective glowing defence against most attacks. When the opportunity arose, the axe-bearers behind would weave in between their less fortunate comrades and cause as many fatalities as possible with their two-handed axes known as *breidox*. This would be reinforced by the charade of spellbound flaming arrows hurtled over their heads.

"The Witches have left the main gates and are forming their defence beyond the next ridge," said a muscly scout who had returned on horseback.

Jolla assessed the distance with great concentration as the sun began to set over the hills. "Good," he said. "We will continue as planned. Be sure your men are in place. No one advance until I give the order and remember... " Jolla stood in his stirrups to address his men. "Remember!" he shouted to everyone who could hear. "No one kill the Qwein. She must not be harmed." *Unless by me*, Jolla thought smugly.

"Of course, chief," the soldier turned as he kicked his legs and made a clucking noise, sending his horse into a quick gallop. Within seconds a dusty haze clouded him as he readied his platoon of men for battle.

The chanting army marched on and, advancing into the

neck of the valley, saw a wall of black in the far distance. This line appeared several people deep and around five hundred paces wide. This view was hazy as, not far ahead, lay an enormous expanse of vertical water. The great divide at Synchnant Pass had been severed many times before by Oddvard, but Jolla had yet to complete the opening of the god's barrier himself.

As the men reached the edge they stopped and stood aside to let Jolla through on horseback. A man rode behind him with an unconscious woman drooped over the rear of his horse.

As Jolla dismounted, he unsheathed his sword and waited anxiously as the soldier carried the woman to the edge and awaited further instruction. He nodded, and the soldier placed the woman's head through the water. He felt a strange pull on the body as the woman's soul was being severed from her physical form. Jolla swung his axe around over his head and brought it down savagely on the woman's neck, causing the barrier of water to dissolve from the point the woman's head entered it. Crimson blood was sucked from the severed neck into the wall of water, creating veins of red throughout the retreating barrier. The men rushed to cross the border, knowing the opening would last only a few minutes. The return trip would mean finding another victim to sacrifice, but with the way the battle was expected to go it should be relatively easy to find another.

***

Magatha crouched behind the protection of a moss-covered boulder. Far below them, in the foot of the valley, the enemy crossed the great barrier. Magatha mused that even if she knew the incantation to open the wall of the gods, her people would never sacrifice a life to pass through it.

In the distance a faint line of black and purple blocked the way forward. Magatha knew the line to be at least twenty soldiers deep, yet her eyes could not confirm this at such a distance.

"They are in place," she heard someone yell. Silence gripped them, a silence felt throughout the valley as they awaited the ferocious storm ahead. Magatha's breathing was rapid and her heart pummelled in her chest. She watched the scene below with intense concentration waiting for their sign. Far down below a cry of horns erupted and a heavily-clad soldier dropped from his horse by Jolla's side, removing a long spear from his master's horse.

Magatha could see the spear had to be at least nine feet long. She knew it as *gungnir*, named after a Norse God of War. She had once tried to remove it after it had skewered the ground ahead of her, her intention to see how they reacted if it was thrown back, but it was cleverly engineered. The pins holding the head to the shaft had obviously been removed prior to throwing. As she yanked at the solid ash shaft, she found herself toppling backwards as the spear fell into two pieces.

She was brought back to the situation as she saw the chief wave his arms over the man's head in small, quick circles and an orange light flared from his open palms, through the man's body and into the spear, lighting it with an unnaturally bright glow. The man turned toward the Witches, who were now only a few hundred feet away, and marched towards them. He held the spear at arm's length and showed no signs of fear or fatigue. Magatha knew what this spear symbolised and readied herself for action.

The Sorcerers often called upon their God of War to begin a battle. By launching a spell-cast object into the oncoming enemy, they believed they would be blessed and the battle successful.

As the spear punctured the ground just ahead of the Witches, a small ring of flame erupted around it and the spear was swallowed by the ground. Magatha hadn't seen this before, and she rubbed her chin as she tried to decide what trickery this could be.

An array of screams and magic shot into the sky from the spear to create an electrifying dome of pure power around the battle as lightning-like charges fired toward her village from the point where the spear disappeared.

In the distance she could see blurred patches of light as rooftops and defences were set alight. The Sorcerers charged at the Witches' front line of defence, a mist of blood mingling with charges of magic from either side.

They could hear the tortured screams of many in the distance, but still they waited, hugging the ground in an attempt to grow roots and be fixed in relative safety. Suddenly three turquoise blue flares rose high into the sky before fizzing into a shower of burning sparks. That was their signal. The signal that meant the Sorcerers were finding it harder than they probably expected to penetrate the Witches line, and gaps were beginning to show in the Sorcerer's defences.

Magatha's troop climbed to their feet and began stealthily down the hill at an angle into the valley to try and come up behind the Sorcerers. They held their swords low to the ground, the raw magic implanted within them glowing red.

As they hit the valley floor, they spotted the back line of Sorcerers about two hundred yards ahead. Spreading out, they charged at their targets, fingers already miming the spells for fire and destruction.

***

Jolla had hung back during the first stages. This was mainly for protection. His line of bodyguards waited slightly ahead of him.

He watched as his men savagely ripped the Witches to pieces. He had noticed he'd already lost quite a few men and the Witches seemed to be putting up a good fight. He knew his King had always seen his men as expendable, though, when a greater cause required it, so he wasn't deeply troubled by the losses.

As he stood in his stirrups to see better, he heard a faint rustle behind him. He knew immediately something was wrong, and kicked his horse into motion before even looking back. A line of a hundred or so Witches had approached from the rear and, with the majority of men entangled ahead, he had no choice but to fight.

"Attack from the rear!" he roared as several of his bodyguards scrambled between him and the enemy. He pictured Craller, the Rune of Fire, and propelled his open hand toward the approaching Witches. Magatha spotted this and began to form the spell of protection with her left hand, her sword occupying the right and the fly now in her pocket.

Jolla unleashed the blow and a wave of blue fire rolled from his open palm, singeing any surviving plant life ahead. Magatha continued her run, her defensive spell casting a blue orb around her. She noticed that many of her comrades hadn't spotted the attack early enough and fell to the ground in shrieks of agony as the spelled fire burned their flesh and souls.

Jolla looked on as the surviving Witches continued their run toward him and his men, and a smile formed at the greatly diminished numbers. Swirls of magic lit the sky beside him as his bodyguards joined in the fight. This gave Jolla the chance to catch his breath after his last spell, which he hadn't intended to consume so much energy.

"Die!" Magatha screamed as she approached the outer ring of men. She was surprised at her lust for vengeance given her earlier conversation with Captain Balla, and she jumped a few feet from the ground between two bodyguards, spun in the air, and removed both men's heads in one fatal swoop. The magic from her sword glistened with their blood as their decapitated corpses fell to the ground with a thud.

As Jolla ducked beneath a stray spell he saw rebound off a soldier's shield, he took cover behind his startled horse. Looking around to regain his bearings, he spotted a scrawny, black-clad Witche devouring his men as though they'd never laid hands on a weapon.

"At last!" he spat through gritted teeth, "We meet on this dark night, Witche Qwein. King Oddvard will surely take me as one of his own after this."

Magatha looked up as she kicked a corpse she had just skewered off her sword. She recognised Jolla immediately from their previous encounters, and knew this was her chance. If she could take Jolla down now, his men would surely flee without the control of a leader. A more worrying thought came to her about the whereabouts of Oddvard, and she immediately thought of Niamh.

She began to run toward him, sword held outstretched ahead of her. Her left hand created the shapes of immobility and weakness. If she could take Jolla alive, maybe it would show his kind how powerful they really were.

As she picked up her pace, he sank to the ground with his legs crossed, his cape swooping around him in a breeze nobody else could feel. As mayhem exploded around him, he sat in a relatively calm pose and placed his blade in the soil ahead of him. Placing both hands face down on the trodden ground, he pressed his fingers slightly under the surface of the soil and his eyes rolled back.

Magatha knew this must be some Sorcerer trick, but took it as an opportunity to attack while he was less aware. She began to swerve to her right in the hope of catching Jolla from the side, but noticed an electric green light pulsing from the ground into his fingers. She hesitated for a second then continued her run, her hands now performing spells of eternal torture – a fierce and demanding spell in this situation but, despite her desire for peace, she didn't want to take any chances now.

He rose to his feet with what seemed like no effort at all, almost puppet-like, and stared straight at Magatha. His eyes now glowed green like embers of evil. He aimed his fingers at Magatha and muttered something under his breath. Magatha felt a weight in her stomach like nothing she'd ever felt before. The pain began to grow and she skidded to her knees only feet away from Jolla, her sword falling to the ground, her face scraping across the rough ground.

She began to vomit blood and rolled onto her back, the spells in the sky seeming inappropriately beautiful to her. She saw Jolla lean over her and felt his rigid, muscular fingers grip her throat.

"Tell me where the necklace is, Witche!" he grunted, the green flames licking at her cheeks. The pain had become excruciating now, and she wondered how he had done it with such little contact.

"Never!" she screamed, a patch of dark red blood now beginning to appear at her abdomen. Jolla lifted her even further from the ground by her neck, her body lolling weightlessly below.

"Your fate here is clear, Witche. It will be far less painful if you cooperate. I need to get that necklace. You do not understand the powers you are meddling with and the potential they have for destruction. It will not benefit your kind tonight."

Magatha began to panic. She could sense the battle around her slowing as Jolla's men seemed to be overpowering her own. She felt around on the ground for her sword but realised she was too high to reach anything. She frantically felt in her pockets for the brooch. Maybe if she could hit him with it hard enough it might do enough damage for him to drop her.

She placed her hand in her pocket and felt warm, viscous liquid cling to her fingers. She was sure she hadn't dropped it. She felt further inside and realised the cause of her pain.

Her finger pressed gently into the goo and a sharp stabbing sensation gripped her whole body. The brooch was inside her; she could feel it writhing under her skin, fighting to get out. She yelped in panic and disgust and Jolla dropped her to the ground laughing.

The laugh rose in volume and echoed throughout the valley. "Come now, Witche, I am tired of these games. All I need to do is make the fly enter your brain and you will tell me all I need to know. It would be a far less painful death for you if you just cooperated now."

Magatha struggled to summon the energy to raise her

head. After a few seconds she gazed into the sickening green eyes and sobbed. "I will never tell you! NEVER! My time here is over anyway." She sank to the floor sobbing.

Without a hint of emotion, Jolla raised his hands to Magatha's head. A green light shone blindingly from his hands into her temples, lighting her veins green and causing her body to convulse violently. After several minutes she fell with a thud to the trampled ground, silent, the back of her clothes ripped and burnt. Jolla stood back as the fly pulsed green through her skin and began to move up her spinal cord and into her brain. As it punctured her brain, Magatha let out a deep gurgling sound and blood began to seep from her ears and nose. Jolla lifted his hands and Magatha's body sat up like a limp puppet, her eyes the same electric green as his.

"Tell me now, Witche. Tell me where the necklace is!" he yelled, his mouth only inches from her face.

Even though Magatha's mind was still alive in what appeared to be her now dead body, she could not prevent the words escaping her mouth.

"The necklace can be found where the three lines of Witchecraft cross and the power of the land is most intense. It is occupied by humans, one of which holds the Necklace of the Sea," she said in a monotone voice. Her head occasionally twitched so violently that her neck could be heard cracking from several yards away.

"The necklace must be returned to the gods at the point they were separated, an island to the north of Ysrir and the farthest point north on this land. Here the evil your people brought on this land will be repaired."

Jolla's body loosened and his eyes began to return to normal. He re-sheathed his sword and began to walk away toward his horse. "That is what you think," he said, mainly to himself, and laughed.

As he mounted his horse, he scanned the horizon. Scores of Witches lay dead all around him. It appeared he had lost several of his own men, but the survivors were already checking the bodies for valuables and weapons.

One soldier dragged a struggling Witche by the feet toward the great water barrier. Overall, it had been a successful encounter. "Men, let us return to Adiabene where we will regroup and plan our next move. I have what King Oddvard requires."

"But, chief, the Witches's defences are almost destroyed. Their army is flattened. Surely we should advance to the town and finish what we started?" asked a heavily armoured bodyguard.

"They will not recover from this blow and their Qwein is dead. We have more pressing matters to attend to. Come, ride with me and I will tell you all. We have news the King will be extremely pleased with. We must get word to him immediately. After this, we will not need to bother fighting with the Witches. They will be destroyed in one fatal swoop."

As he turned, he unsheathed his sword once again. "I waited a long time for this, Witche. You should hope my master has as much mercy with your daughter." He brought his blade down in a large swoop and removed Magatha's head cleanly, causing it to roll a few feet from her body. The men behind him cheered.

Magatha watched from afar as her head bounced across the floor with a quiet thud. She noticed the swarm of people heading toward a white light behind her. She hadn't actually seen the light yet, but somehow she knew it was there. She turned and started walking, occasionally spotting the semi-transparent appearance of a soldier she recognised walking beside her.

The light caused the back of her eyes to hurt as she neared it, but she continued on, looking around in all directions. Where all the pale faced soldiers were walking, almost unconsciously, toward the light, Magatha was frantically looking this way and that.

Just feet from the light and the entrance to a long, white tunnel, Magatha stopped. She had spotted what she was looking for and sprinted through the clusters of people to what looked like a small hole of nothingness. *Oh no, you don't. It's not my time yet,* she thought as she reached the black hole.

She plunged her hand deep within and pulled the opening wider. Struggling to squeeze through, she wriggled her body until only her feet and ankles were visible and then disappeared through the wall.

Chapter 16

As they ran, Niamh noticed the sun already approaching the tips of the mountains in the distance. The smoke still snaked across the sky beyond the next hill. Her muscles burned with cramp. They had been running for too long, acid seeping through her muscles as she tried to keep a steady pace. As she looked up she noticed Henry pulling further and further away.

"Henry, wait!" Niamh gasped.

"No time. Come on. We can rest in a while," he said breathlessly.

Niamh pushed through the initial pain and scrunched her face as she ran. The pain dulled to a pulsating ache that was uncomfortable but bearable.

As she noticed Henry gaining even more speed she turned it into a game. As she jumped and weaved between the long rushes and grass mounds she mentally tracked the distance between herself and Henry and tried to close it. She was more stubborn than competitive and she knew she could do it.

Henry continued his rhythmic gallop, occasionally glancing back to make sure Niamh wasn't lagging too far behind. They knew they probably wouldn't make it by sundown, and Samhein usually started at around seven or eight o'clock at night. They had to try, though. Whatever it was Niamh's mother was worried about had to be bad. She didn't scare easily.

After about an hour of jogging, the pace had definitely deteriorated. Niamh imagined Henry was now a little embarrassed to be jogging a few feet behind her, and she was now running with a smug grin on her face. She was pleased Henry couldn't see it, though.

Henry eventually gave in. "Wait, Niamh," he panted. "We should stop for a rest, get our strength up. Maybe have a bit of food."

Niamh had already slowed to nearly walking pace when she spotted a log a few feet ahead. She stumbled over to it with exhaustion and sat down. Henry slumped beside her and gasped for air. His chest was tight and they sat for a few minutes trying to catch their breath.

Niamh felt inside her cloth satchel and found some food Patch had left them. Breaking a round piece of crusty bread in half, she passed some to Henry.

"You think we can make it?" Niamh asked after they had both devoured their food.

"Honestly? No," Henry said. "We can do our best, but it will be sundown soon and we still have a fair way to go."

They both jumped as a shriek so penetrating that they were scared their ears might burst erupted all around them. They covered their ears with their hands and looked around frantically, the sound converting to pain as it reached their brains.

They heard wails and yells echoing in the valley ahead as they noticed the sun disappear behind the hills. It was sundown.

"We didn't make it, then," Henry said.

"Doesn't sound like it. I'm guessing whatever made

that noise is probably what my mother was hoping we would avoid."

Niamh knew the history of Samhein better than most. Her family had always been at the head of the table at the great feast. Niamh wasn't supposed to go, being a child, but she and Henry always managed to sneak in under the canvas tent. Samhein was the night of death when Witches would summon the spirits that had passed and, so the story went, the dead walked the land.

A sudden realisation of where the scream had come from suddenly hit them.

"Are we still going that way, then?" asked Niamh, pointing in the direction of the shriek, which they were both sure had stopped now. Their ears seemed unwilling to accept this and continued to ring and buzz in the aftermath.

"Yeah, let's go," Henry said as he got up. As they set off toward the faint lines of smoke, they noticed the light had dimmed extremely quickly. It was now nearly pitch black, the dark grey clouds shielding the moon.

They jogged for a while longer before spotting movement in the bushes up ahead. Something was moving away from them at great speed.

"Wai..." Henry went to shout but was stifled by Niamh's hand.

"What are you doing?" she whispered. "We don't know what that is. It could be anything. It could be what we are trying to avoid you idiot!"

Henry jumped on a nearby rock and tried to look out after the retreating creature. "I think it might be a human," he attempted quietly as though not wanting to voice his opinion in case it was horribly wrong.

"Hey!" Henry yelled through cupped hands.

∗∗∗

Trialla stopped, stunned. She was panicky, knowing she should have been back well before now. She knew she should have set off earlier but the solitude of the lake, the quiet ripples reflecting the last of the sunlight, was too relaxing compared to the mayhem she was going to face at home. A night of torturous screams and hammering on her walls if the creatures caught her scent hiding in her home.

They couldn't have made it this far from the village already. She'd only just heard their cries but she definitely heard something then. Her heart raced as she ran through the bushes and jumped at a tree. If she couldn't make it back to the village at least she would be safe, if uncomfortable, up a tree for the night.

"Hey wait!" she heard again. "We won't hurt you." As much as she knew the nightly beasts would kill her if she was wrong she was drawn to the friendly, masculine voice. She knew they couldn't talk, but was it far enough past sundown?

Niamh and Henry pushed through the prickly thorns of the knee-high bushes and into a clearing. Up ahead they saw a small figure walking through a sudden mist that had fallen like a heavy blanket, the lack of light making it hard to see the approaching outline.

"Hello?" Trialla dared. "Who's there? Speak!" she demanded, holding her mining pick up high.

"It's OK," Niamh said taking over. She thought a female voice might ease the fright clear in the slowly approaching girl.

As the three of them came within a few feet of each other, they all sighed and felt a great relief as they realised there was no obvious threat.

"Who are you?" Trialla asked cautiously.

"We're friends. I'm Henry and this is Niamh. We are just travellers looking for a village around here," Henry interjected. They didn't want to get into the whole story and they still didn't know who she was. He also knew Niamh was likely to give something away if left to ramble for too long. Niamh gave him a glare, knowing exactly what he was thinking.

"Who are you?" said Niamh looking back at the stranger.

"My name is Trialla. I'm sorry, I really can't stay. I must get back to my village. You should go too. You're not safe here," said Trialla.

Henry and Niamh looked at each other, Magatha's words clear in their minds. They could see Trialla was obviously petrified of something, although she looked like she could take care of herself.

Henry noticed she seemed quite well built and strong for a girl, and she had approached complete strangers in the mist and dark. Henry could also tell it wasn't really them she was afraid of, as she kept looking anxiously into the woods around them.

Trialla turned to run into the daunting trees behind them when Henry laid a hand on her shoulder. "Wait, please. We have to find a village. Teare Gro, it is called. Do you know it?" he asked.

Trialla looked astounded. "Why would you be looking for my village? Where are you from, travellers? Are you from Lertha?"

Niamh thought for a few seconds, knowing she couldn't possibly know the correct answer to give. "No, we are from a lot further afield than that," she attempted.

"You're all the way from Hunts Town?" asked Trialla, amazed.

"Yeah, near there," Henry interjected, again looking over at Niamh. They knew this girl was probably human based on the fact they were so close to a human settlement. They also both knew this girl was definitely not a Witche and probably not a Sorcerer.

"What are you so scared of?" asked Niamh.

Trialla seemed to suddenly snap back to reality, worry etched across her tired face.

"It's my people. It's a long story. There is a curse on my people. I have never been as far as Hunts Town, so I guess your people are unaffected. It is not safe there after dark."

Henry looked up at the sky, "Like now, you mean?" he asked.

"Yes. I should really go. My village is the Teare Gro you seek, but I would not wish it upon anyone after dusk. You would be safer with me, though, I suppose. We need to get to my hut. Please, do not hurt anyone. No matter what. Please."

Henry and Niamh looked at her questioningly.

"Please," she repeated as she spun on her heels and headed for the trees. The low-hanging branches made it difficult to see the weaving path she was taking, but they managed to keep up. After about fifteen minutes of ducking and weaving between trees, bushes and rocks, they came to a large wooden wall circling row after row of small huts. The wall towered above them, and what they assumed to be guard platforms stood empty. It was too quiet for a village of this size. As soon as Henry had thought this, a howl came from the trees behind them. Trialla spun, fear clear on her face.

"Run!" she screamed.

Chapter 17

They sprinted through the open wooden gates at speed. Niamh soon realised there had once been horses here. She leapt over the partially-devoured carcass of a white stallion and tried not to focus on the horrid taste in the back of her throat as she was nearly sick.

She began to ready spells of protection and defence after Trialla's words earlier. As she glanced to the side she noticed Henry doing the same, his left hand on the handle of his sword. He looked over at Niamh as they ran. They could both sense the fear in each other and in this girl. They could also feel the danger her mother had warned of, getting closer, its breath on their sweating necks. This was not a safe place to be.

As they ran, Niamh noticed a silvery-looking tree shrouded in mist up ahead. She almost stopped to look at it in amazement. The visions her mother told her had come true. They had predicted she would see this tree. She dallied only for a split second until fear overcame her astonishment and she picked up her pace again.

They weaved through the maze of shanty town huts in pursuit of Trialla. She obviously knew where she was going. They hoped she did, anyway. They took a sharp corner into an alleyway. Lines of rope spread from hut to hut, creating a webbed effect. Wet clothes with old red stains hung at random to dry. They had both noticed the mist had descended once again, obscuring their view in the cluttered alley.

As they ducked under the first line, Trialla skidded to a quick halt. Niamh ran straight into the back of her, and Henry used all his strength not to fall as he cannoned into the pair of them from behind. The reason for the abrupt stop soon became clear as Niamh let out a yelp of surprise.

Ahead of them were three people. They couldn't be described as people, Niamh soon realised. Their skin was white and flesh hung from them in bloody, rotten chunks. Their eyes were empty purple sockets, their clothes nothing but tattered rags.

They shuffled as though they had never walked before, feet dragging behind as an afterthought. The one at the front wailed as though attempting to speak, and scraped his hand on the wall of a hut. The back of its hand was severed on a piece of sharp railing, and blood spilled to the floor. Niamh cringed as she saw this but the figure seemed unperturbed.

"Quick!" Trialla shouted as she hopped on the spot and darted down another alley. Niamh and Henry ran after her and the figures wailed behind them. Henry bounced off the wall of a hut as they left the alleyway, and he tried to keep up with Niamh and Trialla.

As they rounded another corner, they skidded to a stop again. More creatures blocked their path. They looked around at the surrounding pathways. The figures seemed to be flocking toward them, their own presence acting like a beacon.

Henry unsheathed his sword and stepped ahead of the two girls.

"No!" shrieked Trialla, pulling his hand down. Henry was startled, but this was more from worry about the sharpness of his blade and it being so close to his leg.

He fired an angry look at her. "What else do you suggest? I don't think they're here to make friends," he said in a sarcastic tone.

"No, but they *are* my friends. I might refer to them as 'creatures', but that is so I do not connect them with the real people they are in case I have to kill one of them," she said.

Henry took a moment to think about this, then realised he didn't have much time to decide what to do. He didn't understand her response. He sheathed his sword again, and said, "What do we do, then?"

As much as she didn't want to hurt her friends and family, Trialla always knew it might come to this. It didn't look as though there was much choice. The creatures closed in from all directions. The three targets in the centre closed in back to back and began to weigh up their options.

"We don't have much choice, Trialla," said Niamh as she held her Staff out at arm's length and cast a spell of protection around them. The blue orb grew and pulsed around them.

"What is this?" gasped Trialla, "Magic?"

"Good one, Niamh," Henry said as Niamh realised her mistake.

Trialla attempted to push free of the orb and her hands pierced the outer glow causing it to shrink and disappear. "Wait!" yelled Niamh. "It's protecting you. You are safer in here."

Trialla was trapped between death and magic. She didn't know what to do. The lesser of two evils did seem to be the new travelers, but how was she to know it wasn't them who had put this curse on her people in the first place?

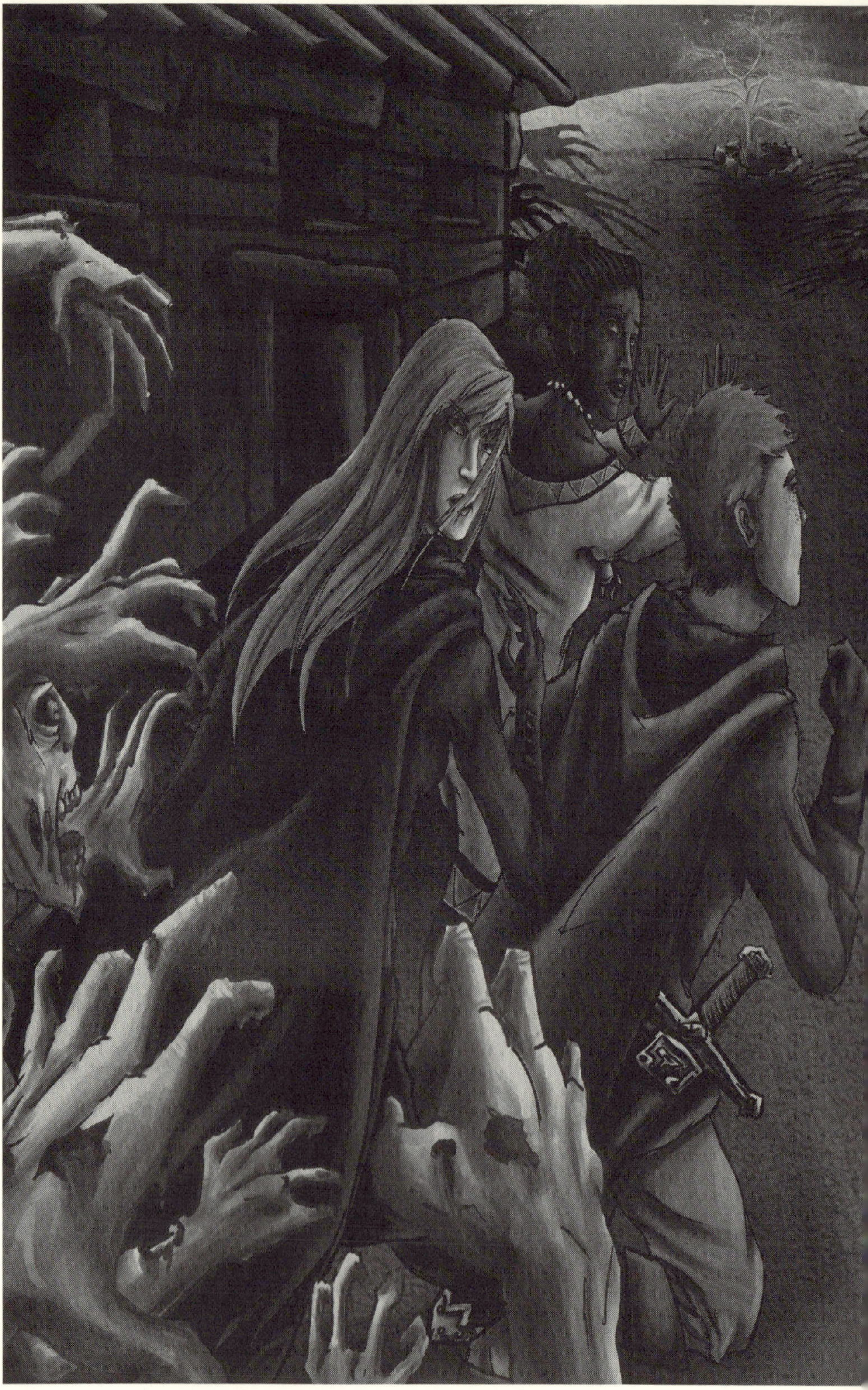

As she was deciding what to do, a bloody hand came down on her shoulder. Yellow nails dug into her skin and drew blood. She cried out and looked to the travellers for help.

As Henry and Niamh surged forward, Staff and blade in hand, they felt a sudden pull from behind. The creatures yanked at their shoulders and pulled Niamh to the ground. More came from behind as they felt claws scratching at them, wails and cries coming from their rotten, stinking mouths.

The mist began to thicken, the sudden fog seeming to tighten the air. Henry felt his chest close in and lost sight of Niamh in the mass of fleshy bodies.

"Niamh! NIAMH!" he shouted as he hacked through the dropping corpses with ease.

As Trialla looked up and frantically lashed out to get free, she saw something dart from an alley. *This is it*, she thought. *The final blow.* She closed her eyes and prayed. Suddenly, a weight lifted from her and she opened her eyes.

A creature had rammed its side into the pack of blood-thirsty creatures on top of her. She leaped to her feet and looked around. Ahead of her were three struggling bodies on the ground, and standing beside her was the attacking creature. Its right cheek hung from the bone by threads of purple vein. Trialla cowered but held her pick tight in her hand, ready.

The creature turned, bones cracking as it did, and dived at the attackers on top of Niamh and Henry. After a few minutes of scrapping, skin flapping loosely as they scratched and fought, Henry and Niamh struggled to their feet. They were injured but not badly, and their arms and faces stung with fresh scratches and cuts.

Niamh looked at Henry while cautiously backing away from the creature. It had saved them, but they were unsure why. Trialla had never seen one act like this.

"NO!" shouted Trialla, but she did not stop Niamh walking toward it.

Niamh edged a bit closer and stared it in the eyes, or the sockets. "I think it wants to say something," Niamh said. "It keeps staring at me." The creature stood motionless, its rotten head on one side, looking in the direction of Niamh. It continued to stare.

"This has never happened before," Trialla stated whilst looking around frantically for more creatures.

"What's going on, Trialla? You said you know these people," Henry said.

"They're my family and friends. They're not like this during the day, though. It is a curse. Maybe it's like the shine you used before," suggested Trialla. "They go back to normal at day break."

"Daaaaay breeeaaak!" howled the creature. "Saaaaafffe tthisss waaaay, Niiiammhhh." The creature turned and began to hobble down the alley toward the village gates.

Trialla stood motionless. "They've never spoken before either," she said. "Ever."

They took a few tentative steps forward and then began striding after it. Henry stayed at the rear with his sword held high. He had already cast a new blue orb. He looked at Niamh to make sure she was doing the same, when he noticed her staring at the creature ahead.

"It knew my name," she muttered. "How did it know my name?"

They made it to the gates without encountering any more creatures and headed out of the village and up the edge of the hillside. The creature clearly struggled with the climb. Its decaying flesh repeatedly got snagged on rocks and brambles.

Niamh climbed behind, never taking her gaze from it. Henry remained at the rear and spotted a few creatures circling around behind them. They kept their distance, obviously aware of the new threat leading their prey up the mountain. They showed evidence of basic animal instincts and, with one showing itself as a leader, an aggressor, it became dominant over the rest.

They reached a ledge a few feet square that led to a small crack in the hillside. "We're going in there?" asked Trialla, pointing to the cave. "With that?" she spat. "You don't know what they're capable of."

Henry noticed Niamh had already followed it into the opening, casting a light spell as she did to create a small floating glow ahead of her. "Niamh, wait!" Henry shouted as he ran after her, leaving Trialla to follow behind cautiously. A cry came from lower down the slope and she hurried after them.

About twenty strides inside the cave, the passageway opened up into a damp, dripping space. High above was a small crack that revealed a small slither of moonlight. Against the back of the cave was the creature, stood facing the wall, swaying and groaning. Niamh was standing beside it, staring.

"Niamh, get away. What are you doing?" Henry said, rushing toward her.

"Yooouuuu arre saaffe," groaned the creature. It turned to look at Niamh, blood dripping from its face to stain its chest. It was clear this creature had once been a woman. Trialla now thought she recognised her as Chella, a cloth weaver from the other side of the village.

"She's called Chella," Trialla said.

"Nooo. Nottt Chellaa," it said.

"I think she's afraid," Niamh said.

"How did you know my name?" Niamh asked it, speaking slowly and loudly as though speaking to someone who didn't understand the language.

"Niiiaaammhh. Maaaggaaathhha," it said, turning to face Niamh.

"How does it know your mother as well, Niamh?" Henry asked. He was disgusted by its appearance and smell. The stench clogged his throat and made him want to heave.

"I think... I think somehow it *is* my mother," Niamh said. She didn't know why she knew this. It was just a feeling – a sensation she got the first time she saw it. It was the way it looked at her. How could this be? Some kind of Witchecraft she had used because it was Samhein?

"Mother?" she asked tentatively, not sure whether she wanted an answer. "Is that you? How're you doing this?"

The creature, even though it had no eyes in its raw sockets, stared at Niamh and said, "Yeessssss. I... I... I have paaaasssed oovvveeerrrrr. I... I am dead, Niiiaammmh."

Niamh was stunned by this. Her eyes began to fill up.

Her mother couldn't be dead. She was the most powerful Witche on Ysrir. She was her mother. How dare she leave her parentless; how dare she die on her!

The creature went to place a fleshy hand on Niamh's shoulder, then retracted it as it sensed her flinch. "Evverrrytthiing haaappens fforrr a reeeasssson. Tthhhiiissss iiiisss myyyy paaarrrt. It iisssss only a hossst, I aam innn noo paaaain."

Niamh wiped a tear from her cheek and looked at the floor. She had to fight the urge to hug the creature – her mother. It was repulsive, the smell unbearable. But it was her mother. 'It' was a 'she' – a 'Qwein'. They had their differences, but she still loved her; still looked up to her.

Niamh hesitated, then wrapped her arms around the creature, the blood seeping into her clothes, the skin feeling loose in her hands. They embraced for a few minutes, then Magatha pulled away. "Iiii mmuuusssstt ggo. Yooou wiiill bbeeee ssaaaaffffe heeerre ttiiillllll mmoorrrrnniing. You have done well to come this far. I am proooud of yoooou, Niiaammh," Magatha said. Niamh felt a lump growing in her throat. Her mother had never said that before.

Magatha hobbled over to the cave entrance and put a bony hand on Henry's shoulder as she passed. Henry backed away, stunned. Trialla watched in amazement. She had never seen anything like this.

As Magatha turned to leave the cave, a creature appeared in the entrance and ran at her, ramming her to the ground.

"Get off her!" Niamh yelled as she ran at the new creature and jumped on its back, pulling loose flesh away as easily as when eating a chicken leg.

"Leeaaaave the children aloooone," the new creature spluttered.

This left Niamh, Henry and Trialla utterly confused. The creatures they had seen as vicious and scary all seemed to be falling over each other to protect the three of them.

The two creatures rolled around on the floor, pulling at loose body parts, then seemed to stop. The new one was face down on top of Magatha. They fell silent. The silence ate away the tension as the two creatures remained locked, staring into each other's bloodied, lifeless eyes.

They abruptly stood and embraced as old friends might. Niamh was sure a tear fell from the left socket where she assumed her mother's eye was supposed to be.

"Isssss itt reaaally you?" Magatha stammered, placing a bony hand on the new creature's shoulder.

"Yesss, it haasss beeeeen too long, Magathaaa," the new male creature said.

"Therrrrre issssss someone I wannnnt youuu to meeet, Niammmmmhson," Magatha said as she turned to look toward Niamh. "This isss ouuuur daughterrrrr, Niamh."

The new creature's eyes bored into Niamh and seemed to see right through to her very soul. Realisation struck her with more force than lightning, and she sobbed. It was all too overwhelming. Surely this couldn't be the father she had longed to know? The one person in the world she wished she could spend just two seconds in the company of?

Niamh looked up through teary eyes and said, "Father, is it really you?"

"Yeesss. It seemssss there issss so much that I have missed. A daaaaughter I... I neeeevver haaaad the chaaance to knowwww," he said. He rounded on Magatha and said, "I thougggghtt yoouu were deead, Magathhaaaa. Iii searchhhed for an eterrrrnity inn the nexxxt plaace, butt there wassss noo signnn of youuu, Magatha. He wailed as he held out his arms and stepped toward Niamh. She fell to the ground, sobbing, and hugged the creature's calf.

"I only wisssshh I could haavve got to know you properly, Niaamh. See youuuu grow up innnnto the amazzzzing young Witche you havvvve clearly becommme," her father said as he stroked her cheek and wriggled free of her grip. Her mother passed her too, running her fingers across the top of her daughter's head as Niamh continued to sob on the floor.

As Magatha got to the cave entrance she stopped and placed an arm around Niamhson's shoulder. She looked towards Niamh and said, "I love you, Niamh," and they headed out into the night, letting out an ear-piercing scream from somewhere down the hillside.

"NO!" Niamh screamed, running after them. "I love you too! I love you too!" As she got to the end of the ledge, she couldn't spot either of them. "I love you too," she whispered to herself as she knelt down and cried in the mist.

Henry and Trialla both came out to comfort her, hearing her crying echoing in the cave. They were scared for Niamh, and, selfishly Henry thought, also for the attention her crying might attract.

Henry knelt beside her and wrapped his arms around her neck. "Look at me," he whispered. "Look at me." Niamh struggled to hide her tears and lifted her head to meet his gaze. "She's gone. They both are." Niamh wept harder. Henry saw the tears highlighting the deep blue of her eyes in the glow of her magical light.

"I know," he replied. "It's OK. Let it out." There was an awkward silence when Henry struggled to find words to say. Niamh put her head on Henry's shoulder and continued to cry. "She was proud of you, Niamh. She loved you, and at least you got a chance to meet your father," Henry attempted. This lifted Niamh's mood slightly as she pushed away and rubbed her eyes. "We should get back inside," she said as she walked toward the cave. "I want to be alone for a while."

"Is she OK?" Trialla asked Henry once Niamh had retreated to the depths of the cave.

"No, but she will be. She was never close to her mother, but she wanted to be. She'd never met her father until now as well. Well, kind of her father, I suppose. He died years ago in the Great War before she was born."

"The Great Wa...," Trialla began, but gave up, knowing this was all too much for her to take in.

"We should check she's OK," Henry said.

Trialla followed him, looking out to her village as she did. *Well, this is new,* she thought as she went after Henry.

They found Niamh curled up in a corner, her head resting on her satchel. She was gripping the Staff of Light tightly in her arms. Henry checked that she was asleep, then sat down against the opposite wall. Trialla joined him.

"How long has this been going on?" Henry asked.

"As long as I can remember," Trialla replied. "It has never been like tonight, though. They've never spoken and they've never protected me before. How could she have known Niamh? How could it be her mother?"

Henry thought about this for a few minutes. "I don't know," he said. "But she was dead. Maybe when people die they inhabit these people before they pass over or something. I don't know. I thought it was just because it was Samhein."

"Samhein?" Trialla asked looking puzzled.

Henry knew she was already wary of them and didn't want to scare her any more, but he was too tired to think of more lies. "It is a celebration of the dead. Witches speak to people who have passed away. It happens once a year on this night," he explained.

"Oh, Halloween," Trialla said. "That was yesterday in my village." Trialla contemplated this for a while, wondering why this would happen, twisting her black hair through her fingers as she thought. "What are you? Where are you really from?" she asked, studying Henry's handsome face for signs of lying.

"We are Witches from a village called Rusalimum beyond the Wooden Realm. Our people have been fighting with a neighbouring race of Sorcerers. I have never come across your race – humans, we call you – but Niamh's mother has in secret. Niamh's ancestors were actually from a human settlement many, many years ago. I expect if we could see back in time we would find many of our people probably are, actually. We once lived in harmony together. There are restrictions in place on Ysrir preventing races from mixing now," Henry said.

"Why?" Trialla asked.

"The gods didn't want the races to mix because it had

always ended in war in the past. From what has been happening recently I would say they are pretty close to the mark. The Sorcerers have abused this land for many years. They came from some far-off land in the north, centuries ago."

Henry continued to tell Trialla of the fighting gods, the fleeing villager and the necklace.

"We are looking for this necklace so we can return it to the gods and return our land to peace."

"Wow," Trialla said, playing with the necklace under her cotton blouse. The necklace began to eat what little light there was in the room and started to glow. The emerald in its centre seemed to increase the light in the cave tenfold.

Henry looked at the emerald a little closer. It was encased in a tear drop of intricate metal work, which hung from a silver chain. The emerald was mesmerising, clouds of mist swirling in its many-sided reflections.

"How did you get that necklace?" Henry asked suspiciously.

"It has always been passed down through my family when a girl was born. You don't think this is the necklace you are seeking, do you?"

"I think it could be, yes," said Henry, staring at it. "I think we may have been brought together in this way by the gods. We need to return it to them. Niamh's mother said we need to give them back what is rightfully theirs. They are angered and we need to right all our wrongs. This is the only way," he pleaded. He knew an object as beautiful as this would not be given up easily – especially one that had been passed down through so many generations.

Trialla immediately handed Henry the necklace. "Take it. If the gods are angered, maybe they are doing this to my people. Have you seen anything like this before?" Trialla asked, a sad, thoughtful look in her eyes.

"No. It would take extreme power to do this. I do not believe this to be the work of Witchecraft or Sorcery. Thank you; this will help. I really should rest. This is only half of our journey. We can speak more tomorrow."

"OK," she said as she laid back to sleep. She looked over at Henry's muscular back and closed her eyes, falling into a half sleep for fear of more creatures getting in during the night. It had been an interesting evening. She felt naked without the necklace, but it could be the first step to freedom, she thought, as she closed her eyes and tried to imagine a normal life.

Chapter 18

Niamh woke, her back aching from the cold, hard floor beneath her. She opened her eyes and looked around. The cave was eerily light, with a watery mist floating in the shafts of light coming from the hole above.

Something was wrong. Niamh could sense it. She looked around to see Henry asleep. As she looked closer, she realised he was lying alongside Trialla, his hand around her shoulder. Niamh edged closer and tapped him on the arm.

"Henry, wake up," she whispered, then put her hand over his mouth so he would not wake Trialla.

Henry opened his eyes and darted an embarrassed look at Trialla. She had not woken. Niamh glared at the back of Trialla's head whilst Henry changed his clothes. "What's all this, then?" she asked, waving an arm toward Trialla.

"What do you mean?" Henry replied. "I fell asleep."

Niamh could tell from the look on his face that it was innocent. "I must have been sleep-cuddling or something," he said, and Niamh couldn't help chuckling.

Her eyes widened as she suddenly realised what was wrong. "My dream!" she yelled, waking Trialla. "My dream was different!"

"What's going on?" Trialla asked sleepily, rubbing her eyes.

"It was different this time. I didn't drown. I mean, I was in water and swimming around, but I didn't go under. I just…" Niamh's eyes darkened and she turned, dropped to her knees and vomited. "It was… It was horrible. I think I preferred it when I was dying."

When Niamh turned around again, she noticed Henry running in from the outskirts of the cave. "Here. Have this," he said, offering her a large, green and orange spiky leaf in his open palm.

"What is it?" Niamh asked.

"A Croneborium leaf. I learned about it in Mrs Vlemicks's class while you were off ill, ironically."

He took the leaf from her again, ran his finger down the spine and snapped it as though breaking its back.

"Drink this," he said, offering it back to her. Niamh held the leaf in the air and watched as thick drops of pulpy water dropped to her feet. She held it above her mouth and let the ice-cold, viscous liquid drip onto her tongue. She tried to swallow but found it difficult. "What is it?" she coughed.

"Mrs Vlemicks said it relaxes you if you drink the water straight from the cracked leaves. I recognised it on our way in last night. It's everywhere."

"Yes, we often use it in medicines as well," Trialla offered making Niamh feel a little left out.

Niamh felt her stomach relax instantly, and sat down, sweat dripping from her forehead. "It was horrible, Henry," she said, holding her arms out for a hug. Henry knelt down and wrapped his arms around her. Niamh glanced briefly at Trialla and noticed her look away.

"I was floating in the water and I felt things beneath me. As I looked down I saw faces, Henry!" she cried. "Faces! It was horrible. I saw your grandmother, Elicia from school, the headmistress – hundreds of dead bodies beneath the surface staring at me. I didn't know what to do. I tried to swim, but I kept..." Niamh put her hand to her mouth. "I kept kicking the bodies underneath me. It was dreadful. It felt so real."

"Niamh, it's OK," Henry said, stroking her hair. "It's only a dream. They'll stop eventually. Everyone gets them. You just need to stop thinking about it before you go to sleep or else you're bound to dream about it. And with everything that happened here last night... Come on, I'll sort you some food. Trialla, how long do we have to wait before it's safe to go outside?"

Trialla briefly stepped outside to look and returned, nodding. "It should be fine now, I think. The sun has been up for a while, I guess, so it should be back to normal. I can see movement over the village walls. Come on, I'll introduce you to my family."

Niamh and Henry shared dubious looks. "Sounds fun," Niamh said quietly, receiving a sharp look from Trialla.

When they reached the village walls, there seemed to be more of a buzz about the huts. The sun shone through the occasional cloud now that the mist had lifted, and people moved about collecting fallen objects and sweeping outside their huts.

As they walked through the town they noticed nothing out of the ordinary. The people looked like any other normal people, although there was definitely something that said they weren't Witches. Neither Niamh or Henry could decide what it was that was different; they just didn't 'feel' like Witches.

Niamh noticed that there seemed to be no evidence of the night before. "Are these the same people?" she asked.

Trialla glanced around, smiling occasionally as people caught her eye. "Yes. They are not evil people, you understand. It is not their will to be like they are. That is why we need to fix this. Whatever you do, don't use any of your light stuff here. They might not be as understanding as me."

As they passed the huts where Henry had hacked at the creatures, he noticed Trialla stop and stare at the bloodstains on the sandy floor. He didn't know if that meant they were now properly dead, but he could tell she was upset.

They continued on, and as they all stumbled through a small hut door, Henry reached for his sword. The image of a very large man startled him, but this fear was soon overcome by Trialla jumping and wrapping her arms around his neck. "Pa," she wailed. "I'm so glad you're OK."

Niamh noticed an obvious uneasiness about Trialla's family. They were visibly shaken, but Niamh got the impression Trialla's father was trying to hide it. She remembered how Trialla had explained that they forgot everything about their night-time transformation, and suddenly realised she had a lot in common with these poor people. She, too, often woke unnerved and uneasy.

After Trialla had finished hugging and kissing her family, she began to introduce them. She introduced Niamh and Henry as travellers from Hunts Town in search of shelter. They were explorers sent to discover what was beyond the village boundaries.

Jonna laughed, his large chest booming with the crackling noise. "Good luck, little ones! I have seen men ten times as strong as you return in tears after trying to escape this land. We are here for a reason, my friends. It is not our place to argue."

After their brief introduction, Trialla explained what had been going on again. Niamh and Henry were surprised at the fact that it was nearly word-for-word the story she had told them. Niamh felt a small pang of pity as she thought of how such a young girl, even though she appeared slightly older than them, had been coping alone with this terror.

"But that is not the most fascinating bit, Pa!" she said with excitement. "Henry and Niamh have been searching for my neck..." Realisation about what she had said suddenly dawned on Trialla. To reveal what her new friends sought would raise many more questions. It was simpler to lie, although she hated lying to her family.

"...Have been searching for the most northern point of the village. I thought I could take them. Please, Pa-Pa?" Trialla pleaded.

Jonna looked unconvinced. "I don't think so, Trialla. You know we do not venture too far from the village. You don't know what is out there."

Trialla knew her father was stubborn, but she also knew how to convince him. "Please, Pa. Please. I won't be gone long, and I've had to deal with so much on my own I think it would do me good to get out of the village for a little while."

Jonna seemed to consider this for a few minutes. "OK, but you know we cannot pass Lark Rock, so stop well before it."

***

Later, the three of them sat for a meal of lamb and carrots around the central stove with Trialla's family and discussed the horror possessing them by night. Trialla didn't want to upset or worry her family any further, so didn't mention all the events of the night before and left out references to the walking dead. She decided it was something they wouldn't want to hear.

After a hearty meal, Jonna and Trialla's brother Anag left to help rebuild some of the huts damaged during the night before. Trialla's mother left the hut to wash the clothes and try to get the stench of blood from them once more.

The three of them were left in the hut alone. Trialla crossed the room and placed a small wooden stool behind the door.

"You have the necklace?" Niamh yelled. "When did you find this out?" she asked, turning on Henry. Henry cowered back a little and looked at Trialla.

"Last night, while you were sleeping. It was given to her by her mother. I think it's what we've been looking for, Niamh."

Niamh, now feeling even more left out and isolated, snatched the necklace from Henry's hand and held it to the light coming from the fire. As much as she was angered by them leaving her out, she couldn't fight the beauty of it. The cloudy emerald shimmered in the light.

"It's beautiful!" she exclaimed. "And you think this is the one?" she asked Henry after several minutes of staring, mesmerised, into the glassy depths.

"I really think so. From what Trialla told me it sounds like this has been passed down for centuries in her family. It also seems to go misty when she is in trouble, which could be related."

"Plus, my mother said... " Niamh had not thought of her mother for a couple of hours. It seemed like a dream now, and she was so tired. She felt immediate guilt at not having grieved for her more today.

Niamh composed herself, fluttered her eyelashes a few times and continued. "My mother said that the Sea God could summon a mist to ward off danger. There was nothing *but* mist last night when we arrived."

The air was cool now. They sat at the table with cups of warm lemon and discussed all that had happened so far. They were well aware of the dangers that could lie ahead, but were just relieved to have lived through this one.

After a few moments' silence, each one thinking of what was to come, Niamh stood. She opened her satchel and removed the rolled piece of cloth from a glass tube.

As she rolled it open, silver dust glittered from its surface and fell to the ground to disappear beneath the table. Again, the map seemed to look different. There was more land visible to the north, and a mountain that Henry was sure hadn't been there last time. As far as they could tell there was still no northern coastline.

"It looks different," Henry stated. "Look. This mountain is new and... here. This river wasn't there last time as well."

Niamh thought this must have been their tiredness. Maybe they'd not looked properly last time, but Henry was right. "The Wooden Realm has gone too," she said, pointing to the bottom of the map. As she pointed, the lines shifted and the whole map moved upwards. The Wooded Realm appeared where Niamh's finger touched the cloth. They all stared intently, fascinated by this new kind of magic.

Trialla, too, was fascinated, but was also wary of this new cloth. She still couldn't trust what she didn't understand, so kept her distance from the edge of the table.

"Well, that's novel," Henry said, smiling at Niamh. "Put your finger at the top. See what happens."

Niamh slid her finger up and, as expected, the map panned to the north, revealing a river dissecting the land from east to west and a mountain range beyond that. After the mountains came the coastline. The ocean was shown by a series of thin, silvery-blue lines swaying in the light.

"It's amazing," Henry said. "Where is the island we're going to?"

Niamh scanned the surface for anything just off the coastline. She swept her hand left to right to see what was beyond the edges. "There!" she shouted, pointing at an island off the northern coastline.

Trialla, feeling a little braver, leaned in behind Henry. Just off the coastline, about half an inch on this map, was a small round piece of land with a black circle and a white triangle within it.

"What does that mean?" Henry asked pointing to the symbols on the island. Niamh tried hard to remember the books she'd borrowed from her mother's study. Symbols of Witchecraft and religion were explained in great depth. Most of them Niamh couldn't understand, but she liked to draw the symbols when she was bored in class.

"I can't remember. I think the circle represents eternity, everything coming about to where it began, and the triangle..." Niamh stood staring at it and scratched her head. "I don't know."

"Well, that is where we're heading, then," Henry said. "We should go soon." He turned to Trialla and smiled. "Thank you for welcoming us into your home. I hope everything goes well in the village. You never know, maybe this will cure them," he said, looking at the necklace.

"I'll walk you to the border," Trialla said, looking a little upset to be seeing them off. She had spent all of her life trying not to get too close to people in her village. She had few friends except for her family. She found it easier that way. If it came to it, she thought it would be much harder to kill a friend than a face you pass in the alleys.

"You should stay here," Niamh said. "You heard what your father said. It is not safe."

Trialla slumped back into her chair and laughed a sickly laugh. "And you think it is safe here, do you? I spend my life defending myself from far worse things than the edge of a village." She put her head in her hands and wept.

Henry looked across at Niamh. He could sense that she felt helpless, as did he. What did you say to comfort someone whose family turned into the living dead every night? It wasn't exactly a normal occurrence.

He placed his hand on her head and knelt down to eye level. "You can come with us, OK? You have to be careful, though, and we have to go now. You need plenty of time to be back before dark."

She wiped her eyes and stood up, turning away quickly so they did not see her upset. "I'll pack you some food."

Once packed, the three of them set off out of the village gates, around the circumference of the wall to the north side and down a winding path through nettles and brambles. They had an initial fright as Chella passed them, and Henry was sure he heard Niamh say, "Mother?" in a rather hopeful voice. It was returned by nothing more than a quizzical look and a smile.

It wasn't a pleasant path, but Trialla assured them it was the quickest way. They meandered through the overgrown wilderness for nearly an hour until the path widened into a mud track and, directly ahead of them, they saw a small mound and the vast horizon behind it.

They had never even imagined Ysrir was so big, but this was astounding. They reached a clearing with a small hill in its centre. The mound ahead of them was only a few feet from ground level, and at the top was a small, grey granite rock.

As they approached it they took a wide circle around the base of the hill, following Trialla's lead. Trialla was clearly trying not to look at it as they passed, darting quick glances to check if they had passed it yet.

"This is Lark Rock. It is believed to be dangerous. We are to be careful near it, as it is told it possesses a deep evil that man is not supposed to wield. Look, it has strange pictures on the side."

Niamh studied the rock with great concentration as they passed. She looked back to Henry, who was trailing behind, and saw that he too was staring at the rock.

Although most of their classmates wouldn't recognise it, they knew it was Witcherock. Niamh had seen it several times in her mother's paintings of Witches Mount, and she knew that, one day, she would have to visit it herself to summon the Spirit of Seirim.

Niamh could see in Henry's eyes the same realisation that Witches must have once inhabited this area and, probably, had been accepted as her mother had said. The 'pictures' as Trialla had described them were obviously Witche runes. *Maybe there are still Witches here now that we don't know about,* Niamh thought.

Trialla had continued to speak about the history of their land, but Niamh and Henry had not been listening. They thought it best not to mention the history of the rock to Trialla. She had enough to deal with at the moment. They both fought to catch up with her and her tales.

They jumped over a wooden stile and weaved between several pointed stakes protruding from the ground. It was obvious that people were not supposed to cross here easily. As they exited a patch of dense spikes, they felt the now familiar grip of frost pulling their hearts to the ground. They had not even spotted this barrier. They staggered for a second and fell to their knees beside Trialla, who had just experienced the same thing.

To Niamh and Henry's surprise, Trialla was ecstatic. "I've never been able to come this far before!" Trialla said, astonished. "I've always had to turn back before Lark Rock. It was always unbearable. Like a weight pulling my heart to the ground through my skin. I've always run back, but now I feel fine. I got the same feelings, but it didn't seem as bad somehow."

Trialla edged forward further, cautiously at first, and slid between the next lot of wooden spikes. With the last of the spikes in sight, Trialla began to speed up and emerged with a triumphant leap. "I've left the village!" she shouted with joy. "This has never happened. Nobody has ever left the villages heading north as long as I can remember. Obviously, long ago people must have or else how would my necklace have come from the north?"

Trialla thought of the necklace in Henry's pocket and wondered at the powers that must live within it. Had it helped her escape the village because she now had a part to play?

Henry noticed she was looking around in all directions to take in what, to her, was alien terrain.

"Maybe this is just the right time for you to leave," he said. Looking at Niamh, he caught her staring fixedly at the tip of her mother's Staff, the afternoon light reflecting from the amber sap and enclosed milky globe.

As he watched, waiting for some reaction to what had been said, he saw Niamh pulled further and further into the shimmer of the globe. To his surprise it began to glow yellow, getting brighter and brighter until he had to shield his eyes from the burning light and heat emanating from it.

Niamh dropped the Staff and fell backward on the grass, looking at her blistered hands in surprise.

"What...?" Niamh managed before light shot out in an arc of colours from the inner globe, the Staff being propelled upright and standing, unaided, on the grass. Beams of colour continued to pour from the tip far into the sky, creating several rainbows ahead of them.

The intensity of the light had diminished a little and Niamh backed around the Staff towards the safety of Henry and the defensive orb he had cast.

"Wait! Come hither, you!" she heard. It was not a voice she recognised. It was a high-pitched, squeaky voice that sounded a little too fast for normal talk. As she turned to look around she saw nobody.

"Hey. Are you kidding me?" came the voice again. "It's not my fault. Hey! Down here!" the voice squeaked.

As they all continued to look around, Niamh let out a little squeak of her own as she jumped with fright. Leaning against the base of the Staff, looking nonchalant, was a tiny green creature. Its body was minute and scaly. It wore no clothes, had glistening scales like a fish and a small, lizard-like head. Its eyes shone with amber fire and it had ridges up the side of each arm. It stood staring, one leg crossed over the other, looking down the length of its arm at its small talons.

Henry kept the protective orb going whilst he began to slowly unsheath his sword. Niamh and Trialla stood frozen. They had never seen a creature like this. It looked menacing and vicious, and its voice was disturbing. As they watched, it leapt up to the top of the Staff and sat on the inner globe, legs crossed, looking at them expectantly.

"Well, who died?" it asked.

"Who what?" said Henry.

"Who died? D i e d?" he said again as though speaking to an infant who couldn't grasp an instruction.

After seeing them still struggling to comprehend the situation, he interrupted the silence.

"Look, I'm here now unfortunately. I can't get a second's peace. I've been summoned because a Witche Qwein died and there is an heir who is not trained and in need of my help, which I am guessing would be... " The lizard creature studied them all, slowly pointing his scaly talon. "You," it said stopping at Niamh. "Your mother would be Magatha, her mother Ariota, hers Jerrialla, hers..."

"OK, we get the picture," Niamh said. "Who are you?" she asked, looking at the new arrival with mounting suspicion.

"I am the Watcher. Every Witche Qwein dies eventually, although some seem to take a lot longer than others. Their spirits are bound to the Staff of Light."

He tapped the globe beneath him a couple of times to make sure they were keeping up. He wasn't used to dealing with mortals, and noticed they never seemed to grasp things easily.

"When a Witche Qwein dies, their spirit and wisdom comes to the Staff. They are allowed to pass over and rest, but their duties never end. Their knowledge and power is channelled through the Watcher to aid any heir who needs help or is unprepared for what is to come. I'm guessing that means you need help, and I'm the one to do it," he said, jumping to his feet and doing a little dance, finishing with a little clap and two hands pointing toward his head.

"Wait, wait. So you can speak to my mother even though she is dead?" Niamh asked.

"Oh no, you funny-looking little munchkin. I have her knowledge. Her instincts. I recognise people she once knew, but it is only a sense of *déjà vu*. When did your mother die?" he asked.

Niamh looked around to find something to focus on. She wasn't going to cry, she was stronger than that. "I don't know," she managed, her voice wavering slightly. "Recently, though, I think."

"Just as I expected. That's marvellous!" the creature said, jumping on the spot clapping, its oily skin stretched over its bony skeleton as it jumped. Niamh felt a sudden anger boil at his disregard for her feelings.

"I was summoned to you, but I haven't felt your mother's passing yet," he said. "Either she died recently or she was delayed passing over. Either way, I am here to help, but I cannot help you with your mother's intuition for a while yet. You should fill me in on what you children are up to," the Watcher said. "I'm guessing it has been centuries since I was last needed. There definitely seems to be less around than when I was here last," he said looking out over the landscape ahead of them. In the far distance were four gigantic peaks. A snowy cap had formed on the mountain peaks and they all wondered if they would find an easy route through. *Probably not,* Niamh thought pessimistically.

As they walked and spoke of what had happened and where they were going, Henry now carrying the Staff at arm's length, Niamh hung back and watched the group meander down a rocky hillside.

She felt suddenly less alone than she had when they set out from Rusalimum. She missed home and wondered if she would ever see the lush grass of her village again.

At the outset this had seemed like a fun adventure and a chance to explore an otherwise foreign terrain – a story they could tell and re-tell in vivid, exaggerated discussions back at school. Now she was becoming more unsettled at the responsibility and danger involved in returning this stupid thing.

They had a long way to go yet, and she knew it would take all her strength to cover a good distance before night fall. She put her head down and marched on.

Chapter 19

Jonna grunted as he heaved a large wooden timber back up against the outer walls. All around him men worked to strengthen their defences. Jonna was unsure if keeping the village folk in when they changed was such a good idea for his daughter, but the public had voted in favour, reasoning that they could do untold damage to themselves outside the walls.

He jolted as he felt a sudden stabbing pain in his ear. As he turned he realised there was obviously much that he didn't understand about his world. A small black insect about as big as one of his hands was flapping near his ear, sharp claws clear on his miniature fingers. Jonna was even more startled when it began to speak.

"Where is the Witche child?" it demanded in an authoritative tone.

"I... I don't know what you're talking about or even..." Jonna looked around sheepishly, "...or even if I am actually having this conversation. Surely this is my imagination through lack of sleep?"

Oddvard sent a white bolt into Jonna's chest, which would have left most men writhing on the floor. Although it had little effect on Jonna's hardened muscular build, it did, however, reassure him that this was actually happening.

"Who are you?" Jonna asked, backing away from the creature slightly.

"It is of little concern to you. What is, though, is the whereabouts of... "

Jonna watched, gobsmacked, as the small insect fell to

the ground with a thud and lay motionless. He was unsure whether it was dead. He leaned over and poked it with the end of his stubby finger.

"You OK, little fellow?" he whispered, and prodded it again.

Jonna was thrown back off his feet and into the outer wooden defences as the small creature suddenly sprouted to a naked man, slightly larger than normal. The man stood there for a few moments and studied himself.

"Interesting," he rasped. "Very interesting."

He extended an open palm toward Jonna, who was instantly lifted from his feet and pinned against the wall by what felt like an invisible hand around his neck.

"Where is the Witche?" Oddvard asked with obvious impatience in his angular face.

Jonna looked genuinely confused. "What is this trickery you are placing over my eyes?" he asked, looking worried now. A group of villagers was beginning to gather at a distance, indecision clear on their faces.

"The child!" Oddvard spat. "The Witche girl and her young male companion. They came for the necklace."

"Niamh, you mean. What on earth could you want with that poor little girl?" As soon as the words had left Jonna's mouth, he realised his mistake. This man obviously didn't want to help her on her way.

Oddvard strengthened the grip holding Jonna's throat to the wall as Trialla's mother came running from behind, screaming. Oddvard grabbed her by the face as she ran past and threw her against the wall beside her husband so hard that her head splintered the wood. She fell to the floor in a heap.

"And the necklace? Does she have the necklace?" Oddvard spluttered in a frenzied rage.

Jonna knew of his daughter's strange necklace and knew it would be a big coincidence if it was this he was speaking of. However, this man was obviously powerful in a strange, evil way. He looked down at his wife crumpled on the ground below him and screamed inwardly. To Oddvard's surprise, Jonna broke himself free of the spell with sheer brute force before Oddvard recast the spell, pinning him to the wall by his neck once more.

"The *necklace*?" Oddvard roared.

"I know of no necklace, Witche scum!" Jonna fired back in a strangled voice. Unknowingly, he had just cast the worst insult possible, and, as he was to find out in the seconds that followed, the final words he would ever speak.

Having finished with the giant of a man, Oddvard spun on his heels and headed for the crowd of onlookers that was now trying to flee his path. He had to assume that if they left the village they must either be in possession of the necklace or have discovered its location. Either way he was heading north.

As he neared the rows of huts, he shot waves of fire down the alleyways, burning fleeing villagers and setting rows of hanging clothes alight. He suddenly realised he was enjoying the fact that they had no control over the land's power and were, effectively, defenceless. 'Easy prey,' he sniggered to himself.

Oddvard was enjoying the look of terror on the human faces around him. His magical supremacy was obviously a sight they hadn't seen before. He turned to face the way he had come and fired a blue bolt of flame towards the silver oak tree near the village gates.

He stopped and watched as it exploded into an enormous mushroom of smoke seeping up into the clear sky, lines of molten silver fire shooting off in all directions. He turned and continued to walk. As much as he was enjoying wielding his power over these pathetic, helpless animals, he had more important things to attend to. He headed through the huts and toward the north side of the village. He could smell the power close by; almost taste it.

***

As Niamh and the others stopped at the edge of a steep gorge, they looked down at a fast-flowing river racing below. They tried to catch their breath and eat a little *wicci* bread for strength.

"So you're telling me the Sorcerers have broken through the gods' barrier?" the Watcher asked incredulously.

"They managed that a long time ago," Niamh explained in a knowing tone.

"A long time ago for you, maybe, flesh-ball," the Watcher shot back.

"They're trying to regain power over Ysrir like their ancestors did. Niamh's mother..." Henry stopped short, realising he was reminding Niamh of a painful event that he had been doing his best to avoid. He had gone too far, though, faked a cough and continued, "Niamh's mother said they once ruled this land, but I can't believe that."

The Watcher let out a long, low whistle. "It seems a lot has been happening since I was here last."

As the Watcher jumped back onto the tip of Niamh's Staff, they suddenly realised Trialla wasn't standing beside them anymore. They glanced around and saw her running and stumbling back the way they had come.

"What's she doing?" Henry asked.

Niamh realised immediately what she was doing, as she saw a cloud of blue and black smoke rising from the direction of her village as the sound of an explosion hit them and a hot gust of air. "Trialla, wait. Hey, wait for us!" she called after her.

Niamh and Henry managed to stop her before she had made too much ground.

"Get off me!" she screamed, shrugging them off.

"Look, everyone dies. Even me. It's supposed to be fun," the Watcher added with what Niamh guessed was supposed to be a chirpy smile. It came out creepy and Trialla shoved him off the top of the Staff.

They all stood silent, trying to contemplate the rubbish the Watcher had just spouted as he dusted himself off and made his way back to the staff grumbling.

"Look, Trialla, I'm sorry but there is nothing you can do. It's too late," Niamh attempted. "Magic at that scale can only be the work of a Sorcerer. All you can do is hope they escape unharmed, but if you return then you too could be killed. You also don't know if you can make it back through the barrier. You've come through this way, so who is to say that returning the other way will not kill you?"

Henry realised from the smoke on the horizon that her parents were unlikely to have survived and that, more worryingly, the Sorcerer couldn't be too far behind them now.

"We can't hang around here, Niamh," Henry whispered while Trialla stood rooted to the spot, fixedly looking at the distant remains of her village.

"Come on, Trialla. Come with us. It'll be OK," Niamh offered.

"OK? OK! My family could be dead. What would you know?"

Trialla caught the piercing glare coming from Niamh as she spoke these words and suddenly dropped her head in shame. Not only had Niamh lost her mother and father, but she had witnessed them return in such a dreadful way.

Niamh turned to storm off, tears welling in her eyes. She wanted to cry more since the night her mother came back, but had felt she couldn't let herself down like that. She was stronger than that. Trialla grabbed her shoulder and pleaded, "I'm sorry. Really I am. It's just... It's my family."

Niamh was angered, but she could also sense the pain and anguish in Trialla's voice. It was a position she'd been in only the day before, and she knew the hurt it caused even if she didn't show it openly. For a split second Niamh even thought this might bring them closer together, then dismissed it as dreadful. *The poor girl's parents might have just died and you're thinking of making friends,* she thought.

As the silver streams began to fade away and the cloud of smoke settled in the distance, Henry urged the girls to continue walking. They figured the Sorcerer couldn't be far behind and they had achieved so much already. Niamh wasn't going to let her mother down now.

"We need to move. We'll go down the banking and cross the river. Once we get a bit past the other side we can find somewhere secluded and check the map. We need to make some distance because we'll have to sleep and eat at some point. I'm guessing Sorcerers need to do the same," he said, looking at Niamh as though she might know.

"There is really nothing we can do against the Sorcerer, Trialla," Niamh offered. "If we could, we would. We need to finish this now. It might be the only hope for your people."

"OK, let's go," Trialla said reluctantly as she skidded down the edge of the banking toward the raging water below. Both Niamh and Henry saw a new spark in her eye. It was one of determination and anger. Whether or not this was a front, they did not know, but Henry was just glad to be moving again. As much as he wanted revenge on the Sorcerers for taking his family away, he knew returning the necklace was more important.

***

As Oddvard left the northern walls, he reached Lark Rock, laughing as he passed it. He knew that the land would soon be rid of the disease and he would be the most powerful being on Ysrir. His head swam with thoughts of conquering neighbouring continents and the scale of his reign as King. He would go down in history as the most powerful King of the Onjanaha line to have walked the land. His face would be carved in the castle walls.

A shriek from above caused him to jump slightly and, snorting with an embarrassed sigh of relief, he signalled to his raven to descend onto his arm. The claws dug deep but Oddvard didn't wince. To retreat was a sign of disrespect to his trusted messenger.

As the raven passed what it knew to its master, his lip curled into a menacing grin. "About time too, and good riddance," he cackled as he continued on his path, shaking his head and laughing.

Chapter 20

As they reached the base of the steep mudded bank, they stood still, shocked by the force of the river. The water made a deafening roaring sound, the rapids in a constant race to exit the steep valley first.

Niamh stood staring at the passing, foamy current. *This can't be happening*, she thought. Of all the things she hated, it was water she hated most. She wondered now if it was because of her mother. She'd always hated rain and thunder. *Maybe it's hereditary,* she thought to herself. Hereditary or not, she would not be crossing the river.

"I can't," she muttered as Henry and Trialla had gone in opposite directions looking for a shallower passage. "I can't!" she shouted a little louder. Henry heard this and stopped, facing away from Niamh. He took a couple of seconds before he turned and walked back to Niamh.

"Look, Niamh," he said. "It's simple: we have to get over this river. The only way back is through whatever it was that... " He looked around to make sure Trialla was out of earshot and continued in a whisper. "Through whatever it was that destroyed the village back there. I think I'd take my chances if I were you."

"But you don't understand," Niamh began, but Henry interrupted.

"Look, we have little time. I'm sorry and I know you hate water, but we have to cross. There is no other way. Come on." Henry grabbed her hand and turned toward the water. She yanked it back and stood shivering.

"Niamh, we haven't got time for this. I'm not going to

die because you're scared of a little water. Now COME ON!" he yelled.

As they turned, Trialla was waving for them to come toward her. They could just make out her soft voice shouting about a shallow spot. When they arrived they could see the fast-moving pebbles being carried along the riverbed in an endless cycle of rocks weathering down to sand.

"This doesn't look too deep," Trialla said passing a cautious glance at Niamh. "You OK?" she asked. Niamh swallowed hard and held her head up. "Of course I'm OK. Come on, then, if we're going."

She began walking towards the water, but subtly managed to push Henry ahead of her.

"Here," he said to Niamh, holding out his arms. "I'll give you a lift, if you want."

The relief in Niamh's face was instant. She jumped up onto his back and swung her arms around his broad, muscular neck. He grabbed under her knees and set off for the water.

Through all the commotion and trying to convince Niamh to cross, they had failed to spot the loose lumps of mud that had started to roll down the banking toward the river behind them. They were too late.

Chapter 21

Oddvard struggled toward his prey, their small outlines shimmering knee-deep in the rushing water. He could see they were finding it hard to keep their footing. Oddvard tried to pick up his pace down the crumbly slope.

As he reached the base, staggering slightly, he brushed himself off and strolled towards the water. He knew they wouldn't make the far side before he got to them.

"Stop wriggling, Niamh!" Henry snapped. He was nearly a quarter of the way across, but finding it increasingly difficult to stay steady with Niamh trying to keep her feet out of the water.

"Lean forward more! Niamh, what are you doing?" he yelled. They struggled on the spot for a moment and Niamh clenched her arms around his neck, even more terrified.

"I'm sorry. Don't drop me!" she pleaded, but it was too late. Henry's left knee buckled as he lost his footing. Waist deep in water, he felt the weight of Niamh falling backwards. He turned back toward the shore and attempted to keep her aloft but, in doing so, stopped dead with terror and let them both fall under the water.

As Niamh hit the cold rushing water, the last sight she saw was a tall, angular face bearing toward her, his arms outstretched and a sinister, evil look on his face.

"Nooaghasgdg," she gargled as her head dropped below the water level. Her nightmare returned. She was trapped beneath the surface. All around her was as black as night, and she could feel the current brushing against her face, threatening to take her further from safety.

She needed to breathe; her lungs cried out for air. She knew that if she opened her mouth she was dead. *Maybe I'll wake up soon,* she thought. Struggling for a few seconds, she tried to regain a perspective on which way she was trying to go.

She had obviously reached deeper water, as her body now spun in somersaults. Her nightmare was real. She felt what she could only assume was a dead body under her feet, and kicked at it hard. This was her nightmare, and it was really happening. She had accepted that this was probably the end. *But this is different,* she found herself thinking through the panic. There was light up ahead. There wasn't normally a light.

She found herself being pulled toward it. She fought back, kicking and punching under the water, but it was no use against such a strong force. She found herself thinking, *Oh, it's that light.*

After what seemed like hours, she felt the sensation of cold air over her face. Spluttering and flailing her arms, she realised she had broken the surface and was still very much alive. The sight she saw next left her wondering if that was actually a good outcome to the situation.

Towering above her, with a long outstretched arm clinging to the back of her neck, was what she could only imagine to be a Sorcerer in what appeared to be ill-fitting rags from one of the clothes lines in the village.

Frozen, she tried to clear her eyes from the water now blurring them. This couldn't be happening. They'd travelled so far. They'd done so well. Her mother had been proud of her.

She wriggled and fought nearly a foot out of the foamy

water as the Sorcerer cackled insanely.

"Well, well, well. How I do enjoy a good game of catch." He leaned in closer to her face and sniffed comically. Turning away and shielding his face in his shoulder he said, "A Witche, of all things. Disgusting."

Niamh wriggled some more, but realised it was hopeless. The Sorcerer was clearly bigger and stronger than she was, and any chance she had to escape would be through wit or sheer luck – two things she happened to be good at.

Looking around, she searched for Henry and Trialla. *Where could they be?*, she thought.

"What have you done with them?" she demanded. "Tell me! If you've hurt them, I..."

"What, little Witche? What? Please entertain me with what you think you could possibly do now against me, Oddvard, King and Ruler of Ysrir. Even you can't dispute my dominance now your mother is dead." An evil smile flashed across Oddvard's lips.

Niamh hung staring, unresponsive.

"Oh, you know, then, do you? Big loss, I expect. Well, no matter. My men said it was a painful and gruesome death at least. I suppose you can take comfort knowing she was in extreme agony and pleading for her life when we took her head."

Niamh exploded, her arms and legs lashing out in a violent fit – a fit that let out all her anger and grief at the loss of her mother and all the things she'd wanted to say but hadn't. All her exhaustion from the journey so far, and all her hatred for the Sorcerers for all they had done to her people.

After several minutes, Oddvard still stood staring at her with what looked like slight admiration. He held her at arm's length while she swung dangerously in the air. Several jabs caught his forearm but caused little pain. She eventually drooped, her head hanging low. "I'm ruler of Ysrir now," she cried. "Me, not you. You don't deserve it. You are evil."

Niamh looked up at his eyes, and beyond his shoulder saw Trialla suspended against the far banking, her arms and legs pinned against the loose mud.

"Where's Henry?" she yelled with what little energy she had left. "What have you done with him?" she demanded.

Oddvard simply laughed, the reflection of the rushing water vivid in his large olive eyes. "Child, it is not I who have killed your little friend. He washed downstream when you pulled him under. I expect he is miles away by now." Oddvard looked at her wickedly and plainly said with no emotion, "I expect he's dead by now. Oh yes, quite dead."

Niamh seemed to hang her head even lower, the pain in the back of her neck no longer registering from the Sorcerer's rough grip. It was her fault Henry was here. It was her fault Henry was probably dead. A million images of Henry's face flashed through her thoughts; thoughts of them at school, playing at the harbor, thoughts of them re-enacting great battles and adventures in the comfort and safety of their village walls. She had lost her mother and only friend in the same week. Life couldn't get much worse. *Was it even worth living?* she found herself thinking.

A voice entered her head – a familiar voice that she had completely forgotten about: *"Of course it is, you stupid girl. You are Witche Qwein of Ysrir. Who else is going to rule your people and help them survive, eh?"*

She noticed the Watcher was nowhere to be seen, but he was right. She raised her chin high, crossed her arms and screamed, "I'm the ruler of Ysrir now, and you will never defeat my people!"

The outburst seemed to catch Oddvard by surprise. He stumbled backwards slightly, then regained his footing. "You are a feisty one, aren't you? You would have made a competent leader, I suppose. Let's get to the point. You have something and I want it. You can give it to me or I can take it. Either way you *are* going to die."

Niamh noticed an icy emphasis on the word 'are' and felt a shiver run up her neck. For the first time in her life she truly didn't know what to do.

***

Several hundred years ago a rock had plummeted down the hillside and splashed into the river about a thousand feet further downstream from where Oddvard held Niamh captive. It was this rock that had saved Henry's life.

After plummeting headfirst into the fast-flowing river with Niamh, he had been plunged deep under the freezing water. He had risen to the surface just in time to inhale a mouthful of pure air after he had been winded underwater by what he assumed was Niamh kicking.

As the spot where they had fallen began to get rapidly smaller, he saw the figure of a large man holding Niamh in the air. Trialla was nowhere to be seen. He had to do something.

He spun around to face the flow of water and saw a rock approaching fast to his left. Unsheathing his sword, he managed to wedge it under the riverbed in front of the rock, giving him a temporary branch to cling onto. He also managed, to the despair of the Watcher, to ram the Staff of Light deep under the loose pebbles. Once he managed to secure his back against the rock, the rushing water arcing in a v-shape around the base and his feet, he had time to think.

Using the sword and Staff in separate hands, he clawed his way along the riverbed upstream, using them to jab at the bed and give him something to grip while his body floated just under the surface of the water.

It took all the strength he could muster and then more still. The Watcher sat happily perched on top of the Staff, giving Henry a quick commentary of what he could see when he came up for air. From what he could decipher over the rushing water, he had little time. He had contemplated getting back to the edge and running upstream, but he was sure this would lead to him being spotted. He would be no use to Niamh and Trialla dead.

As he approached them, he could see the back of a man's feet under water, buckles shimmering occasionally as beams of light managed to dissect the foamy surface of the river. This was it. He had to think quickly.

***

Niamh had to buy some time, but how? "I have the necklace," she said. "You can have it if you want, but you should know it's cursed!"

"Foolish girl! Do you really think anything would stop me in my search now? Even if what you say isn't a nonsense attempt to put me off, I'm sure I could counter anything a *Witche* could put on it."

It was all she could think of. What else could she do?

Then it hit her. She ripped the necklace from her neck and revealed it to Oddvard. The change in his look was immediate. His eyes widened. His nostrils flared and his lips arced into a broad grin.

"You know little of the destruction this could cause, girl," he said.

Niamh held her arm out over the river away from Oddvard. "I'll drop it!" she screamed. "I swear to Seirim I'll drop it."

Oddvard's expression changed to one of thunder – a face Niamh imagined he wore when in battle.

"I am not playing, little girl. GIVE IT TO ME!" he roared, his yellow teeth dripping with saliva.

Oddvard knew that if dropped and eventually lost to the depths of the sea, it would be safe for a long time. However, objects such as this rarely presented themselves, so he had to have it. He had two agendas here, and one was power. With it no one could stop him, not even the gods. His people would be free to roam the seas once more.

"I will ask you one more time, child. Give me the NECKLACE!"

A white-hot searing pain unleashed itself on Oddvard – a pain so excruciating that his brain didn't even know how to process it. He couldn't even tell where it was coming from. All he knew was that he wanted to die. Surely this Witche didn't have powers this great?

Oddvard stumbled again as his head went fuzzy. Small yellow and green dots crossed his vision. He had no choice but to let Niamh fall. He had to stop the pain. As he looked frantically around, he spotted slivers of crimson rushing through the water, colouring the foamy current pink. To his horror he realised what had caused the pain: protruding from where his left foot would be was the handle of a sword, glimmering bronze and silver in the light under the surface.

He stood, woozy, as he watched the Witche girl being helped to the far side by the boy she called Henry. Their other little friend was already waiting after the pain had shocked Oddvard into loosening the spell he had over her.

He knew he had to stop them. He knew, but he could do nothing about it. His foot was skewered to the river bed. Every attempt to move resulted in a raw, masculine scream. He felt sick with pain and could tell he was losing blood fast. He knelt in the water and tried to pull it out, but screamed again. He was in too much pain to conjure a simple relief spell. As he stood again, everything went white. He felt as though he was spinning, and he felt the icy crispness of running water against his face. He could do nothing to stop it.

Niamh reached the bank and frantically began scrambling up it. Henry caught her and put his hand on her shoulder, the Watcher looking around with excitement.

"Good show!" he hissed.

"It's OK, he's gone. I think he passed out," Henry offered, looking warily downstream.

Niamh looked around, trembling, and saw the occasional flicker of silver beneath the water where the sword stood, a thin trail of blood flowing downstream.

"But he was stuck, wasn't he?" she asked as they rejoined Trialla and began up the banking at a hurried pace.

"Are you joking?" Henry replied. "Did you not see how sharp the blade was? I expect he'll have soldiers carrying him to the battlefield from now on, if he survives."

"Ahem. You're welcome, by the way," the Watcher interjected.

"What for?" Henry and Niamh said in unison.

"Well, first of all for making you get some backbone, girl. Second, for suggesting that Henry here use the sword to pin the Sorcerer to the bed." The Watcher held his head high awaiting his praise.

"No, you didn't!" Henry yelled. "You didn't help one bit. You just sat there insulting my swimming and telling me we probably wouldn't make it in time."

"Well, what about the Staff? You used that, didn't you and that's mine—"

"Will you two stop it! What are we doing just standing here? We need to move. Come on," Niamh instructed.

"Are you not going back for it? The sword, I mean," Trialla asked.

Henry stopped and looked back. From his elevated viewpoint he could now see more of the blade glimmering in the sunlight through the water. He thought for a minute. He had loved that blade. He had never been allowed things like that back home. It made him feel like he was part of the Witches Front.

"No," he said eventually. "I think I might be getting a sudden fear of water."

"Ha!" Niamh said aloud as she reached the top of the bank. The Watcher looked up and sniggered. "Now you might look for Sorcerers behind us instead of arguing when I don't want to go near water from now on," Niamh added matter-of-factly.

Henry felt the need to defend himself. He opened his mouth to reply, but thought better of it. You couldn't argue with Niamh anyway.

They took a quick glance around to make sure the Sorcerer had really floated downstream, and turned to see the next stage ahead. There was a relatively easy trek to the base of four enormous snow-capped mountains. Niamh could smell the end. She could go home and grieve the loss of her mother. She could rebuild her life. *What will I do on my own?*, she thought.

As they started picking up pace again, Niamh put an arm around Henry's back and looked deep into his eyes.

"Thanks," she said awkwardly. "I thought I'd lost you for a minute."

Henry didn't reply but kissed her on the top of her head while they walked. He put his other arm out toward Trialla, who was glad of the physical comfort and affection as they carried on to what they hoped would be a quick end to this mess.

Chapter 22

The journey so far had been far more tiring than Jorgan had expected. After reaching the Great Barrier, and making his way easily though the Wooded Realm, Jorgan had reached a frozen lake – not a frozen lake by normal standards, but a vast ocean of semi-transparent, semi-solid liquid.

He stood for nearly an hour trying to decide the best path of action. Jorgan apparently took this characteristic from his mother, who had always told his father to think things through properly, apparently: "A problem acted upon rashly is a problem exacerbated, but a problem thought through rationally is no problem at all". *That's the only decent bit of advice my father ever gave me, and it wasn't even his advice,* Jorgan thought bitterly.

He knew that if he followed the shore of the lake and attempted to circumnavigate it, it would lead to several days more travel. Could he afford this delay? He thought not. The sooner he picked up the scent of the Witches' trail, the better. He knew he had to reach a point farthest north of a settlement marked as Teare Gro according to what he had overheard his father telling his advisers. He pulled a circular object from his pocket and flicked his wrist to open it. The lid sprang backward, revealing a small sheet of glass. Jorgan began to spin slowly on his heels until a beam of sunlight ricocheted off the glass surface and angled directly over the lake. "Due north," he stated out loud to no one in particular.

Flicking the lid shut again, he continued to study the frosty surface. Retreating back to the dry-stone wall behind him, he watched a leaf blowing in the wind as he concentrated hard.

"Of course!" he yelled, and scurried back toward the

edge of the Wooded Realm. He returned an hour later with two small sections of bark about the length of his thighs, and several lengths of vine knotted together and rolled over his right shoulder.

He sat down beside the lake and removed his long velvet gown. He began threading the vine through holes that he had punctured in each corner, and then placed it to one side. Then, placing the pieces of bark on the ice, he put his feet in them and stood tentatively. *This will do fine*, he thought.

Everything was in place. All he needed now was a good gust of wind. Jorgan knew once he was a few hundred yards away from the edge that the ice would be far thicker and would definitely hold his weight to the other side. If the wind kept up then he would ride the bark as far as he could. It beat walking, after all.

He pulled a small blue marble from the back of his left boot and looked over his shoulder. His face contorted as he worked something out. As he studied the space behind him, he began muttering, "Distance..., erm, yes, that should do it. Mmmmm, velocity squared over gravitational acceler....yes yes." He pulled his arm back and launched the marble behind him.

As he faced back toward the lake, he steadied his feet on the bark and threw his gown in the air as the marble exploded and a sharp gust of warm wind thundered behind him.

He felt it pull at the gown and his feet slowly start to slide over the ice. *Spread the mass*, he thought to himself. *So obvious when you think about it.*

He knew he could work out the time it would take at this speed to reach the other side, but he needed to concentrate on avoiding the rough patches of ice. He knew it would be at least a few hours, anyway.

Chapter 23

The cold was excruciating. It was the kind of cold of multi-level hell, described in books. Niamh curled her arms around her legs and let her hair fall over her knees in the hope that it might create a sliver of warmth. The three travellers had never fully dried and warmed up from their trip across the river.

"Well?" she snapped at Henry as he returned with the Watcher on his shoulder, the two of them bickering and provoking each other. "What's the plan?"

"Yes, oh knowledgeable one, what's the plan?" chortled the Watcher.

Henry walked over to the pair and moved his hands in a quick movement of symbols as a blanket of steam fell around them, causing the ground to hiss and steam.

"Thanks," shivered Trialla.

"Yeah, thanks," Niamh grumbled after a few seconds of expectant stares from Henry. She had tried that spell several times while Henry was away but couldn't unfreeze her fingers enough. 'Maybe your light stuff doesn't work out here,' Trialla had offered. *What does she know anyway? Maybe it doesn't, though,* she had thought until Henry dismissed the theory with his heat spell.

"Henreee," Niamh pleaded in a fake extended sob. "Can we just go?"

"Yeah, I think we should. I've looked around and we have a few options. We can go around all four mountains on either the left or the right. It will take a while, but it would be the flattest option."

The Watcher had jumped back to the Staff beside Niamh now and curled up like a small kitten obviously unaware of the plummeting temperature.

Henry waited a second to make sure they had both been listening and had actually absorbed what he was saying. Even he found it a little hard to concentrate with the cold eating away at him and giving him earache.

"Or we could go through one of the three gaps between the mountains. This would be a rocky, difficult path, and there is always the danger of falling rocks. However, if anyone is trying to follow us, there seem to be a lot of caves and crevices to hide in and there might be a bit of warmth for when we need shelter."

Both Niamh and Trialla looked at each other then at Henry pleadingly.

"Wait, wait. The third option is over the mountains. There seems to be a path winding up the side of each mountain and, I guess, back down the other side."

"What!" Trialla exclaimed. For a second it took Niamh by surprise and the Watcher raised one eyelid to see what the commotion was and then returned to his sleep as a grumpy cat might when not in the mood for play. Trialla had seemed so timid and eager to please until now. Maybe the strain of the journey had toughened her slightly.

"Well," said Henry in a tone suggesting all would become clear soon. "The obvious route would be through one of the gaps, but that is the problem. It's obvious. If we are followed into one of the valleys there are only two ways out: forward or back. Anyone following is bound to think we took the most direct route. If we're up there," he spun and pointed but quickly retreated his finger back under his robe, "then we can see anyone following below and we have the advantage of height."

"But no cover from the wind, rain, snow... cold!" Niamh said with a certain quality added to the last word that Henry hadn't heard in her voice before. He could tell she was genuinely scared. She had had enough.

"No," he replied. "No cover from the cold, unless the wind is coming from the east or west, because the mountains should guard us a little."

The three of them stood for a while under the cover of an aged tree as their brains calculated their need for warmth over their need to get to the other side.

"Let's have a vote. What d'you think, Henry?" Trialla asked.

Both girls spun toward him and he felt an immediate need to decide. But should he decide in favour of his gut instinct, or what he knew they both wanted to hear?

"I think we should, erm... well, for the best advantage over..."

"Just pick one, you fool, or I'm going," Niamh snorted.

"Up the mountain," he said, and regretted it immediately from the looks he received. "I'm more worried about crazy Sorcerers than I am about the weather."

"Whatever he said..." the Watcher interjected drowsily.

Henry began to feel a slight affection for the small lizard-like creature at this comment, until the Watcher completed his sentence.

"...I want to do the opposite," he stated. He smiled at Henry and went back to sleep.

"OK," Trialla said, blatantly ignoring what the Watcher had just said. "Well, I disagree. I think we should go through the mountains and make camp at the first cave we find. We need a fire. We're no good to anyone in this state."

"Fine," said Henry, feeling a little betrayed and ganged up on. He knew what was best for them, but what should he do if they voted against him? He thought maybe Niamh would come through for him...

"Let's go, then. Through the mountain it is," Niamh said.

"What! But what about the..." Henry hung his head and sighed as he watched the back of Niamh and Trialla heading toward the middle valley, the towering hillside causing an uneasy darkness and the Watcher bobbing along beside them, smirking.

***

Jorgan felt the air rushing through his hair and his cheeks were now cold from the frosty wind. His invention had served as a far better aid than he could ever have imagined. He looked down and saw a herd of cows grazing about one hundred feet below and looked up quickly, a brief wave of vertigo rolling over him.

He didn't particularly like heights, but flying was a different story altogether. He'd never felt so free. He felt like an eagle or a hawk, soaring this way and that without a care in the world.

His wind spell was obviously more powerful than he'd given it credit for, and after picking up great speed skating across the ice, he'd felt the ground disappear beneath him and his cape pulled him up into the air.

He'd been airborne now for several hours and the mountains were nearing rapidly. He wasn't sure of the best route through the mountains, but he hoped he could keep enough height to at least fly though them. He would have to be careful not to get stuck halfway up one, though. Coming down was always more dicey than going up.

***

Henry continued to sulk at the back of the group whilst Niamh and Trialla led the way a little up ahead.

"How're you ho-ho-holding up, Tri-rialla?" Niamh asked through chattering teeth. She knew she was cold, but this was emphasised on seeing how blue Trialla's face had become.

"O-O-O-OK. We should stop soon, I thi-i-ink," she managed.

Niamh could see a crack in the hillside ahead. She hoped it would be a decent enough cave so they could build a fire and maybe get a little sleep. Even if it was just a protruding rock, it might give a little shelter from the icy blast gusting through the valley ahead.

The four of them clambered over loose rocks and soil, slowly snaking their way through the ravine. Niamh noticed at one point that she could lean forward without falling due to the sheer force of the gale.

The Watcher, to their delight, was having far more trouble. He had already been blown back through the ravine a few times now, his sharp talons scratching along the rocky floor in search of grip.

As they reached the crack in the hillside, the weather changed and all three of them nearly fell forward with the shift. A great flow of wind came rocketing up the valley from behind, throwing them off balance. The Watcher tumbled forward this time onto a large rock just after the cave. They managed to stay upright and scrambled inside. The effect was immediate relief. The warmth hit them and began to slowly thaw out their arms and legs.

From inside the cave they saw branches, dust and even small rocks tumbling past, all caught up in the rampage of the sudden shift in weather.

"Do you think it's always like this here?" Trialla asked of no one in particular.

"I hope not," the Watcher sulked, rubbing his knee through gritted teeth.

"Who knows?" Henry replied. "I expected it to be windy, because the valley will channel the wind down its path, but this is a bit extreme."

All three sat there a while whilst Henry conjured a small fire and they began to warm their hands.

"It stings," Trialla said. "Near the fire, I mean."

Niamh turned toward her with a look of surprise. "Are you joking? We've just walked for Seirim-knows how long, come face to face with a Sorcerer and managed to pass through some of the most feared parts of Ysrir, and you're telling me a bit of heat hurts?"

Henry took Trialla's hands in his own and started blowing softly on them.

"It's because you're too cold. My gran always said if you get really cold, don't let yourself warm up too quickly no matter how much you want to. You'll only pay for it when the chill monster gets you."

"That's silly," she said, laughing out loud.

"No, it's not, it's true. Look, you put your hands over the fire now. See, it's because I warmed them up for you." Henry went to move away and Trialla put a hand on his. "Thank you," she said.

Niamh made a tutting noise in her throat whilst the Watcher mimicked being sick. Niamh got up and walked over to the entrance. Leaning against the wall, she casually looked back over her shoulder to find Henry and Trialla sat separately. She was about to return to the fire when something caught her eye. Something flew past the cave entrance, making a whooshing noise in the wind. As she looked she thought she caught a glimpse of purple racing past and then nothing. The wind behind it seemed to die down again.

"Quick! Look!" she yelled as she raced outside to see what it was. Henry and Trialla followed behind, wondering what the commotion was. Henry secretly wondered if Niamh had done it on purpose. This thought soon evaporated as he watched a skinny figure surrounded by a red orb being dragged through the air at great speed. The object pulling him seemed to be a shimmering purple-black sheet of some kind.

"Wha...?" Niamh attempted, but Henry put his hand over her mouth to silence her and motioned for them to go back in the cave.

"What was that?" Niamh attempted for the second time. "It was a Sorcerer, wasn't it?"

"I expect so," Henry said. "I've never heard of anyone flying before, so that would be the best bet."

"How did he...?" Trialla began, but was quickly interrupted by Henry.

"We've got to go. That didn't look like the one from the river. Who knows how many there are? There could be more on the way. I knew we should have gone up the mountain!" Henry yelled. He knew it was pointless getting annoyed now, but it made him feel better. This journey hadn't turned out anything like he expected it to. He was cold, hungry and tired. He wanted nothing more than to get home to a nice warm bed and eat his gran's mutton stew. Well, maybe there was something he wanted more, but before he could think any further he was interrupted by a sharp pain in the arm.

"Don't you dare say I told you so, Henry! Don't you dare," Niamh said as she punched him in the arm again. "We were cold and tired. We want to go home too, you know," she said, and Henry was sure he saw the slightest glimmer of a tear in her eyes.

He sighed heavily and walked to the entrance, looking tentatively around the corner to see if anyone else was approaching. "I know," he said, finally returning to the fire. "We should go, though. Whoever it was will be out of this valley before us, and if they're heading for the same place that means they'll be there waiting for us. Worst case, they could be waiting at the end while another one comes in from behind. Either way," he waved his hand dismissively, "I think we should go."

"What if they're not after the necklace? They might live near here," Trialla added with a look that betrayed her lack of confidence in her statement.

"I doubt it. Not with our luck," Niamh said as she picked up her things and headed out after Henry. The comment worried Niamh a little, though, as she had not considered the thought of different Sorcerers occupying this part of Ysrir, or new races they didn't even know about.

They picked their way through the valley, occasionally ducking into caves and behind boulders when they felt a shift in the wind. They continued single file with the Watcher keeping an eye on the surrounding sky and hillsides. Henry kept glancing up anyway, just to make sure he was doing a good job.

It was nearly dark when the valley seemed to open up, and it took several seconds for them to realise that the sparkling in the distance was in fact the last of the sunlight bouncing off the sea. They had nearly made it.

"It's getting too dark to carry on, I think," Henry said.

"At least it's downhill," Trialla added.

Out in front of them lay a lightly sloping downhill meadow that seemed to rise and drop like a calm sea in the wind. The dark green suddenly turned to black as the meadow dropped over a cliff edge into what was obviously the sea.

Overhead, seagulls circled looking for food and gave them a fright. Despite the initial shock, it seemed the flying Sorcerer was nowhere to be seen. They ducked back inside a cave near where the valley opened up, and fell asleep immediately.

***

Nearly a hundred miles down shore, a horse was galloping through the night, jumping hedges and streams, darting between trees and galloping over meadows. The horse was shattered, but the rider pushed it further. He had lost enough time already.

His foot still ached with pain, but he had managed to stop the bleeding. They were going to pay for that one. After falling into the murky depths of unconsciousness, Oddvard found himself washed up on rocks further downstream. He was so far downstream, in fact, that the mouth of the river was in sight and, beyond, the vast blue of the northern sea – a sea for which his people had yearned for for centuries.

Chapter 24

Magatha had been wandering the battlefield for what felt like days, surveying the carnage the Sorcerers had caused. The shock of seeing her own head on the ground again shocked her at first, but she felt no pain and always knew it might end this way.

Recent events in the human village felt like a dream to Magatha, but she knew it had happened. She knew she was already dead. What she couldn't understand was why she had ended up roaming the battlefield once more and had not passed over yet. Just as she had begun to wonder if she was destined to walk the battlefield for all eternity, a bright light began to grow in the distance. It was an almost blinding light, and Magatha pushed against the flow of people that had suddenly materialised around her – a sea of men, women and children being pulled toward the light. Magatha fought it. She could feel the pull deep within her soul. She knew she was on borrowed time now, but she wanted to live. She wanted to help her only daughter.

She fell to her knees, the rush of people trampling her feet. No one was talking or crying, their faces solemn and eyes unfocused. Eventually it was too strong to resist, and she felt herself being dragged into the ebb of the crowd as her final thoughts were of her daughter who, she knew, must now be close to her goal.

***

Niamh awoke feeling refreshed - as refreshed as she could be given her nightly torture. Her dream was hazy, pieces not quite fitting together. She creased her forehead in concentration as she tried to connect the dots. Whatever had happened she knew it didn't feel as bad. There was definitely water, and definitely drowning people, but it didn't seem as frightening. She had slept better on the cold, stony surface of the cave than she had in days, weeks even. She sat up, shook the haze from her head, and rubbed her eyes. "Henry," she called out, then heard Trialla stir beside her. "Sorry," she whispered and made her way to the entrance.

She found Henry sitting by a circle of rocks cooking what looked like some kind of boar with three tusks on a spit. The Watcher sat cross-legged beside him with his eyes closed.

"You hungry?" Henry asked. "We shouldn't stop long just in case, but we haven't eaten properly in a while and we need the energy."

Niamh didn't even thank him, but grabbed one of the legs he had de-boned and placed on a nearby rock before she began to devour it.

"Mpfanks," she spat as the warm meat soothed her insides and burned her throat and the roof of her mouth slightly. After swallowing the piece she was eating and looking slightly embarrassed, she said, "What's he doing?" nodding toward the Watcher.

"Not a clue. He was prodding me with a stick and trying to steal the food when he went all quiet and just sat down, humming."

After a curious look, Niamh said, "We're nearly there, Henry." There was a long pause and then, "Sorry."

"Why are you sorry?" Henry asked, looking confused.

"For getting you into this mess. It was my fault we had to do this. I thought it would be fun. I thought we would be home long before now."

Henry studied her, puzzled, then said, "But your mother said I had an important part to play in all this. Just as important as yours, she told me."

Niamh appeared slightly reassured by this. "Maybe it was because you killed the Sorcerer at the river."

"Maybe," Henry said, looking doubtful. He didn't know much about Sorcerers, but he knew his people hadn't been at war with, and he hadn't lost his parents to, a race that died or gave up so easily.

Several minutes went by during which they said nothing. They just sat quietly thinking of what they had accomplished and what may still lie ahead.

"Do you think Trialla is alright?" Niamh asked. Although she had been feeling jealous, she could still sense that Trialla was deeply troubled. She was lost in a world that no longer had meaning or purpose for her. She was going along with somebody else's quest, having lost everything of her own to it already.

Henry didn't know if she was alright, but she was strong. "Yeah, I'm sure she'll be fine once this is all over. Maybe she could come back to Rusalimum with us afterwards?"

Niamh knew this was a point where her jealousy should have been bubbling. She should have been shouting and yelling at Henry – shouting her feelings and demanding he tell her his, but she hadn't the energy anymore and why should she bother? It wasn't as though Henry was hers or even that she was sure she liked him in that way.

"Yeah," she said, putting a hand on his shoulder and heading off to wake Trialla up. "Why not?"

"Ah, that feels better," The Watcher sighed, licking his lips. "Your mother has passed over. She took her time, didn't she?"

Niamh glared at him for several seconds before asking, "So what does that mean? Is she gone forever?"

"Yep, certainly is. No chance of coming back now. No, no, no."

"So, do you feel different? How did you know?" Niamh asked, feeling her dislike for the Watcher grow every minute.

"I just know. It's like you suddenly feel full or like a thirst is quenched. I fear I am now on borrowed time, though, and will be leaving you shortly." Niamh got the distinct impression that the Watcher expected them to be sad about his imminent departure.

Niamh needed a little time on her own to think, so went and sat looking down the meadow out toward the distant sea.

Once they had all been awake for a little while and eaten breakfast, they gathered their things and started down the sloping meadow. The grass was long and tickled their ankles and the sun was beating down on them.

The contrast could not have been greater between the weather over the last few days and the beautiful midsummer-like day they were enjoying now. The sun seemed to melt away all their tensions from the last day, week, even years, and they felt their age again. They were actually enjoying themselves, playing chase through the fields and trying to leapfrog old crumbly dry-stone walls.

They soon crossed the meadow and realised that they hadn't even noticed the distance they had travelled. Henry looked back and saw that they were now well over halfway to the sea. Up ahead they saw the meadow carry on sloping downward. The grass swayed in the cool breeze and a small incline appeared down to the cliff edge. "Not far to go now," Henry shouted back to the two girls following behind him and chatting conspiratorially.

Henry continued down the grass and felt a sudden pull from behind. As his back hit the ground he heard the laughter of Niamh and Trialla fading into the distance and the slow burning sensation of itching seeds down his neck and back. He sat up and watched them running off, laughing. Getting to his feet, he chased after them whilst trying to dislodge the itchy seeds from beneath his clothes.

He finally caught them and pushed them to the floor. As they tried to pull him down he stood, breathless, looking into the distance.

"What?" Niamh asked. "What is it?" she asked again as she sat up and looked ahead. Straight ahead of them, over the edge of the hillside, they could now see a beautiful twinkling sea swaying back and forth, the light shattering the surface and reflecting blindingly in all directions.

It soon became clear that this was not what had caught Henry's attention. As Niamh and Trialla got to their feet, they followed his gaze down the slope ahead to a rocky shoreline and a small stretch of water separating the mainland from a small, circular island. The mist from the crashing waves obscured their vision, but there seemed to be some sort of buildings or statues at the top of the hill. They could make out something large and grey, and they studied it, each seeing different shapes in the hazy fog.

"Well," Niamh said. "This is it. Let's go fulfill our destiny."

"Do you believe in that? Destiny, I mean," Trialla asked.

Niamh thought about it for a minute – really thought about it – and replied, "My mother did, and she was never wrong about anything."

Chapter 25

The air now seemed somehow lighter, and the grass crisper. The sea air billowed from the rocks ahead and fresh ocean spray met the three young travellers as they scurried down the rocky face. They occasionally slid and clutched at exposed tree roots as they lost their footing.

On any other occasion the fresh scene might have been comforting, but the circumstances no longer seemed to be in favour of Niamh, Henry and Trialla. To them the colour had drained from the vast shoreline, and the sea seemed a devilish shade of black and white. The grass looked somehow bleak to them now.

They didn't once look back, as they knew what horror would meet their gaze. As they neared the water's edge, rocks exploded into thousands of razor-sharp splinters.

"Go! Go!" Henry pleaded as he passed Trialla, who had stubbed her toe on a rock.

About a hundred yards down shore, at the top of the incline, the Sorcerer from the river had appeared.. His eyes blazed with the reflections of spell after spell as he unleashed a wave of attacks on the fleeing Witches. He felt a fury he had never felt before. If the Witches returned this item, all would be lost. He couldn't afford to let that happen. It shouldn't have come this far.

As Niamh reached the water's edge, the sloshing water creating a sheep's wool-type covering for the beach, she heard Henry yelling.

"Niamh! What are you doing?" He screamed. "Your orb!"

She snapped back to the situation and noticed that her defensive orb had failed. She quickly moved her fingers and muttered a few words under her breath as she pulled Trialla closer to cover her.

A milky-blue orb grew around them as a red flame flew past to their left and ricocheted off the water's surface, sending shards of fractured light in every direction.

Oddvard was now stumbling down the cliff edge, his stallion collapsed with exhaustion behind him.

"The water's too deep," Trialla said. "We can't cross yet. What are we going to do?" she shouted over the crashing waves.

Henry looked back and quickly attempted a spell to litter the Sorcerer's path with boulders. All he managed was a shower of sand, but it did slow his progress for a minute, as he was partially blinded.

Niamh was staring, wide-eyed, at the surface of the water. *Not again*, she thought. The Watcher jumped to attention on top of the Staff and pulled Niamh's ear close.

"Repeat after me," he said as he whispered some incantations into her ear.

Following them closely, Niamh raised her hands and began twisting and turning her fingers as she repeated what the Watcher told her.

Up ahead, Henry and Trialla were cowering from the barrage of spells Oddvard was unleashing on them. Henry attempted to cast some back, but found it too difficult to concentrate on maintaining his protective sphere and attacking at the same time.

Straining to ensure she didn't mispronounce anything, Niamh pressed on with the spell, eyes clamped shut in concentration. She recognised parts of the spell, or at least the language, from books in her mother's normally locked study.

She suddenly heard a lack of instruction from the Watcher and opened her eyes, worried that she might see him dead. What met her eyes was probably a more shocking sight, as the sea in front of her was beginning to part. The sea bed was now wet like a beach on low tide, and towering waves held back on either side. The Watcher was nowhere to be seen.

"Thank you," she whispered as they swiftly headed across the shallow valley of crashing water.

They found that they needed to strengthen their defensive orbs often, and, twice, Oddvard's spells bounced off the vertical surface of water on either side of them, illuminating an expanse of underwater nothingness around them.

Henry glanced back to see the Sorcerer walking calmly towards them. Henry noticed in the panic that the Sorcerer had actually stopped firing to inspect the intricacy of the spell he was witnessing as he studied the waves either side of him.

Henry managed to pull himself onto the shingle beach of the island and saw Niamh pushing Trialla up a gravel path not far ahead. Once all three of them were only feet away, they heard an enormous crash and felt ocean spray tingle the back of their necks, the fresh scent mingling with the burning smell of recent explosions. Looking back they saw a wave towering over them, the aftermath of Niamh's spell caving in on the Sorcerer.

"Run!" Henry yelled as all three pushed their muscles through the intense strain they were already under to outrun the immediate danger of the mini-tsunami.

As they tried to run up the final stretch, arms flailing wildly, they felt the sudden bite of the cold again, its malicious teeth stinging their bare legs. They all knew there was little they could do to defend themselves against the cold in their damp clothes.

For the time being, it appeared they had lost the Sorcerer. They put their heads down and ran even faster, clothes clinging to their wet, blue-tinged skin. The weather grew suddenly worse, the sky now a murky grey with an eerie tint of orange. The approaching storm left an electric tingle in the air as a warning to anyone who might be standing in its path.

The ever thickening fog now meant Henry could only see a few feet ahead and could barely make out the back of Niamh's sprinting figure. He could only guess Trialla was up ahead.

Henry chanced a quick look over his shoulder and almost stumbled as his feet got caught up in what seemed to be some purple rags or a sheet on the ground.

He realised what this probably was, and, even worse, who it belonged to, but had no choice but to carry on. He tried to call out to warn Niamh and Trialla, but found the wind was against him too. As he yelled, he couldn't even hear his own voice properly, and the gales sucked the breath from his lungs.

As they reached the top they were met by a magnificent sight. They ran into the centre of twelve stone pillars. They all surrounded a central slab, laid on its side. As they neared the flat slab, they found themselves subjected to twelve piercing stares – twelve godly faces carved into the inside edge of each stone pillar.

Spinning around, looking for what they needed to do, their attention was drawn to the slab in the middle of the circle. It was about waist high and easily twenty feet long. Running her hands across the surface, Niamh studied the ancient rune marks and symbols for a clue about what to do next. Henry stood guard trying to search the suffocating mist.

"I don't know what to do!" Niamh screamed, holding the necklace aloft. "It's here, take it. We don't want it anymore!" she yelled as she fell to her knees, sobbing. Henry quickly reinforced their defensive orbs.

The rain lashed against Niamh's bare face as she heard it: the sickly sound of death approaching, its deep, crackly laugh filled with nothing but hate and malice.

Niamh didn't even look up as Henry attempted to shield them by spreading his arms and backing slowly into the girls.

As he scanned the twelve haunting slabs of stone, he noticed the mist parting as the dark figure approached.

"Well, little Witche, you will not get the better of me again. That I can assure you," Oddvard spoke softly as he neared the three of them,

As he limped to the central slab, his rigid features became clear. He knew they had nothing left to match the skill wielded by this Sorcerer. It appeared he was almost invincible. Henry backed further still into Niamh and Trialla, pinning them against the cold, slippery surface of the aged, moss-scented rock.

Henry began to look frantically around like a cornered

animal searching for an escape. The only alternative would be to fight, but he was confident it would only end one way.

"Come now, boy," Oddvard said. "You know you cannot defeat me. Why make this more difficult than it needs to be? Move aside and give me the Witche girl and the necklace. You will not suffer greatly. My battle is not with you at the minute." Oddvard calmly stopped feet away, the mist distorting his angular features.

Trialla cowered, sobbing, and until now Niamh had not even looked up from the necklace clasped so tightly in her hand that she'd pierced her rain-soaked skin.

Before Oddvard had given a second for Henry to consider his options, he raised both hands out to each side and Henry felt the wind knocked from his lungs as he was flung violently against one of the outer slabs, his head crashing against the stone figure's weathered bottom lip.

As he hung in the air, he noticed Trialla pinned against the slab opposite him, her head lolled against her chest. Oddvard advanced, arms outstretched, toward Niamh.

Niamh stood quickly with new-found energy, and stared straight at Oddvard, feet apart, necklace still clenched tightly in her palm.

"Give it to me, child. I tire of these games," he said, dropping Trialla to the floor in a crumpled heap so he could extend his open hand to Niamh.

"You do not understand the power you wield in that little trinket," Oddvard said in a more hushed, pleading tone. The wind whistled and howled between the slabs, and the pelting horizontal rain had now solidified into small pellets of ice. The daylight had skulked away, and the eerie gloom of the storm had set in.

"You do not deserve the power this holds. Your people don't deserve it. You've brought nothing but war, torture and misery to this land. Too many people have died at your hands. Tell me, why should I give this to you?" Niamh demanded, her eyes boring into his so fiercely that he nearly looked away.

"Stupid girl, you really don't understand the power for destruction this necklace can bring. My opinion of you Witches gets lower and lower with each encounter."

With this revelation, Oddvard sprang at Niamh, Henry dropping to the ground as he lowered his other hand. Oddvard grabbed Niamh by the shoulders. He picked her up with hardly any effort and threw her across the top of the central slab, her arms grazing along the carved surface. She came to a rolling stop about halfway along, and found the Sorcerer already looming over her. She tried to make herself a defensive orb, but he was on her too quickly. He pressed his muscular hand against the side of her face and began to crush her into the slab. With his other hand he bent her arm behind her head and began trying to prise the necklace from her fingers, her grip on the necklace as strong as a hand in rigor mortis.

"I have had to watch as your people have sucked the power from the very ground," he spat. "You have been shown time and time again that this is our land. You do not belong here on our soil, but no matter how many times we come to defeat you, you remain – sometimes even stronger than ever. Well, I am sick of this plague. Your people disgust me. You have no right to even breathe the same air as me." Oddvard dragged her limp face close to his.

"Maybe I should let you return the necklace," Oddvard

continued. "Let the gods deal with it and let my people rebuild their lives without the fear of being infected by your stench." Oddvard prised her struggling fingers apart and took the blood-soaked necklace from her grip. Holding it aloft to try and study his prize in the little available light, he began a spell to finish the Witche girl off. His fingers moved rapidly and he mumbled things under his breath, all the while his gaze fixed on the necklace.

"I'm sure this won't be as much fun as killing your repulsive mother, but it will definitely sit highly with my most favoured kills," he said as he lifted his now glowing white hand over his head to strike.

"Stop!" came a cry from behind him. "Let her go."

Oddvard would have enjoyed nothing more than to finish his strike and watch as the only heir to the now extinct Witche throne burned, and he would have had he not recognised the voice as his own son. He dropped Niamh, and she quickly scurried over the edge of the slab and back toward Henry, who was attempting to creep along the edge unseen.

As Oddvard turned he saw, to his amazement, his own son walking along the slab towards him.

Chapter 26

"That is enough, Father. What have you become? She is only a child."

Oddvard swiftly picked Jorgan from his feet and threw him against an outer slab, where he landed on his side.

"How dare you take the side of a Witche over me, your King?" Oddvard said as he spat on the ground beside him. "What have *I* become? Me? Look at yourself. I can only imagine what trickery you have used to get yourself here, but you are out of place. You are not worthy of dealing with matters involving gods. Go home and I will deal with you later, boy. Why, I would have killed anyone else had they spoken to me the way you have." Oddvard turned to walk away with a tut of disgust.

"I am not scared of you, Father. Not anymore. If this is the kind of ruler you are, if this is the kind of coward you are..." Jorgan immediately realised the repercussions of what he had just said. He flinched as Oddvard turned and his fist crunched against the side of his head, blood spurting from his lip as it burst violently. Jorgan fell to the ground, holding his face and looking at his father.

"A coward? Boy, I have had to endure fighting and killing all my life to protect our people; to make a better future for our people. But the only thing that makes me realise I am no coward is the fact that I have faced the one thing that makes me sick to my stomach every day of my life and have stopped myself doing anything about it. Do you know, there hasn't been a day pass since your mother's death that I haven't wanted to kill you for what you did to her? I've fed you, clothed you, and God only knows how much I have tried to train you so one day you might even actually fight back when I did try to kill you. You make me sick. You might think me a coward, but I have had to look the murderer of my soulmate in the eyes every day and do nothing. Do you know how hard that is?"

A new silence gripped the air and clung, not wanting to let go. The sound of the crashing waves, the rain, and even the ringing in Jorgan's ears seemed to be more subdued after these words. He knew his father blamed him for his mother's death, and he knew he had always been ashamed of his lack of warrior spirit, but to hear it spoken in such a spiteful way shocked him.

"I came to try and help," Jorgan managed at last, a slight waver in his voice. "I wanted to show you I can be a warrior, that there is no reason to be ashamed of me. I just wanted you to see what I can do and be... be proud of me."

***

Niamh and Henry had managed to retreat to find Trialla regaining consciousness and helped her up. They didn't know what to do now that the Sorcerer had got the necklace. They had come this far, and there was no way they were going home without finishing what her mother had set them to do.

They stayed low to the ground and tried to decide what to do whilst Trialla began to regain some of her balance and the muffled feeling surrounding her head eased slightly.

***

Jorgan still sat cowering on the floor at the base of an outer slab with Oddvard towering over him, arms swinging in the rain.

"I should kill you now, boy, for this, but I don't. Do

you understand the restraint that takes? You sicken me. You are no son of mine!" he shouted as he turned to walk back toward the shoreline.

Jorgan sat for several seconds mulling over what had been said. He was better than this. He would make a better leader than his father was. Ruling a people didn't depend on being able to fight or kill children. It was about respect and having the respect of your people.

He sat, legs twisted, looking tearfully after his father. He felt a wave of emotion from anger to hate, anxiety to fear. Without even realising it, he was on his feet and found himself hurtling towards his father, arms outstretched.

He bowled Oddvard to the ground and, rolling several times entangled, crashed into the opposite stone slab. Jorgan was lucky enough to land on top of his father and he began to punch him in the face, over and over, the blood mingling with the misty air to create a crimson glow around them. Oddvard struggled to regain control and could taste his own blood from his open lip as he struggled to free his arms from under Jorgan's knees. He'd never seen his son so enraged before. And he liked it.

After a few minutes, Jorgan tired and leapt to his feet, backing away hesitantly, the courage and anger he had felt only seconds before ebbing away. It was being replaced with fear, guilt, and the thought that he may have just given his father the final provocation he needed to kill his own son.

Oddvard got to his knees then stood up, wheezing. His twisted grin was smeared with blood, his teeth dyed pink and his nose dripping to the sodden ground. The two of them stood, staring and panting, looking at each other until Oddvard laughed. This slowly extended into a booming laugh. When his fit subsided, he shook his head, wiped the blood from his mouth with the back of his hand and said, "It's a start, boy. It's a start."

Oddvard turned once more to walk away, this time slightly more conscious of what was happening behind him. Jorgan held out his hand, and what looked like a small silvery butterfly with an enormous tail fluttered to his hand from his own pocket as he smiled. Oddvard realised his error and spun on his heels with great speed to see Jorgan smirking back at him, the necklace in his hand.

"Don't toy with me, boy, not now!" Oddvard snapped, with a hint of impatience in his voice. "This is not a time for foolishness. Give it back to me," he snarled revealing his pink teeth once more.

"What did the runes tell you? That night with Trioso, I saw you. What did they tell you?" Jorgan asked.

"Boy, if you knew, I assure you that you would not be wasting my time now with these pranks. Do you not understand the power you hold within your hand. The power to destroy the world is held in that tiny gem, and we can't let them have it. The whole world could be destroyed like that," Oddvard attempted to click his fingers, which resulted in his rain-soaked hands making a dull thud. "Give me the necklace and go home," he continued.

Jorgan stood his ground more from uncertainty than bravery. He watched as Oddvard began to raise his left hand. To his surprise, it was not he who was the victim of his father's magic, but the young Witche girl.

Niamh felt herself pulled into the air, Henry trying to pull her back by her feet as she went. Oddvard stood, his left arm vertical now as Niamh hung twenty feet above him, arms and legs dangling.

"The necklace," he repeated.

When Jorgan made no move, Oddvard lowered his arm in an arcing movement to his other side, and Niamh ricocheted off a stone slab to the solid earth below. Henry and Trialla looked on in utter terror.

Oddvard noticed the young Witche boy retreating from the circle of slabs into the shadows, but he was confident the boy posed little threat now.

Jorgan tried his hardest to keep his gaze fixed on his father, but he couldn't help a quick glance to see if the girl was hurt.

"Ha! See!" Oddvard yelled. "This is your downfall: compassion. She is merely a Witche, you fool. Do not pity her, feel sorry for her, or care about her. You should be bubbling inside with the urge to kill her. Your heart should be yearning to see her blood spilled on the ground she sits on now as her face turns pale and lifeless. Here," he added, as though it was an afterthought, "let me show you."

Oddvard walked past Jorgan towards where Niamh now lay on the floor. He knew he could goad his son into fighting, into becoming a mighty warrior one day. Maybe today was that day. *Does he have it in him to kill this vermin, though?* Oddvard wondered.

As the looming figure approached Niamh, sheltering her from the rain, he felt a sudden snag. He looked down to his hands and found them bound so tightly in velvet thread that he felt clumsy moving them.

"What's this...?"

Jorgan threw another ball at him, which seemed to alter

direction of its own accord and then explode into a web of yellow and white, enveloping Oddvard in an intricate net of razor-fine wire. The wire began to twist around his face in small strands until the bottom half of his face was completely covered, leaving two small nostril holes for breathing. He fell to the ground with a thud. He suddenly began to feel claustrophobic and frustrated, especially as his hands were bound, preventing him from using any powerful spells.

He struggled and squirmed like a fish on dry land, but it was no use. The more he fought, the tighter the net became.

As Jorgan approached him, he noticed the thin lines of red that had appeared as the wire began to cut the surface of his skin.

"Let me tell you something, Father, I have done nothing but try to live up to your expectations. To become what you ask of me. But I am a failure. You tell me every day, and maybe I am, but I'm going to teach you something today. Something I wish my mother had taught you. Humility."

Jorgan stepped over his father, who struggled to free himself but found the wires to be too deep now to move at all. Instead he listened. He heard the trampling of feet moving away from him, the cracks of lightning above, and then his own son say, "Witche, what is your name?"

"Niamh," she said, standing. "Witche Qwein and Ruler of Ysrir," she added after a second, intending to intimidate and show her courage, but her voice betrayed her a little on both accounts. She was still unclear on what exactly was going on, and this was evident on her face.

"Please," Jorgan said. "Forgive me." He knelt swiftly, bowed his head and took her right hand, kissing it.

"I believe this belongs to you," he said, returning to his feet. He held out his hand, and the small butterfly fluttered and dropped the necklace in her hand before returning to his open palm. Niamh now realised the long tail the butterfly seemed to have was in fact the necklace chain. The bulk of the necklace was gripped underneath its reflective body which, Niamh soon realised, must have been a strange concoction of magic.

"Let this, please, bring peace," he said, stepping back a little as though he expected it to produce some immediate effect. Behind him Jorgan could hear his father's muffled screams and shouts of despair at the thought of the Witches having his precious object – the object he probably cared more for than his own son.

"I don't know what to do with it!" Niamh shouted at the retreating Jorgan. She would have been happy with an answer from anyone.

Trialla came and joined them, wary of Jorgan as she passed him, and held out her bloody hand to Niamh. Niamh dropped the necklace into it. As the blood and rain began to cover the necklace, many colours shifted and danced inside. Her blood soaked into the necklace to create a red haze inside its beautiful centre.

Trialla felt a tingle in her hand and opened it quickly. Her natural instinct was to drop it as fast as she could. She didn't understand any of the powers that the others seemed to have, so was unsure whether things like this were supposed to be happening. She found the glowing necklace wouldn't drop, and seemed to be stuck to her downturned palm. It began to pulse with a bright light and remained stuck.

She felt the tingle again, and found her hand being pulled away from her. Before long she could no longer resist the pull, and was forced onto her feet and around the central slab. She seemed to be doing a lap of the outer carved stones until she halted at one, her palm facing directly at the engraved face.

She suddenly felt her knees buckle, and her hand plunged below the surface of the mud and under the slab. She was shoulder-deep in soil, and Henry and Niamh grabbed her feet as the right side of her face touched the ground despite her efforts to twist her head away. Henry remembered the horrors of being pulled through the mud by Patch, and it wasn't something he'd wish on anyone.

She began to feel the tingle subside, and realised her hand was now free. She struggled to stand, and gawped as she watched the hole she had just made close up around the only object she had ever treasured, swallowing up the only hope she'd had that maybe someday again her people might be free to do as they pleased and go where they wanted, as they had when this necklace had first been worn.

Niamh, Henry and Trialla stared at the giant stone slab as Jorgan joined them slowly from behind. No one was sure what to do next, when a low rumbling noise began to shake the floor beneath their feet. The shrieks and cries of Oddvard could barely be heard as the noise grew louder and the slabs began to resonate at an extremely high pitch. The four of them fell to the ground, clutching their ears, hoping for anything that would make it stop. Suddenly it did stop, a few bits of loose rock tumbling from the slabs as the aftershocks continued and eventually ebbed away.

They all stood, Jorgan quickly glancing back to check on his father, and stared at the slab. It looked different somehow. The rock still looked almost the same. The colour seemed the same, but the weathered face carved into the side seemed to have more character.

"It moved!" shrieked Trialla. "Look," she added pointing.

They stared, motionless, for a few seconds and Niamh was about to make a sarcastic comment when she thought she saw a flicker of light in the figure's eye.

"Don't be sil—" Henry began, but Niamh raised her hand to him to silence his remark as she slowly edged closer to look up at the slab's aged face. She studied it closely for what seemed like many minutes, no one behind her daring to interrupt. The rain had eased a little, but it still made looking up at the slab difficult and disorientating.

Eventually Henry said, "It's just the rain. You can barely see the thing anyway in this light. Do you think that's it? That is all that needs to happen?"

He waited for an answer, but found Niamh had either chosen not to answer him or was so enveloped in studying the face that she hadn't even heard him.

"I said..." Henry began when a great creaking noise thundered through the sky. The low bass tone was like the movement of great mountains or the creaking of ancient trees. The four of them continued to stare up as Niamh staggered backwards in shock and fright.

"It... It moved," Niamh stuttered. "Why is the rock moving, Henry? I'm pretty sure rocks don't generally do that."

As they eased their way slowly backwards, the face began to crunch and move, the mouth stretching open and creaking as though stretching out an ache. The large, bulbous eyes blinked a few times with what seemed like slate eyelids, and the marble eyeballs seemed to roll back into the stone a few times until the pupils focused down on the four figures before it.

The face was surreal, as though the giant had been encased in the rock with only the tips of his features remaining.

He seemed to look around for a while, scanning the horizon and studying the characters below him. He stretched his stone jaw once more before saying, "I have waited many years for this moment. Answer. Who stands before me with the gift of spirit? Who returns my essence at such a high price?"

Niamh felt a surge of courage bubbling within her and was about to step forward until the words replayed in her head. What did he mean, 'at such a high price'?

Henry eventually said, "I would like to return this necklace as a gift from the Witches, the Sorcerers and the Humans of Ysrir," looking across at his companions. "We want peace in our land and return this necklace to you as a kind of payment in the hope that you might help us."

The slab face seemed to be chewing rocks while he listened as he munched his mouth in circular motions. "What is your name, little one?" he asked.

"Henry, and this is Niamh and Trialla and..." His mind scanned for a name but came up blank.

"And Jorgan, son of Oddvard, King of Ysrir," Jorgan offered when he saw Henry was clearly struggling.

"Ah," the head replied as it looked disapprovingly

down at Jorgan. "The mighty Sorcerers from the north. You have brought much distress to this fair land with your ways. Time and time again you have been punished with drought, famine and disease, yet you continue with your evil ways. Are you here for redemption, boy, or do you have a more sinister motive that you are yet to reveal?"

Jorgan knelt and lowered his head. "I have no sinister motive. I agree that my people have made mistakes, but I am not an evil person. I just wanted to show my father that I can be a good warrior, that there is reason to be proud of me."

"PROUD!" the face groaned, parts of the slab cracking from its mouth. "There is no credit in war. There is no reasoning behind killing and death and destruction. Your people came to my land and took from it what was not theirs. I have been entombed for centuries because your people value greed and possession over peace and happiness. Do you have anything to say in your defence? Is there anything that could be said?"

Jorgan remained on one knee, unsure how to progress. It was true that his people had caused much distress in the past, but he had been no part of it. If anything, he had tried to prevent his father from going to war on many occasions.

"There is nothing I can say in defence of my people," Jorgan added as his head sank even further into his chest.

"Can you help us?" Niamh said as she stepped forward and placed her hand on Jorgan's shoulder. "We are hoping for peace. We have come a long way and are tired of running and fighting. Is there anything you can do to help us?" she pleaded.

The face seemed to scrunch in intense thought as it made clucking noises. Eventually it said, "You were chosen for a reason, little ones. You have returned the essence of my spirit to me, and for that I am truly grateful, but the ultimate reason was not simply to reunite me with the gods. It was to prevent me from being lost forever.

"Many times have we tried to control the people of this land. There have been many races come and go, many different colours, shapes, species that have walked, flown and swum the surface of this beautiful place, yet not once has there been an even mixture of peace and harmony.

"It has become clear that there is no correct balance to be achieved. There is no restriction we can put in place that will give a constant peace. You have the perfect resources to live a harmonious life. There is nothing stopping the inhabitants of this planet living in complete paradise, except the people themselves.

"Why is it that you always seek out misery? Why do you choose destruction and war over peace and tranquillity?"

The face seemed to pause here to let the group think over what it had said. Just as Trialla was about to offer an answer, he continued, "There is no right and wrong combination here. We have tried everything within our power to create a peaceful world, but you are always working against us. You are divided by land, possessions, even by which god you worship. We are as a whole; you should not worship one of us. You worship what we have created, the power we possess. Even the great barriers have had no effect. You even sacrifice your own people to get around that."

"But *my* people are not evil, sir," Trialla shouted, retreating slightly and shocked at her own outburst.

"Are they not? Your people used to torture those they thought Witches because they followed a different god;

because they looked and acted differently. Is this not evil? Your people slaughter innocent animals and trees for clothing, for tools. How is this not evil, young girl? You may not be evil yourself, but as a whole your species is."

Trialla stepped backwards, slightly ashamed and also angered by the slab's comments. Her people did what they needed to survive. When had they ever been told it was wrong to eat animals?

"Your people are paying for their sins as we speak. The people of your village live a torturous life by night, and wake with half-dreams of death and destruction."

"Yes!" Trialla wailed. "Then you know why I ask your help. Do you know what evil causes this?"

"Of course I know what causes this. It is you, your people. You bring these things on yourselves. When your people die, they are not permitted to continue on their chosen path – to the other place – if they have caused others pain or have sinned in any way. But where do these people go, then? They do not deserve the peace that lies ahead, and they have no right to return to where they have come from, so they stay suspended between worlds. They are nowhere during the day and continue their existence and live a half-life at night, but even your people have taken to killing during this time. They are confused and scared and return to their natural instincts: to kill and to eat. Even the gods cannot punish their own people because their need to sin is too great."

"But why? Why do you cause such pain? Surely you can stop this happening? Why won't you stop this?" Trialla sobbed, tears tickling her cheeks.

"Because this is the only way. There is little hope of them passing over, yet they simply cannot cease to be. They cannot go from living to nothing, so they must still exist somewhere. The only place for them to exist is in the bodies of people who sleep. This is not just a case of punishment. There is simply nowhere else for these souls to pass to."

"But why does this only happen to humans, then?" Niamh ventured, although secretly thankful it did.

"You are all paying in your own way. Has your village not recently recovered from drought? The Sorcerers from famine?"

"But surely we are meant to hunt and kill? If you gave us these natural urges, then surely it is your fault?" Niamh attempted to shout over the slowly increasing winds. As the words left her mouth, she quickly realised what she had just done. Surely accusing a god of being at fault was not the smartest thing she had ever done?

To her surprise, the Sea God seemed speechless. He opened and closed his mouth, but nothing came out. Eventually he sighed a huge, stone-crunching sigh, and was silent.

"Please help us," Niamh added in a pleading tone. "We do want to live in peace, but how? Tell us what we need to do!"

"It is true," the Sea God began, and then stopped again to think. "It is true some fault must lie with the gods. We did, as you say, create all species with certain attributes – attributes that we later regretted and attempted to rectify, but the will of your races seems too strong. It seems that by giving you free will it has inevitably led to your downfall on numerous occasions, but I do intend to help you." The slab scrunched his face in concentration again.

"Neither have we escaped these mishaps unscathed, little one," he continued. "Us lower gods have been cast here in this way until we could bring together all races for this decision."

The ground began to shake, and loose parts of the slabs began to crumble to the ground. The waves could be heard crashing against the rocks below, and Niamh pulled her cloak higher around her neck to try and gain at least a little shelter from the now vicious wind.

All four of them found they had slowly backed toward the central slab. All that could be heard above the crunching of stone and wind was the occasional whimper from Jorgan's father, who still lay curled on the floor. Jorgan cast a glance in his direction to make sure he was still OK.

The Sea God unscrewed his face and blinked his cold grey eyelids. "I call to order the final session of the gods. I welcome you all and am glad to be reunited with you once more, my friends."

Niamh, Henry, Trialla and Jorgan were frozen on the spot. Surrounding them were not only the twelve slabs of stone, but twelve twitching, yawning, coughing and grumbling stone faces – presumably the other gods. The children cowered slightly in the stinging rain and realised that one of the slabs remained motionless, a look of white-washed anguish and pain on its face.

"Are we all present?" the Sea God continued as his bulbous, grainy eyes scanned the circle, his face remaining frozen to the slab as his eyes attempted to view the gods on either side of him.

A chorus of 'aye' rumbled around the four children. It was an earth-grinding, tree-splitting, thunder-cracking acknowledgement that all were present.

"Very well, then. I shall begin. You have been called to order here to complete what should have been done many moons ago. As many of you I expect have prophesised, the time is now upon us. We are confronted by the four races of this land: Witches, Sorcerers, humans and fayeryes."

At this Niamh shot an understanding glance at Henry as he felt the warm buzz of the eggs in his pocket. They also noticed that there was a hint of something in the Sea God's face as he mentioned the Sorcerers, and Niamh was sure it was anger.

He continued. "You are all aware of the paths that have been travelled to get to this point, my own a particularly trying and testing one. And we are all, including myself, sad to see that we are now an incomplete number, with the God of Fire no longer with us. This situation was no doubt set in motion when we met at this spot many centuries ago."

There was a general mumbling of agreement and sideways looks from many eyes around the circle.

"We are at a time of grave concern. My brothers and I believe this to be a significant day in history. For too long have we concerned ourselves with matters of the people of this planet. It has become clear that we have done what we can for the people here, and it is now up to them to control their own destinies, to build their futures on the foundations we set so long ago."

Through the ever-rising whistling of the wind, and the stinging of what now seemed to be hailstones on their faces, the four of them looked up in awe as the gods spoke with such booming voices. They were possibly witnessing something no other person in Ysrir had ever seen before, and all they could think of was home. Niamh and Henry, thought of steaming callaberry juice around a warm fire, the setting sun on the watery horizon as their classmates run through the gates of school to play in the fields, and what would be left when they returned home. Much must have happened since they left, and they wondered if the gods would help them rebuild what had been destroyed over the years.

"We have been asked for help, and, as was originally planned, help will be given. The people of this world have had too many opportunities to build a great future with our assistance, so we offer it one final time."

At these words Niamh felt the gaze of eleven grey faces bearing down on them – faces showing great wisdom, knowledge, anxiety and anticipation. Niamh could tell that what was decided in this moment would help the future of her people for an eternity, but she could also tell this was not a decision the gods had come to easily.

"Which one of you do we address as leader at this grave time?" the Sea God asked.

The four of them looked at each other, not knowing what to say. No one was leader. No one wanted to be leader. How could anyone claim to be leader when they came from such different backgrounds?

Henry turned as though he was about to speak, until Niamh placed a hand on his shoulder. She smiled at him in a way she knew he would understand. He stepped out of the way and managed to smile back. He knew Niamh was the reason all this had begun. However the gods intended to help, he knew that for some reason Niamh was at the centre of it all.

"You can address me," she said, stepping forward from the group, quickly adding, "Erm, sir?" How did you address not only a Sea God but one who was talking to you through what was probably several tons of stone? "I am Niamh Retalla," she continued, turning slowly to address every god. "Witche Qwein of Ysrir, daughter of Magatha and Ruler of Rusalimum and the far reaches of Ysrir."

"Very well," he replied. Looking up again to address the other gods, he asked, "Are we in agreement?"

This time there was a stinging silence as each slab seemed to mull over all other possibilities and outcomes until each one eventually said "Aye".

"Niamh, Witche Qwein, is your group in agreement? Do you seek our help to bring peace to this once great land? Do you accept that this is the last act we can perform to aid your people, and that you will be responsible from this point on in maintaining the peace without our help?"

Niamh turned to look at Henry. "This is it," she said. "We've come a long way for this moment. Everyone OK?" she asked as she looked at Trialla and Jorgan. When she got a general nodding of agreement, she turned back to face the Sea God, her neck aching from looking up, and nodded. "Yes, we want peace in our land once more," she said as Oddvard began to thrash and groan again in the distance.

"Fine," the Sea God boomed. "Thank you for your presence and agreement in this matter," he said, addressing the other gods. "Your work here is done, and let us pray that this will, one day soon, bring peace."

At this the other slabs began to shriek and cry in agony as the faces began to crumble and fade as though time had speeded up and the wind had finally won the battle to weather them away like pebbles in a stream. They finally crumbled to nothing and left several dry patches of grass.

"May you find peace and tranquility, Niamh, Qwein of Ysrir, and may your reign be a prosperous and happy one. You will be safe here. The destruction will not touch this island," he said, and his face too began to crumble.

"What? Wait!" Niamh shouted in a firm, authoritative voice. "What do you mean, destruction? You promised us peace. You said you'd help us!" she yelled looking frantically at the others.

"We are helping you. This is the only way. In destruction will come peace and new beginnings. There is no hope for your people at present. There is far too much evil that cannot be reversed now it is in motion."

"But what do you mean?" demanded Niamh. "What do you mean, destruction? Killing people? Surely by killing everyone you are as bad as us. You can't kill everyone!"

The Sea God, still crumbling and cracking, said, "But we can. If it is to help the greater good, then we simply must do it. With the agreement of all the gods and a majority of races, we have a duty to do it. You said yourself you just wanted peace. Well, now you can have it."

"But, but... " Niamh began as the others simply looked on in horror.

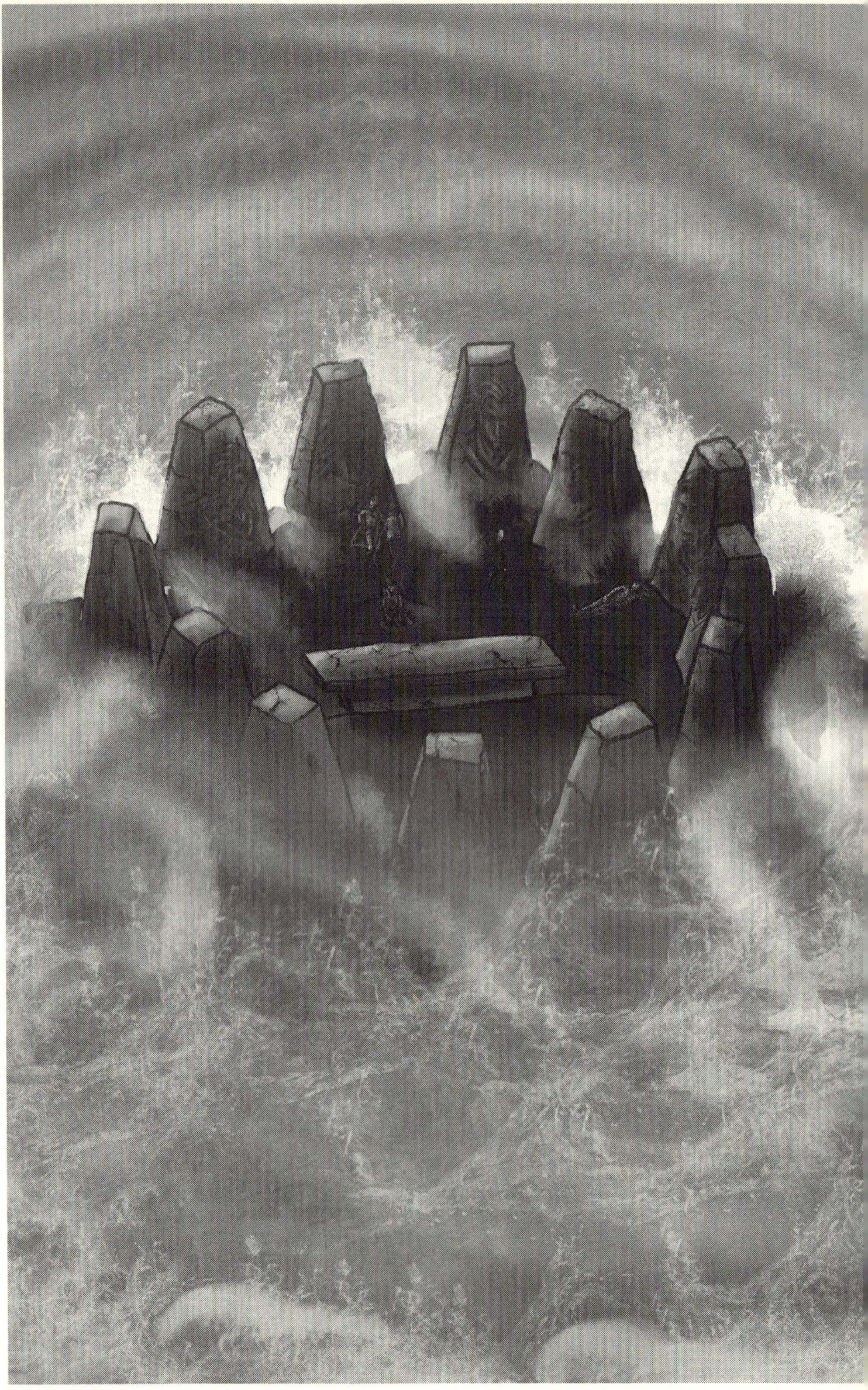

Chapter 27

Jorgan sprinted towards his father. "Father, Father, you've got to help us," he pleaded.

Oddvard, still entwined on the floor, simply laughed, the wires still cutting as he moved. "Help you?" he said as Jorgan freed his mouth. "Why should I help you now? I told you not to meddle, but you just disobeyed me again. You're a disgrace. This is what the runes told me, boy. This! There will be a new beginning with the coming of the waves. Do you not see what I've been trying to do?"

"But... I thought you wanted it to help in the war," Jorgan said.

"Of course I did. I knew the powers that necklace held. I knew what would happen if it were returned, but I also knew that with it no one could oppose me. Not even the gods themselves."

"Then why didn't you just say? Why didn't you tell me this would happen?" asked Jorgan.

"Because you wouldn't have believed me. You'd have just assumed that the only reason was to finish off the Witches. You'd have immediately thought the worst."

Jorgan dropped his gaze and thought for a moment. It was true. Even now he wondered whether his father hadn't told him so that this could happen. There had to be something in it for him if everything ended this way.

"So what can we do? There must be a way of stopping it. Help me, Father. I need your help."

The wind was now nearing gale-force strength, and the

waves were licking the sky closer and closer to where they stood. The water level had risen and had already nearly reached where the outer circle of slabs stood moments before. In the distance they knew it must have reached the top of the hill that they clambered down, but they couldn't see anything because of the dense fog and mist floating in the air.

Henry looked at Niamh and Trialla. What else could they do? He had to think. There must be something they could do to stop this. Did he want to stop this, though? Maybe the Sea God was right. What if this is the last hope? What if everyone would kill each other eventually if things stayed like this? And what about Trialla's family? Surely they couldn't go on living like they were if they were still alive? He turned to look at Niamh, who was sobbing on her knees.

"You can't kill everyone," she sobbed. "You can't just kill all those people."

The waves rose and began sloshing around their ankles as the fog seemed to clear and the mist vanished. As it lifted, they were confronted by an even more terrifying sight: surrounding the circle they stood in, reaching just behind where the Sea God's rocky form stood, was an enormous mountain of water. It seemed as though they were standing right in the centre of a gigantic tornado of water. On all sides the water encircled them, and the vast cylinder of air above them reached to the heavens.

The water seemed to keep rising, and Niamh could see the odd glimpse of what she hoped were sea creatures, her mind immediately racing back to her dreams. *Maybe they're bodies,* she thought. *Maybe they're all dead bodies, suffocating under the water.* She was now white with panic as she had been every morning on waking in a cold sweat from the terrible nightmare that was now partly coming true.

Nothing held the water in place, yet it kept rising. The only safe place seemed to be where the four of them stood now. Jorgan stood and walked toward the edge. He came within a few feet of it, and could feel the wind blowing as it spiralled around them like a huge vortex with them in the middle.

Jorgan heard a groan from behind him, and saw his father moving slowly across the floor. He was being sucked towards the edge by an invisible force. Jorgan dropped to the ground and began pulling at his father's feet as the others rushed over to help.

Oddvard was thrashing and crying with fear, his arms and legs still bound.

"Get this stuff off him!" Henry screamed at Jorgan.

"I can't," he replied. "It'll wear off in a couple of hours. There's nothing I can do."

They pulled with all their might until they saw on Oddvard's face the look of defeat. He knew he had no place in the new world. This must be the way it ended.

He looked up at Jorgan, who was still frantically struggling to pull him back. It was a look filled with questions, love, hate, jealousy, anger and pity – a look that conveyed so much regret that no words were needed. As Jorgan returned the look, he smiled, a tear dropped from his cheek, and he let go.

Oddvard's body was sucked straight through the surface without letting any water in, and began spiralling around and up the wall of water.

"Look!" Trialla shouted, grabbing Henry's arm. "Look,

it's nearly gone."

As they turned, they saw the last few remains of a face carved in stone many centuries before. As they all looked up with a mixture of hatred and confusion, the Sea God opened his stony mouth one last time and said, "One day, Niamh, you will understand that this was for the best. From this day forward your new kingdom is known as Tirfo Thuin, which means 'land under the waves'. May you find peace and happiness." At this, the last remains of the now disfigured mouth crumbled to dust and the slab collapsed into a heap that swiftly blew away into the cold night above them.

As they stood, staring all around them, the water began to drop. The wind turned into more of a subtle chill and the rain stopped. Up ahead, through the clearing water, they could make out a distant sun beaming down and refracting into several rainbows.

The water eventually reached the ground around them once more and began to recede down the island and back to normal sea level. They all stared out towards their new land – a land once filled with loved ones and war. People they called friends and enemies. The grass looked so much greener. The flowers still seemed to be in bloom. The sky was now a sloping gradient of white to blue and the sun seemed to dry them through to the bone straightaway.

They were all confused and tired, and didn't really know what to say to each other. Jorgan slumped to the ground with his legs crossed and cried, head in his hands. Niamh gave Trialla a hug as Henry hitched himself up onto the central slab with his legs dangling. He scanned the horizon again. Several birds swooped and played in the fields opposite and dolphins broke the surface of the glistening water between the island and the mainland.

As he sat there he felt a fuzzy warmth beside him. He pulled back his top to see that his sides seemed fine. He placed his top back down and reached into his pockets. As he pulled out the two eggs, the silver and green now pulsating strongly, they suddenly split down the centre. He dropped them to the floor, where they seemed to shatter into silver dust as two tiny fayeryes emerged and fluttered their way up to the stone slab beside Henry. They seemed to grow all the time as they flew, and by the time they landed they seemed not much smaller than Patch and the others had been.

They landed. The male fayerye bowed his head and the smaller, female one curtsied to Henry.

"I am Patch," said the small fluttering fayerye, "This is Meeleo. I hope we can be of service in some way," he said as the colours on his chest changed and glittered. Patch sat down beside Henry as Meeleo took flight again and seemed to test her flying abilities above them.

As Niamh watched Henry intently, she realised that the other fairies must be dead as well. *The Patch we knew must be dead too*, Niamh thought, and then it dawned on her. The vision she had seen in the shimmering ceiling wasn't Henry and Patch, but his son. His heir.

Once everyone had discovered they were OK, they decided they should head back toward the mainland and see what remained of their towns.

"Come on!" Henry shouted back to Jorgan. "We should get across before the tide rises," he said tentatively, trying to gauge Jorgan's reaction to the loss of his father.

"I'll catch up," Jorgan replied as he stood and looked around properly himself for the first time. This wasn't right. His people didn't deserve to die. His father didn't deserve to die. He was trying to save them all. Why hadn't he seen that? For the first time he'd seen a spark of affection in his father's eye, and now that had been taken from him.

As Niamh, Henry and Trialla made their way back up the meadow on the mainland in silence, they stopped to wait for Jorgan. They couldn't see him, so decided to sit for a while. They weren't to know he'd crossed to the mainland and was currently on the road back to Adiabene alone.

Niamh rested her head against a tree trunk and felt her breathing relax. For the first time in days she felt as though she could sleep forever, and she had a feeling that, tomorrow, she'd probably wake from a restful, water-free sleep.

Epilogue

Niamh looked on as, all around her, people strived to rebuild her town. To their surprise, they had actually found survivors on their return trip. Trialla had found three members of her race after they had barricaded themselves within the mountain side. Despite frantically searching, they found no trace of her family.

Niamh and Henry had searched for people they recognised when they made it back to Rusalimum. They found several members of staff had been holed up in an underground chamber of St Guinevere's that even they hadn't known about, but failed to find any trace of Henry's gran.

Niamh watched as Henry lifted a fallen beam from the school assembly hall and struggled to position it somewhere near where the hall would have been. Patch fluttered beneath the beam, attempting to help, his intricate wings pulsating at great speed.

"What a mess," Niamh mumbled to herself as she smiled at Trialla, who was seeing to the injured humans. It would take forever to rebuild Rusalimum. She struggled to fight back a few tears as she thought of her mother and the many responsibilities Niamh herself had now inherited. Niamh felt a pang of guilt at the bitterness she had once built up at her mother's lack of presence in their home. Niamh now understood the enormous task of ruling an empire. She had barely slept since they returned over a week ago.

The sleeplessness was, thankfully, not down to her nightmares. On the rare occasions that she had managed to rest, her dreams were filled with happy memories and surreal, yet not scary, thoughts. After several discussions with Henry and Trialla she now believed her dreams were a warning. Her human blood had caused her to have premonitions in her sleep, and she believed she was seeing what was going to happen if she did nothing.

Her head sank at the thoughts of what did actually become a reality for most of her people. The nightmares she had had to endure must have been nothing compared to the grim reality of it.

She shook her head and tried to smile. Things were different now. She would ensure that the town was rebuilt and everyone pulled together to make it a safe, peaceful place to live. As she thought of all the work that still needed to be done, she downed her Staff and went to help Henry shift some of the rubble.

***

Jorgan splashed through the low tide and scrambled toward the main gate of the castle. *My castle now*, he thought. His anger at himself had continuously risen during his long journey home. Why had he not trusted his father? Why had he not been a better son? A better Sorcerer?

He stood before the gigantic wooden gate, a crack having appeared down its centre. Even his home had been eternally wounded.

He unleashed a power spell and the crack exploded into a hole just big enough for his scrawny frame to squeeze through.

He had been hoping for a much more impressive spell. He'd intended to remove the entire gate, but he would have been happy with at least a bigger hole than that.

He stood in the outer ward and stared in amazement. The castle was barely recognisable; walls crumbled, buildings fallen like soldiers struck down in battle. There was no evidence at all that the barracks and stables had ever stood to his left.

He ran past the granary and through the gate into the inner ward. *Please let it be there,* he thought. As he rounded the angular forebuilding, he skidded to a stop and sighed with relief. His tower stood before him, a little worse for wear but nothing he couldn't fix with some hard work.

The sun beat down on his forehead and he rubbed the sweat away with the back of his sleeve. Something glistened atop a pile of stone and wood. As he moved closer, he recognised the majestic throne standing, slightly askew, reflecting the midday sun.

He clambered up the ruins and turned to assess his surroundings. It was a scene of complete devastation, but it was still his home. He slowly lowered himself into the throne and felt an immediate sense of importance. Of power.

He could almost feel the magic searing up his arms as he sat back and smiled. He thought of his father, his mother, and the number of people who must have died, and his smile quickly faded into a frown of great concentration.

He would avenge his father's death. He would make everyone pay, even the gods, for what they had done to him. His father had been right all along, and he hadn't trusted him. He wouldn't let him down again. He would soon be the ruler of Ysrir, and his father would look down on him with pride.

About the author

I began writing *Tirfo Thuin* whilst living on the Isle of Man in 2004. I had been going through a particularly tough period of my life and had taken to reading many fantasy fiction novels. Finding inspiration in the many myths and legends of the island, and having loved storytelling since a young age, I set out to try and write my first novel.

Whilst this book contains several elements of fantasy, I hope I succeeded in trying to cover some more real-world issues such as war, death, genocide, and love. The intention was to create a story that appealed to non-fantasy fiction readers as well.

I sincerely hope you liked this book. The best way to support new authors is to write reviews and spread the word. If you do not have the time to write a review, I would love to hear from you anyway.

I am very active on Twitter (@TirfoThuin) and on several fiction-writing forums. I also have my own blog (http://andrewbutterworth.wordpress.com) and a site specific to this book (http://www.tirfothuin.com) that I hope you can visit.

Acknowledgments

This novel started out as a one-man-band adventure of sorts whereby I completed all the research, wrote the novel, edited it myself, created the cover art and prepared it for distribution for the many different formats it appears in.

What I soon realised is adventures like this are often better when you get the expertise and help the novel deserves, whether that be professional editors, illustrators or just book clubs that can offer you honest feedback on your work. It is unbelievable the amount of people that are out there that believe in you and want to see you succeed and it is these people I want to thank here.

I would like to firstly thank my wife, Leann, and daughter, Jessica, for putting up with me rambling on about the plot lines, character development, potential twists and the dream talk of book deals, movies and much more. Without them, this book would not have made it this far. I also want to thank my parents and the rest of my family (the B's, G's and Stott's) for reading and re-reading this novel and offering advice and support – even in the cases when fantasy fiction, and sometimes reading fiction in general, is not really their thing (Stotty). I hope you realise you will need to do the same for book two and three.

I also want to thank my editor, Rebecca Keys, for her attention to detail and for helping me spell. Big thanks to Jenna Kay who I think has to be my biggest fan. She has helped so much in the promotion of this novel and even put me in contact with the next person to thank, Hayley Ormerod, for her great illustrations. I am sure she is going to make it far in the art world.

Big thanks also go to Daniel Peplow, Andy Thomas and

Sean Maloney. I have worked closely with these guys in the past on other projects and through a crowd funding project I ran to raise funds for the professional editing and illustrations, these guys pledged an insane amount of money each. I cannot thank you enough for what your contributions have helped achieved and I will forever be in your debt.

Thank you to Welshy for the great work on my mobile responsive website – you are my HTML/CSS hero and thanks to Richie for all his support (and free hosting). I will pay you one day.

Last but not least, a huge list of people who have backed me, contributed funding and just generally supported me in the completion of this novel that I want to thank: Dave Houlker, Jonathan Whiteside, Sheila Kay, Nicholas Teague, Elaine Stott, Ryan Durkin, Tim Marshall, John Cashmore, Gemma Handley, Richie Coss, Emma Robinson, Rick Mather, Ian Stacey, Rune Vagtholm, Damian Stewart, John Askew, Mike Percival, Jacqui Williams, Rob Stevenson-Leggett, Jessica Bolton, Jayne Edwards, Jon Whiteley, Gavin Cooke, Jamie Griffiths, Nicholas Grant, Reece Ward, Elaine Smith and Elin Rossiter.

Bonus Material

A Free Gift

As a big thank-you, I will be sending a signed print of the *Tirfo Thuin* cover art to the first 10 readers to get in touch with a link to a review they have added for the book. Simply complete your review and email abauthor@gmail.com with a link to the review (highlighting your username or review title), and I will get in touch.

The Sorcerer Runes

If you would like to see the Sorcerer runes and their meaning, as seen by Oddvard, simply visit: http://andrewbutterworth.wordpress.com/the-runes-revealed/ and enter the password **niamh**.

A sneak peek at Part II of the Tirfo Thuin Trilogy – out Autumn 2014

Ella, a short human girl with a face full of mud, clambered back through the trees and brambles in a panic. She knew full well she was late home.

She had been playing in the woods and, to any passer-by, looked like she had been ravaged by a wolf. Her long brown hair was all knotted and full of leaves and dirt, her dress was covered in mud, and she had scratches on her face from running through brambles.

She'd had a fun day until her so called 'friends' had set off back to her village without her. They had argued over who was the most scared during the Great Flood, and she had apparently lost so she decided to sit and sulk for a while. It wasn't her fault she had cried so much. How could they show so little compassion? It was terrifying; and her mother died! *Fools! They could have shown some concern at leaving me here on my own as well,* she thought sullenly.

As she neared the edge of the forest a shooting star appeared in the sky; a tiny speck of light with an amber tail streaking through the inky black sky. She watched it flash between the gaps in the leaves above before she emerged from the trees into a clearing.

Lowering her gaze, she made a wish as her mother had always told her to. Her mother had said a shooting star was a warning from the gods and you had to make a good wish to stop the evil it may warn of.

It was her mother she wished for now. Just to see her one more time. To smell her hair or hear her laugh. To get her morning kiss before she left to work in the hot fields.

On looking up, she realised that instead of streaking across the sky in the distance the shooting star seemed to now be plummeting straight towards her.

She ran back to the cover of the trees as an ear-splitting shriek cut through the air and the star struck the ground close to where she had just stood. Ella was immediately thrown against a tree and landed in the bushes beside it. She struggled to regain consciousness and pulled herself to her feet using the tree to steady her. She didn't know how long she had been unconscious for, but she didn't think it was that long. The sun hadn't seemed to move far.

She stood, dazed and cut, and edged toward the large steaming crater feeling nauseous and dizzy. She was unsure what to expect. No one had ever spoken of seeing a real star up close. They were like rainbows – something you saw but could never prove actually existed.

Ella was mindful of the warnings about evil, and hoped her good wish was good enough.

Reaching the summit of the new crater, she recoiled in fear as a steaming white rock unfolded what appeared to be enormous scaly wings from around itself. The creature stood on its dog-like legs that were as wide as the whole of Ella. It didn't seem concerned that patches of its short fur appeared to be on fire.

The creature erupted in a manly roar to the sky, then sagged back to the ground, panting.

Ella felt a mixture of emotions including fear and compassion as the creature struggled to find its feet again in its obvious exhaustion.

It didn't look like anything Ella had seen before, but the wings reminded her of a character in a story her mother had told her long before she died in the great flood.

"Are... are you an Angel?" the girl asked, mesmerised. She had no idea why she had suddenly plucked up the courage to speak to the creature.

The creature whipped its white, bear-like face around to try and focus on the new voice. Ella saw it had a long snout with a shiny black nose and looked like someone had taken a bear, made it white and stretched its face.

It fixed its gaze on Ella's face and seemed to scrunch up its brow in concentration for a while before it said in a deep voice, "My name is Brno and I was an angel, little girl. Once. But no more."

Ella, unsure what to say or do now, stood staring until the creature continued speaking.

"I wonder how the races of this land will fare with no gods to guide you? No gods means no good force and no good force means evil has already won," Brno stated, trailing off in deep thought.

The girl simply stood staring at the angel as it flapped its bony wings twice to hover just above the crater.

The last thing Ella saw was a beam of orange light that Brno fired at her from his paws, killing her instantly. Her scorched body lay smoking in the grass as Brno took flight, his face twisted in a crazed smile, and he headed south with the wind.

Made in the USA
Charleston, SC
08 December 2013